DAEMON WATERS

DAEMON WATERS

C.J. SHANE

Rope's End Publishing

Published by Rope's End Publishing
ISBNs:
hardcover: 978-0-9892216-7-2
paperback: 978-0-9892216-8-9
Kindle mobi: 978-0-9892216-9-6
epub: 978-0-9993874-8-1

Typesetting services by BOOKOW.COM

To our military veterans. May they return home safe and sound in mind and body.

ACKNOWLEDGMENTS

My sincere thanks go out to Diane C. Taylor, Robert Fedor, Lynne East-Itkin, Eleanor Dart, Steve Passiouras at Bookow, and to my ARC team for all your help in bringing Daemon Waters into the book world.

Letty Valdez Mysteries

Desert Jade 2017

Dragon's Revenge 2018

Daemon Waters 2019

CONTENTS

CHAPTER 1

Gus Padillo tossed the packet of C-4 explosive from one hand to the other. He was bored and impatient, waiting for the early evening light to fade into darkness. The C-4 felt like the modeling clay he'd played with in elementary school. Now it was wrapped in plastic and fit nicely into the palm of his hand. Gus had enough experience now with the stuff to know that it wouldn't explode on him. It needed those blasting caps attached to do that. He ground his teeth in irritation.

He was sitting in a pickup truck parked at the back edge of a convenience store's paved lot. His truck was off the pavement in the bare dirt. To the north were several acres of barren desert. Almost no vegetation grew in the sandy soil. Even farther to the north he could see dim lights from a couple of houses that must be at least a half a mile away. The city of Tucson that he had just crossed in his truck was even farther beyond that. Behind the city lights were the mountain foothills where the old man lived. The urban glow penetrated the dusky early evening sky.

The parking lot behind the convenience store was dimly lit, unlike the front of the building which faced out to the interstate highway. In-Out Fast. That was the name of the convenience store and gas station, too. In the rear of the building, a weak, low-wattage, bare light pointed down to the ground exactly over where the back door opened. The door was used by employees to carry trash out to the dumpster twenty feet away.

Gus stopped breathing when he detected a movement at the door. He slumped down behind the steering wheel and stared as the door opened. One of the store's workers, a tall, thin young man, stepped out and lit a cigarette. Beyond the light over the backdoor, shadows took over. Little light reached beyond that limited area. Usually the employees didn't look beyond the light. They just dumped the trash in the dumpster and went back inside. Gus relaxed a little and watched the dude smoke. This cigarette smoker didn't even look up. He never so much as glanced at Gus's pickup. Five minutes later, the worker threw the stub on the concrete back step and ground it out with his shoe. He seemed lost in thought. Probably thinking about some bitch, Gus snorted to himself. The worker went back inside the store.

Gus looked over at the dark gray BMW parked off to the side away from the dumpster. The vehicle had been backed in so that the license plates were not visible. It was empty. This was the old man's BMW. The old man was at the motel next door to the convenience store, banging some sweet young thing who he knew from his office.

Snickering to himself, Gus thought about that pretty blonde who had opened the motel door to the old man. Stupid bitch. Did she really believe the old man would disturb his life for her? Gus had known plenty of privileged white men like the old man. They had money and a certain amount of personal power that they liked to throw around. They figured they could have any woman they wanted for the least inconvenience possible. He'd followed the old man down from his foothills home in the Santa Catalina Mountains, down and across Tucson to this motel on the southern outskirts of the city. He knew what was going on in that motel room.

Gus was a Mexican-American man with a medium built and medium height. He was in his late twenties. He was clean-shaven, his dark hair long, and, at the moment, tied back behind his head. His family called him Gus, short for Augustín, but he preferred Diablo, a nickname given to him by the soldiers in his platoon. Diablo meant "devil" in Spanish. His fellow soldiers called him that because they knew he was a risk taker, fearless, a man who always had your back, a man would not hesitate to kill another human being.

They had seen him do just that repeatedly in Iraq. He liked to think of himself as El Diablo, The Devil.

His little pickup was nothing compared to the old man's BMW. The pickup was old and beat up, a dark-blue color with rust spots on the body although he had to admit that it was reliable. The truck provided cover for him because the yardwork tools in the back made him look like a worker-for-hire, someone those pinche Anglos didn't ever even bother noticing. And the truck was all he could afford. That was going to change, though. He was determined. One of these days and not too long from now, he was going to have enough money to drive whatever car he wanted. A flashy red sports car maybe. Yeah. Red. And fast. Very fast. He could have any woman he wanted then. He would go back to the old barrio in East LA and show his amigos how far he'd come. He'd be back in California where he belonged.

His eyes narrowed when he thought about the owner of the BMW. What a scumbag. The BMW guy, the old man, was well into middle age and sporting a tire around his middle. He had a shit load of money, and he was screwing two women, three if you counted his wife. He got everything he wanted. And he wanted more. Now he wants what I have, the young man growled to himself. Gus ground his teeth again.

Gus thought back over the interaction he'd had with the old man's wife a week or so earlier. He'd just finished banging her when she told him that somehow the old man found out about Gus's plan and his stash. Gus had been hoarding chemicals for a while now to start making the stuff. The original stash was a lucky find, left behind by a drug dealer who had left the state, then got arrested in Texas and shipped off to prison. Gus added to the stash by carrying out a couple of thefts from local pharmacies. That was too dangerous, though, so he quit doing that. He couldn't afford to get caught stealing stuff. His next move was to make a contact that would bring the stuff across the border in small amounts. He paid for whatever amount he could afford. He kept his stash in cardboard boxes marked as "old clothing" in a locked storage unit in mid-town Tucson.

Now the old man knew about the stash, and he knew what the chemicals would be used for. He wanted in on the action. He wants me to share my profits, Gus thought with considerable outrage. The old man has everything, does nothing, and yet he thinks he should get a cut. No fucking way.

But how had the old man found out about the stash? This bothered him a lot. If the old man found out, then someone else might know, too. Did that bitch Gus was screwing tell the old man? After all, she was the old man's wife. Could she have told her husband about the stash? He considered the idea.

Nah, the young man said to himself. She was on his side. She got him that old RV so he could set up it up as a mobile lab to make the stuff. She had that empty house way out on the east side halfway up that desert mountain with no close neighbors. That's where he parked the RV and started his operation. He moved the RV infrequently so it wouldn't attract attention coming and going. He was sure that she wouldn't tell anyone because she wanted in on the action herself. She said she knew a ton of middle-aged ladies like herself who would want what he had to sell.

"They will like it because it keeps them from feeling hungry. They'll use it as a weight-loss drug." She laughed when she said that.

She said she wanted some money from the sales, but mostly, she wanted him, El Diablo. She was what they called a "cougar." She liked younger men. She was older, not as old as the old man, and she was still good-looking. Somewhere in her mid-forties, Gus figured. It made her feel desirable to have a younger lover. She liked sucking his dick, too. Who could complain about that? Not me, he laughed to himself. They had been banging each other for almost six months. They started not long after he did some yardwork and home repairs for her. He was desperate for cash back then. He needed money to make it back to California. But screwing her gave him an opening to making a lot more money. He'd stick around just long enough to do the two big jobs and to sell some stuff. Then he was outta here.

If the old man can have his action on the side, so can I, Gus thought. The old man would be furious if he found out that his wife was banging some other dude. What a dumb ass.

Now, though, things had gotten serious. The old man knew about the stash in the storage unit, though it was unlikely that he knew about the Mexican supplier or about the lab in the RV or the fact that Gus was screwing the old man's wife. Yeah, things were serious now. It was time to take the old man out. Remove him from the scene. That way he couldn't cause any trouble. And that's what his wife wanted. She wanted hubby to be eliminated. She was willing to pay, too.

Gus judged the dusky light was finally low enough to get started. He also figured the old man had his pants off now. He wouldn't be thinking about what was happening to his car out behind the motel. Gus pulled a black knit cap over his head, opened his pickup door and slipped out. He had previously disabled the interior light, and that, plus his cap and dark clothing, made him difficult to see.

He approached the BMW first from the rear. He moved around to the passenger side, keeping low to the ground. He knelt down close to the driver's side door and pulled some duct tape and a box cutter from his pack. He cut off a couple of long strips of tape then reached under the car. He removed the C-4 explosive packet and armed it with blasting caps from his pocket. The plan was to attach the C-4 under the driver's seat. He taped the C-4 securely to the frame. He cut off two more strips and attached them to make sure the C-4 wouldn't get jiggled off. The explosives weighed a little less than two pounds. Not big. Not heavy. Not much. Just enough to do the job, enough to make a huge explosion and to take out the old man.

Gus crawled backwards toward the rear of the BMW, then stopped and looked under the car. He used a pencil flashlight to make sure nothing was visible. Then he turned off the flashlight and closed his eyes. His imagination took over. He'd seen explosions many times when the insurgents' bombs went off. He remembered well the first time he'd smelled cordite after an explosion.

Then he began making the explosions happen himself. A loud bang, a concussive wave emanating outward, then a huge flame of fire shooting straight up into the air. First there was the explosion, the silence that followed, then the screams and the chaos. He liked everything about it. He especially liked detonating the bomb using a cell phone. He was far enough away from the explosion that witnesses rarely even looked in his direction. But he was close enough that he could enjoy the entire spectacle. Most of all he liked the anticipation. He especially liked those two or three seconds when the person first got into the car. He dialed the number, the bomb went off, and the world changed forever. They were all terrorists so they deserved it. His commanding officer never found out what Gus was doing. Or maybe he didn't care.

Yeah, Gus liked the bombs. He liked being in control.

What did they expect? They were the ones who taught him how to disarm and dispose of highly explosive munitions. There were plenty of those in Iraq and Afghanistan. He stayed busy with the disarmament and disposal aspect of his job on every tour of duty, five in all. They even gave him a badge, Explosive Ordnance Disposal Technician. He didn't realize at the time, but he really got off on disarming those IEDs. They could blow up any second. His life was in danger. But he was good at disarming the bombs. He never accidentally set one off.

The Army also taught him how to construct the explosive devices, not just take them apart. He knew how to make several different kinds of explosives in different sizes for different uses. They didn't think about how he could use those skills when he got out of the Army. Later when they found out what a good shot he was, they moved him into a sniper position. That was easy, picking off those insurgents or anyone else who got his attention. He knew he'd killed innocent people, but he didn't care. He never believed they were innocent anyway, even the young ones. They were all trying to kill him. He got there first.

When he was discharged from the Army, he felt lost. The stress, no, the thrill of disarming explosives and of being a sniper, made so-called normal life unbearably boring. When he returned to the States, he felt dead. He sat around and drank and snorted coke and zoned out. Then he saw a movie about a paid assassin. The idea of being an assassin woke him up and made him feel alive. He felt that thrill again just remembering.

Now Gus had a new line of work. He decided to hire himself out as a hit man, a paid assassin. It made him feel powerful to have that kind of control over life and death. But this time, the job wasn't just for pay. It was so he could feel safe, too. So he could get back to California with some money in his pocket. The old man had to go.

Gus had two jobs on tap. He'd been hired to kill two men in Tucson. One of them was the old man. He knew he would have to be extra careful. Take one out with a high-powered rifle. And blow the old man to smithereens. He knew it was dangerous. Two kills in the same town and worse, sticking around to do the drug deal, was risky. And exciting, too. Make money, get plenty of pussy, and watch two old farts die. Yes, he would have to be extra careful. He figured he'd head for California in only a couple of months. He'd get lost in LA then. The cops will never find me, Gus said to himself. Never.

CHAPTER 2

Letty Valdez stared at an open email on the screen of her office computer. The content of the email was from a potential new client wanting her to find a missing person. The email wasn't addressed to her personally. The opening line read, "Dear Private Investigator." She wondered how many other investigators had received the same email message.

The words on the screen said, "Our family needs help in locating my brother Kenny Wilson. Kenny is an Afghanistan War veteran who served honorably in the U.S. Army. He returned to the U.S. and was discharged from the Army approximately eight months ago. He stayed at my parents' home in Maryland for a few weeks after his discharge. It became apparent to all family members that Kenny had become deeply troubled. Whereas he had been an outgoing young man who enjoyed sports and social activities prior to his Army service, he was withdrawn and distant from his family and former friends after returning from Afghanistan. Also we believe he had acquired a drug habit."

Letty shook her head. Kenny Wilson's story was all too familiar to her. He appeared to be another casualty of the Iraq and Afghanistan Wars, no doubt suffering from what had become known as "combat stress injuries," or more commonly, "PTSD," short for "post-traumatic stress disorder." Letty knew all about that. She was a former U.S. Army medic who had served in Iraq. She knew first-hand what "combat stress" meant. She knew what PTSD meant. She could still hear the sounds of an IED exploding and the smell of cordite in the air. She remembered the blood spraying from severed arteries. Nightmares from her Iraq War experiences haunted her nights all too frequently. She figured the bad dreams would always be there. She couldn't forget what she'd seen.

The email went on. "Kenny disappeared one day last September. He left behind a note telling us that he was going to find friends from his platoon with whom he had served. He mentioned in particular a fellow soldier named Rigo. Kenny told us that Rigo lived in Arizona. My brother left his cell phone number in the note, and said he would text us. After he left, he did text our mother but only a handful of times. Then by November, he went silent. We haven't heard from Kenny since, and he doesn't respond to us when we call or text. We don't know if he made it to Arizona or if he found his friend. I hope you can help us find Kenny and tell us that he is alive and well. If your services are available to find a missing person, please call me." The email was signed, "Stan Wilson, Kenny's brother." Wilson's phone number was included in the email.

Letty figured that she had been contacted because of the last paragraph in the email about the connection to Arizona. She guessed that this email went out to every private investigator in the state.

At first Letty hesitated. After some thought, she decided to go ahead. The Army medic in her wanted to help out a fellow vet. She called Stan Wilson and reached him on the second ring. Their conversation was brief. Letty asked for a photo of Kenny. She told him that she would send him a list of needed information that would help her find the missing man. These details included personal data such as birth date and place, military service ID number, dates of military service, where and when he entered and left service, and any other available information. She also asked for any information about the friend Rigo, but Stan Wilson knew nothing more than the name. To Letty, Rigo sounded like a nickname or maybe a shortened form of a longer name like Federigo or Rodrigo. No last name. Or maybe Rigo was his last name.

Stan Wilson expressed gratitude and the promise of any help he could provide.

Toward the end of their conversation, Letty said, "Mr. Wilson, if I find your brother, I will give him your contact information and your mother's contact information. I will ask him to call or text you. I will not give you his actual location, though. Private investigators don't typically give clients the location of a missing person. We don't really know what the client's intentions might be. For example the client may be an abusive husband looking for a wife who fled his control. I hope you understand and accept this as part of our agreement."

"I understand, Miss Valdez. Another investigator in Phoenix told me the same thing. Right now, it would be a great relief to just know that Kenny is alive. He'll have to decide for himself if he wants to come home or if he even wants us in his life."

Toward the end of the conversation, they came to financial terms for Letty's investigatory services. She emailed him the list of information that would help her. In return, she received Kenny Wilson's photo and as much information as his brother had on hand. She stared at the photo. He was young, twenty-five years old, about five feet ten, average build, brown hair, and with a sad look on his face. There were shadows under his brown eyes. She transferred the photo to her mobile phone so she could show it to anyone who might have information.

Now Letty found herself staring at the email wondering what she had gotten herself into. Some of her jobs as a private investigator were fun, like solving a puzzle. Others were fairly routine, such as serving papers that required a person to show up in court, or doing due diligence research for a client involved in a business investment. Occasionally a job turned out to be dangerous. Letty didn't like the dangerous jobs at all. She did not think that someone trying to beat her up or shoot at her was exciting or challenging. But sometimes that couldn't be avoided.

Finding a missing veteran, one who had already been identified as having some serious psychological issues, made Letty feel somewhat uncomfortable. She knew that most, or at least many, veterans came home okay. They readjusted to civilian life with no serious problems. But up to twenty percent of them could not make that adjustment because the wounds of war came home with them. She had deep empathy for these soldiers. Yet Letty knew in her heart that she was vulnerable herself and vulnerable to their suffering.

Combat stress affected vets in different ways. For some, alcohol and drugs provided temporary relief. For others, guns and a willingness to use them was a personal solution. Some of them were flat-out dangerous. She had no idea what she would find if she were able to track down Kenny Wilson.

Letty decided to start by contacting local veterans groups to see if, by chance, Kenny Wilson had registered with any of them. She searched for a while and came up with nothing.

The front door to her office opened and Letty looked up.

"Tío, what a nice surprise."

Her Uncle Miguel Valdez stood in the outer doorway. Letty joined him in the nearly-empty front reception room of her tiny office. She gave her uncle an affectionate hug. She noticed that behind Miguel's substantial girth, there was a young man standing there. Letty didn't recognize him. He appeared to be in his early twenties, slender and smallish in stature, maybe five feet six inches tall. From his brown skin and dark eyes, he was Mexican-American like Tío Miguel and like Letty's father.

"Come on into my office and have a seat," Letty said. "What brings you to Tucson?"

She pulled out two additional chairs. The three of them nearly filled the second room where Letty had her desk, a computer, and a filing cabinet. When she had two visitors, the room was full. Her rented office space also had a small closet-like storeroom and a tiny bathroom in addition to the outer reception room and Letty's interior office. She was sure that her office had to be one of the smallest in Tucson, but she thought it was perfect for her. The rent was cheap, and the view of the Santa Catalina Mountains to the north from her office window was worth a million dollars.

"We're here on business," Uncle Miguel said seriously. "I hope you can help."

"I'll try my best."

Letty really loved her Tío Miguel. He was the brother of Letty's father Ernesto, called Neto by everyone in the family. Tío Miguel had always been very kind to Letty, especially after her father disappeared when she was a child. Neto showed up eventually in Los Angeles. He was a veteran like Letty. Severe PTSD was a constant in his life. In her father's case, the war was Vietnam. Letty's father just couldn't manage life as a husband and father or in a regular job. She had forgiven him long ago because she knew exactly what Neto Valdez had experienced in war.

"This is Francisco. He's the nephew of my ex-wife's cousin," Miguel gestured to the young man at his side.

Letty smiled to herself. The Mexican side of her family was big, and the relationships complex. She had trouble keeping up with everyone. She had never met this young man.

"You can call me Frankie."

"Okay. Frankie it is."

Frankie was dressed casually and wore a dark-colored Fedora hat with a narrow brim. Letty couldn't help but notice that Frankie had many tattoos visible on his body. She guessed that there were more under his clothing. His earlobes were stretched out slightly to hold small silver rings, maybe a half of an inch wide with a hole in the ear lobe the width of the inner ring. Letty's brother Will had told her that the practice was called "gauging." Letty didn't understand all this poking and inking and stretching. It all looked painful. After all the injuries and death she'd seen in Iraq when she was a medic there, she just didn't understand why anyone would hurt themselves voluntarily. She didn't really know what to think of Frankie based on his appearance. She had to admit she hadn't seen any sign of a smart-ass attitude that some people often thought went with his age and the tattoos. She wondered why Uncle Miguel brought him along.

She looked at her uncle.

"Frankie's brother has disappeared. We'd like to see if you can help find him. We think he may be in Tucson."

Letty nodded, thinking that it was unusual to be asked to find two missing people on the same day. "What's his name?"

"Alfonso Miranda, but we call him Al."

"Tell me about this disappearance. Where was Al before he disappeared? When did he disappear? And what makes you think he's in Tucson?"

Tío Miguel sat back and let Frankie take over the conversation.

"We live in Ambos Nogales. Al was staying with me."

"Which side of the border?"

"Both. I mean I live on the U.S. side, but we have family on both sides. My brother and I were born in the U.S. side so we're both American citizens. My mom moved back Nogales, Sonora, to take care of her parents who are really old."

"What do you do in Nogales?"

"I work full time at a grocery store, mainly stocking shelves and doing inventory, plus I do some office computer work. Also I take a class every semester at Cochise College at the Nogales Center. I'm learning computer stuff. I like computers."

Letty nodded.

"I hope to transfer to the University of Arizona someday," Frankie added. He sounded defiant, as if he were resisting the notion that such a dream was impossible for him to achieve.

Smart, ambitious, hard-working, and poor, Letty thought to herself. She felt immediate empathy for this young man.

"I'm living with a couple of friends in Nogales, Arizona. My brother showed up three months ago. He just got out of the Army. He had multiple deployments to Afghanistan. Like at least four times he went over there."

"So your brother showed up one day three months ago?"

"Yeah. He didn't want to stay with our mom. He told me once he didn't want her to see how screwed up he is."

"And is he? Screwed up?"

"Yeah, basically. He's not like he used to be. He used to laugh and joke a lot. He liked sports, the Mexican baseball teams especially. But now, he's different. Al was very withdrawn all the time he was staying with me. He hardly talked at all. Like he was seriously depressed. He just sat around and drank. Alcohol, I mean. He was drunk most of the three months he was there. He had bad dreams, too. He'd wake up shaking and crying in the night. He told me once that he wasn't good for anything anymore, and he might as well go back to Afghanistan and die there."

Letty shook her head. Sounded familiar. "Then he disappeared?"

"Yeah, sort of. He told me a couple of weeks ago that he had a ride to Tucson. He told me that a friend he met when he was in the Army was coming to meet him. Al said he was going a day early and camping out at one of the homeless camps. He wanted to make sure he was in Tucson early so he'd be there when his friend arrived. One day I came home and he wasn't there. I haven't heard from him since then. I tried calling him several times, but he never answers his phone. My mom is really worried so I decided to see if I could find him. Tío Miguel offered to help."

"What do you think, Letty?" Tío Miguel asked. "Is this the kind of thing you do?

"Yes. Sometimes I get missing persons cases." She turned again to Frankie. "Do you have any names of the friends or fellow vets? Or anything to go on?"

"Nope. I don't know about the homeless camps. I guess there are vets staying there." Frankie frowned. "I'm sorry. I'm not much help."

"Unfortunately there are several homeless camps here in Tucson, and there are a fair number of homeless vets, too, so we may have to do a search for him. Let's contact some of veteran assistance groups here in Tucson first and see if anyone has heard from him. If we don't find him at one of their shelters, we'll go to the camps and ask around. There are several camps in various places around town with all kinds of people, not just vets. The good weather here draws them in. Maybe someone might have met your brother or know someone who knows him."

Miguel stood. "So Letty, you'll take care of this? I need to get back home and attend to business." He turned to Frankie.

"You have some place to stay in Tucson?"

"Yeah, there are a couple of guys I went to high school with who live in Tucson now. I've already called them. They will put me up for a few days. My boss gave me some days off from my job. He's a vet, too, so he was sympathetic."

Letty stood. "Thanks, Tío. Frankie and I will start working on this now."

Frankie turned a dark shade of red and smiled. He looked both embarrassed and pleased.

"I want to help, Miss Valdez, but I don't know much."

"You can start by calling me Letty. You probably know more than you think. Let's get started."

* * *

Letty made a short list of veteran groups. Then she started calling. After four calls, she turned to Frankie and said, "No one has heard of Al. You keep the list in case it might be helpful to you at some point." She handed it to Frankie. "So let's try a different approach. Let me make a call first."

Letty called her little brother Will who was at home from school already. Will and his girlfriend Clarice were both college students and enthusiastic bicyclists. They lived with Letty, along with their family's two dogs, in Letty's mid-town Tucson home.

Will answered immediately.

"Hey, Big Sister. What's up?"

"Will, I need to visit some homeless camps looking for a vet. You and Clarice are always riding on your bikes around town. Do you have any locations you can give me for current encampments? They closed down Camp Bravo that was there for a long time south of downtown. Seems like now the camps are always moving from one place to another."

Letty was silent as she scribbled with a pen on a small notepad.

"Good, good. One of them is not too far from here. Thanks so much. If you think of any more, let me know."

Letty led Frankie to her Nissan pickup in the parking lot outside her office.

"There's an encampment just a little south of here." She paused. "Frankie, you should know that just this morning I agreed to help find another veteran. So we'll be looking for two guys."

Frankie nodded.

"I really appreciate this, Letty."

"No problem. After all, we are in the same family — sort of." She smiled. "I guess by marriage, not by blood, right?"

"Yeah," Frankie said. "It's hard to keep track with such a big extended family."

"I rely on Tío Miguel to keep everything straight."

"Me, too."

She drove south on Alvernon Way, turned back to the east and onto a dirt road. She followed the road as far as she could until it became too uneven and filled with ruts. They entered a large undeveloped stretch of desert surrounded by six-lane roads, houses, and businesses.

Letty and Frankie took off on foot. They crossed a gravel-filled culvert with concrete walls and walked across the open, cactus-dotted landscape toward a large grove of mesquite trees. Letty could see several campsites scattered under the spreading and leafy branches of the trees. There were tents and old lawn chairs and various pieces of junk that the homeless people collected to help them survive. The encampment was fairly large and looked like it had been there for a while.

A couple of men and a woman came out when they saw Letty and Frankie coming toward them.

"Hi," Letty said, smiling. "I'm Letty, and this is Frankie. I'm a veteran from the Iraq War, and we're looking for a couple of guys. Both are Army veterans like me." She hoped that by introducing herself as a vet, she could turn away any concern that she might be a cop. If they were vets, too, there would be a connection. She pulled out her smart phone and pulled up the first photo.

One of the men, roughly dressed and with a gray beard, said, "Let's see."

Letty handed the phone to the man. First, she showed him a photo of Al Miranda given to her earlier by Frankie. Kenny Wilson's photo was next.

The older man shook his head. He passed the phone to the others. They also shook their heads no.

"Sorry. We haven't seen them," the woman said. She, too, was older, probably nearly sixty, and had most of her teeth missing.

"Is there anyone else here who might know them? Especially any vets from Iraq or Afghanistan?

"Not right now. There are a couple of guys that served, but they both have a temporary construction job this week."

"Okay. I guess we'll try some other place. Thanks a lot."

Letty and Frankie returned to her pickup.

"How do you know if they are telling the truth or not?" Frankie asked.

"I don't for sure. But law enforcement officers and psychologists say that you can often tell because there are giveaways when people lie."

"Like what?"

"The person who is lying will pause before they answer you. They'll often look away. I mean, not look you in the eyes or even look at your face. Sometimes they will cough or clear their throat or make some other kind of distracting sound. If they do answer, they are often vague and don't have details. Or they will talk a lot and say nothing relevant. Sometimes they come back with a question to distract from your original question. Oftentimes they just look anxious, like they've been caught stealing cookies from the cookie jar. There are lots of ways to tell. These people we just met didn't show any of those signs. They didn't seem to be hostile toward us at all. They seemed very open and showed no signs of avoiding the question. I watched their eyes when they looked at the photos. There was no sign of recognition on any of their faces. I think they don't know anything."

Frankie nodded. "Wow," he said. "That's useful information."

"Why? Do you suspect people are lying to you?"

"Yeah. My girlfriend." He frowned.

"Uh-oh," Letty said.

They were both quiet as they returned to Letty's pickup truck. They headed northwest to the next encampment.

CHAPTER 3

The drive to the next encampment took about twenty minutes.

On the way, Letty asked Frankie if he knew much about veterans and PTSD.

"Not that much. Just what I see on the news. Most of them are okay. I know some of them come home with depression and start doing drugs or drinking. A few of them are violent. I think it's because the military makes them go too many times."

"Yes, I agree with that."

"How many times did you go?" Frankie glanced at her sideways.

"Two deployments. All together I was there for nearly two years. That was too much for me. I was a mess when I came home. No drugs or alcohol. I just stopped talking." Letty had a half-smile, half-grimace on her face. "I guess that's not such a bad thing. Most people talk too much anyway. In my case, I went out and lived with my grandmother on the reservation for a few months. She said I was spirit sick. She didn't bother me at all or force me to talk about what I'd seen. She said the desert would bring me back into balance. Things got better for me after I stayed with my grandma."

"Oh, I forgot. Your mother is Tohono O'odham, right?"

"Yes, and my dad is Tío Miguel's brother. My dad had his own problems with PTSD from Vietnam. Tío Miguel was really more of a father to me than my own dad. Same with my Uncle Mando, who is my mother's brother. Uncle Mando lives on the reservation. For me, it was almost like having two dads."

"Is Al going to be okay?"

"Maybe. Hard to say. He has to decide that he wants to get better and then get some help. He needs that so he won't drink himself to death. Is he ever violent?"

"No, he seems to be taking everything out on himself, not anyone else."

Letty was now approaching a city block in mid-town Tucson. Unlike the earlier encampment under the grove of mesquites in open desert, this homeless campground was in a residential area and covered a much smaller area than the first camp they'd visited. A narrow waterless creek bed called Arcadia Wash ran through the block from north to south. Single-family houses were to the east of the tree-lined wash. To the far west there was a row of houses lining the next street, Arcadia Street. In between the wash and the street with the houses, there was an open area. Trees dotted the area, mostly mesquite and some palo verde. There were no structures at all.

She parked her pickup on the south side of the block. Together, she and Frankie walked on a trail that led to a dirt-packed area. Almost immediately they saw signs of human habitation under the trees. A handful of tents was situated there, and like the other camp, various pieces of equipment and personal items were visible. She could see that some people had been sleeping on the open ground with no tent to protect them. A handful of men sitting or standing under the trees were talking quietly. There appeared to be no women at all. The men looked a lot rougher than the ones she and Frankie had met in the larger encampment earlier that day.

Letty couldn't help but notice that when they saw her, several of the men glanced at her and then looked away with vaguely frightened looks on their faces. She didn't look like a cop, and Frankie certainly didn't either. But these men had been living such a rough life and had been forcibly removed from one place to another so often that they didn't want to take any chances. They had no interest in interacting with her.

One man, about Letty's six-foot-tall height, was standing in the shadows watching her. He had dark hair, was fairly young, and he was wearing a U.S. Army jacket. She approached him. Much to her surprise, he turned out to be the vet that she'd received the email about earlier that morning. Kenny Wilson. She tried to keep a friendly face and not give away that she recognized him.

Letty approached him. "Hi. My name is Letty. I'm a U.S. Army vet. I served in Iraq. This is Frankie. We're looking for Frankie's brother. He's a vet, too."

Kenny nodded and said, "There are a lot of lost souls out there."

Letty pulled out her phone and showed Wilson the photo of Frankie's brother, Al Miranda.

"Yeah, I know him. His name is Al."

Letty looked at Frankie and frowned. Don't say anything, she signaled.

"Is he camping here?" she asked.

"He was here for only one night and then he left. His girlfriend picked him up."

Letty heard a burst of air come out of Frankie's lungs.

"Got any idea how we can get ahold of him?" she asked.

Kenny Wilson pulled a cell phone from his back pocket. "Yeah, I have her number. Her name is Lillian. Real pretty black girl, very sweet." He handed the phone to Letty, and she recorded the number. "She gave me her number when she came looking for Al, and he wasn't here. The next time she came, he was here, and she took him off in her car. I haven't seen him since."

"Okay. Thanks a lot. This is a great help." Letty turned to go. Then she turned back to him and handed him the phone again. "We're looking for this man, too."

Kenny Wilson took the phone and looked at the photo. His eyes went wide, and he turned pale.

"Where did you get this?"

"Your brother sent it to me. Your family is desperate to know where you are and if you are okay."

He shook his head. "They are good people. They don't deserve to have me in the family."

"I doubt they would agree with that. They want you to call them."

"You won't tell them where I am, will you?"

"No. I won't do that. I will tell them that I found you and that I asked you to call them yourself."

"Okay. I'll think about it."

Letty became aware that a man was approaching rapidly on the dirt trail that led into the mesquite grove. He was probably in his early thirties, had longish brown hair, an unkempt beard, and dirty clothing. In other words, he looked pretty much like the other men in the encampment. The difference was that he was scowling, and he looked angry.

"Who the hell are you, and why are you bothering my friend?"

Letty tried to stay calm. She smiled. "I'm Letty. I don't think I'm bothering him. We were just talking."

"It's okay, Rigo," Kenny Wilson said. "She's looking for that vet who was here last week. The one named Al. Remember?"

Rigo. So this is the friend Kenny had mentioned to his brother, Letty thought to herself. Rigo apparently thought that it was his job to protect the camp. Or to protect Kenny Wilson? Or both?

"I think you two need to get out of here. We don't want your kind around here," Rigo said to Letty. He was openly hostile.

"What 'kind'? I'm an Army veteran, too."

"I don't give a shit what you are. Get your ass out of our camp." Rigo thrust his right arm forward and tried to shove Letty.

Letty sidestepped his arm and as he shoved himself toward her, she captured one of his arms, bent it back and up toward his neck. At the same time, she kicked the back of his knees so that he fell to the ground. She used one hand to hold his arm pinned against his back and the other to push down on one of his legs which was extended too far backward against his back. When he tried to move, she increased the pressure which increased the pain.

"Mr. Rigo, you aren't being very nice. I'm going to let you go. We're going to leave now. Don't try to follow us. Understand?"

"Yeah." His words were partly an angry ejaculation and partly a painful groan.

Letty stood upright, letting go of Rigo's leg and arm as she rose.

"Come on," she said to Frankie. "We can go now." Letty turned to Wilson, looked calmly into his eyes, and said clearly, "I don't have anything more to say. You know what you need to know." She turned and strode out of the encampment, Frankie at her side.

Back in her pickup, Letty said, "Let's go back to my office and we'll see if we can track down Lillian and Al. Did you know Al has a girlfriend?"

"No. He never mentioned a woman."

"If we find her, I bet we'll find Al."

Frankie fell quiet. Then he asked, "Letty, where did you learn all that karate stuff?"

"It's not karate. Karate is Japanese. I practice Chinese gong fu. I first learned hand-to-hand combat in Army Basic Training. I decided to continue with martial arts so every time I had a chance, I took a class. Then I met Zhou LiangWei. He's my teacher now. He's the best gong fu practitioner I've ever met."

"I'm impressed. Do you think I could learn? Small dudes like me get pushed around a lot."

"Sure you can learn. Zhou's classes are definitely the best place to learn. But I'm warning you. It's hard work, and it takes a lot of self-discipline. Zhou isn't very patient with you if he thinks you have no discipline. He expects a lot from his students."

"I can be disciplined."

"You'll have to live in Tucson, though. This is where Zhou lives now. He has a martial arts school here."

"That's another reason to move to Tucson."

"Another reason?"

"Yeah," he frowned. "I need to get away from my lying, cheating girlfriend. If I change the scene, maybe I can get over her faster."

"Also you could start taking computer classes at the community college, get a new job and start a new life."

"Yeah, I like the sound of that. It's not so far from Nogales. I can run down and help my mom if she needs it. And my sisters are there to help her, too."

"Sounds like a plan."

By this time, they were back at Letty's office.

Frankie sat in a chair, and Letty sat behind her desk. She pulled a desk drawer open and pulled out a phone.

"This is a burner phone. The number can't be traced and caller ID doesn't show up for this phone. Let's try Lillian and see if she answers.

She did answer, on the second ring.

Letty nodded to Frankie. She sat up straight in her office chair.

"Hi, my name is Letty, and I'm calling from Mama Mimi's Sub and Pizza. We're going to be opening a new shop here in Tucson in about ten days. How would you like to win free sub sandwiches and drinks? All you have to do is answer a few questions about your take-out preferences." She paused then continued, "Great. What's your name? Okay, I'll call you Lil."

Frankie was grinning now.

"Yes, first here are your questions. How often do you order out? Do you usually order pizza, subs or something else? Is there anything you'd like to see on a take-out and delivery menu that you can't get now? Very good. That's all the questions I have. Now I'll give you some options, and you can choose what you want to eat. Our sub choices are ham and cheese, tuna, and a vegie sub with hummus. All come with complete fixings – your choice. Also you have choice of breads. Whole wheat, sourdough or Rustic Italian."

Letty scribbled notes. "So ham and cheese on sourdough. Mayo or mustard or our special sauce. Okay. Tomatoes, lettuce, peppers, pickles?"

More scribbling.

"We have a selection of drinks, too, like Coke, Pepsi, Dr. Pepper, and Arizona sweet tea. Interested? Great. Dr. Pepper it is. Also my boss wants me to interview the man of the house to see what guys like to order. You know, like during a ball game guys like to eat and will often order a delivery. Do you have a husband, boyfriend, or brother over the age of eighteen?"

Letty waited while Lil went to find the man of the house.

"Hi, I'm Letty. What's your name? Al? Okay. I'll ask you the same questions." She smiled and nodded at Frankie.

Al wanted ham and cheese, too, on sourdough with all the fixings, and he preferred sweetened tea as his drink.

"Very good. What's your address?" More scribbling. "That's north of Grant Road just off First Avenue, right? Okay, that sounds easy. We'll be there as soon as we can get your food ready. This will take us about thirty minutes. Thank you so much."

Letty looked at Frankie and said, "Let's go get them some subs. They'll be hungry and pissed off if we don't show up with something to eat. The subs will pave our way. I'll pay for it. Consider it a gift to fellow veteran."

"Awesome. Letty, you're the best. I didn't know you could make up stories like that."

"Yes, it's one of the advantages of being a private investigator. Cops aren't supposed to lie, but I can."

They drove to the nearest sub shop, and the subs were ready to go in about ten minutes. Another fifteen and they were at the house where Lil and Al said the food could be delivered. Letty parked near a tree so that she could be seen from the front window but Frankie could not easily be seen. She pulled a black baseball cap with an Arizona Wildcats logo from her glove compartment and put it on her head backwards so that the logo wasn't visible.

"Here's what we'll do. I'll go to the front door and knock. You stay behind me and go to the side over there so they can't see you when they open the door."

Frankie followed her directions. She approached the front door, and he went to the side where he was not visible.

Letty knocked and the door opened twenty seconds later.

"Hi," Letty said to the lovely young black woman at the door. "You must be Lil. I have your order. Do you mind signing this slip of paper? My boss wants proof that I delivered. He's paranoid. He thinks his delivery people are eating the subs themselves. But don't tell him I said that."

"Sure." Lil stepped out and signed the paper that Letty had used to write down their orders.

"How about the man of the house? Al? Is he here? I need his signature, too, for my boss."

Lil turned and called Al Miranda. He appeared quickly. He looked a lot like Frankie, but he was a little taller, a little older, and looked a lot more world-weary than the young Frankie.

Lil took the sack with the subs and a cardboard tray with the drinks and disappeared.

Al stepped out, and Letty handed him the paper to sign. He looked down at the paper. At the same time, Letty signaled to Frankie.

"Hi, Al," Frankie said.

"What are you doing here, bro?"

"We've been worried about you. Mama asked me to find you. Are you okay?"

"Yeah, I'm doing better actually."

The two brothers walked together toward Letty's pickup and continued talking.

Letty knocked again and called out, "Lil? Got a minute?"

Lil reappeared.

"What's going on?" She frowned when she saw Al with Frankie. "Who's that?"

"I'm a vet. U.S. Army medic. I served in Iraq. I'm also a private investigator here in Tucson. That's Frankie, Al's brother. Frankie asked me to help him find his brother Al. I just wanted you to know that we have good intentions. I know how rough the war was on a lot of soldiers."

"I know all about that myself," Lil said. "I was a Navy Corpsman."

"Really?" Letty smiled. "Then we were in the same business."

"Yes, trying to stop the blood flow and patch up shrapnel wounds." Navy Corpsman served the same emergency medical function as U.S. Army medics.

"Frankie tells me that Al stayed with him a short while and that he drank himself into a stupor every night. Frankie was afraid that

Al seemed to have lost the will to live. Frankie and the whole family are really worried about Al."

Lil frowned then looked directly in Letty's eyes. "Look. Here's how it is. I met Al in Kandahar. I fell in love with him despite the fact that he seemed to be pretty messed up from the war. He loves me, too. So I came here from Philly just as soon as I was discharged. I'm going to take care of him and make him better."

"What about the booze?"

"He's not drinking now. I told him he could choose – me or the vodka. I think he finds sex with me to be more fun than getting drunk."

Letty chuckled and nodded. "I'm not surprised."

"I'm going to get him help. There are resources here in Tucson for vets. I've been looking into local options for treatment. Al is a fine man, kind-hearted and smart, and he's been really good to me. He's so sweet. It's my job to help him get past the combat stress injuries and to live a normal life. I'm determined to make that happen. I'm really crazy about him."

"Okay," Letty said. "I wish every returning vet had someone to love him like that. He has a family that loves him but there's something to be said for…"

"A little action under the covers?" Lil laughed.

"Right." Letty laughed, too.

"How much do I owe you for the sandwiches and drinks?"

"No charge. Consider this a gift from Valdez Investigations in honor of your service and Al's service."

"And thank you for your service, too," Lil smiled. "By the way, you don't look like the white folk around here. Are you Mexican-American like Al?"

"My dad is Mexican-American. Al and Frankie are in my dad's extended family. My mom is O'Odham. We tend to be darker and kind of red."

"What's O'Odham?"

"Tohono O'odham. We're a Native American tribe. We have a reservation out west of Tucson. It's nearly three million acres, the second largest in the U.S. after the Navajo."

"I can see that in you now. Your skin has a definite reddish cast to it, and your hair is black and straight. How come I haven't heard of your people?"

Letty shrugged her shoulders. "We've been here for four thousand years, farming in the desert. Maybe we didn't kill enough white people to get well-known."

Lil hooted with laughter. "I like you."

Letty nodded and smiled. "You, too." She turned and saw Frankie and Al hugging each other and saying goodbye.

"Here's my card. Call me if you need anything."

Lil took the card. "Likewise. You have my phone number."

They both grinned and waved goodbye.

Back in her truck, she asked Frankie, "Everything okay?"

"Yeah," Frankie looked more relaxed. "Al is going to call our mom. And he invited me to dinner to get to know his girlfriend. She seems okay."

"I have a good feeling about Lil. I talked to her a little bit. She's a vet. She was a medic like me. She loves your brother."

"That's good to hear. So she knows what he's been through."

"You want me to drop you off at your friends' house?"

"No, I think I'm going to learn how to use the city bus system. One route goes past your office, and there's a transfer that will take me to my friends' place."

"Don't forget that you can get a student discount on the bus."

They were silent again then Frankie said, "Letty, I can't thank you enough. If you ever need anything, call me."

"Will do."

"I'm serious."

"I know you are. Maybe if I have a computer problem, I can call you."

"Sure. That's my favorite kind of problem."

Letty was well satisfied with the interaction she'd had. Al had been pretty easy to find. Lil was a surprise and a good one. The only nagging thing in the back of Letty's mind was the vets they met earlier in the day. Kenny Wilson seemed very unsure of himself, likely very depressed, without any direction and obviously unmotivated to get help. Rigo, on the other hand, was full of hostility and anger. It was very possible, Letty thought, that Kenny had come under the domineering influence of Rigo. Whether or not Rigo would allow him to call his family was a big question in her mind.

Letty dropped Frankie off at the closest bus stop. Back in her office, she called Stan Wilson, Kenny's brother, and told him about finding Kenny. Stan was relieved. Letty made it clear that it was up to Kenny now to decide if he would call home or not. She told Stan that she'd met Rigo, too, but didn't mention anything more.

CHAPTER 4

Back in her office, Letty leaned back in her chair and closed her eyes. It had been nearly three months since she'd been attacked and beaten by thugs when jogging with Zhou on the Rillito River trail. She still wasn't feeling one hundred percent. Her rib hurt from time to time, a dull but persistent ache. The rib had been cracked by a particularly vicious kick, and the cartilage had separated from that rib during the attack. Everything in that spot at the base of her rib cage was a little tender to the touch. She feared it always would be tender. Sometimes it ached more than usual if she was too active. Sometimes she was really tired, too.

Of course, she admitted to herself that her fatigue probably had more to do with lack of sleep caused by nightmares, not her injuries. She'd had those Iraq nightmares on an episodic basis since she came home from the war. She dreamed too often of that last convoy, the IED exploding, and the body parts. Bullets zipped past her head and finally one hit her. A huge blast of fire and noise, parts of Humvee flying in the air, running, running, running to the head of the convoy, crying out for Chava. She kept running despite the wound to her shoulder. Blood was everywhere. But Chava was never there. He was gone, vanished in the sand. Gone. Blood evaporating in the dry desert air.

When she had these dreams, she often woke up trembling, crying and panting. And exhausted. Since being attacked by those three guys when she was jogging, the Iraq nightmares had come even more often, sometimes as often three nights each week. She had come to think of the Iraq nightmares as demons haunting her. The demons came and went as they wished. She feared that the bad dreams would always be there for the rest of her life.

Her attention came back to the present when the front door of her office opened slightly. Letty looked up. The door opened wider. She could see a woman, probably in her late forties or early fifties, peeking in. She had a hesitant, rather timid look on her face.

Letty stood, smiled and said, "Hi."

"Hi....uh..." The woman seemed very unsure of herself.

"Come in and sit down." Letty waved toward a chair in front her desk. "I'm Letty Valdez. Can I help you?"

"My name is Jennifer Kimball. Everyone calls me Jen." She sat down and clutched her big purse in front of her on her lap.

"What can I do for you?"

"I've never been to a private investigator before. But it seems like a good move right now. I think I need help."

"What's the problem?"

"Okay. I'm just going to jump in. I think my husband may be having an affair. I think he's going to divorce me. And I think he may be hiding assets from me so that when we divorce, he'll get everything, and I'll be cheated out of what is my fair share."

Letty nodded. "That happens sometimes. Let's take each issue one at a time. What makes you think he's having an affair?"

"He's super nice to me, and he is calling me all sorts of sweet names. You know, endearments? The only other time he's done that was about ten years ago. He was having an affair then, too. He broke it off with her and begged me to stay married to him. We still had children at home at that time. But I think he's at it again. I have the feeling that the way he's talking to me now is a cover up. I guess he thinks if he's nice to me, I won't guess. But to me, his too-sweet words set off an alarm."

"Any ideas about a specific woman he might be seeing?"

"No. But I do remember going to his office once unannounced. I was in the neighborhood, and I thought about asking him to eat lunch with me. When I got there, I saw one of the secretary's husbands in my husband's office. The secretary's husband was yelling at Scott. That very day, the secretary quit her job."

"Do you know her name?"

"No."

"How long have you been married to Scott? What about your children?"

"We've been married twenty-six years. We have four kids. They are all gone from home now. The youngest is still in college. The others are finished with school, and they are working. I have one grandbaby."

"Other than his sweet talk, is there any other sign that he may be having an affair?"

"I call him sometimes during the day and his phone is turned off. Occasionally he comes home late. He says he had to work late but he never says why or what he's doing. Also he never wants to make love with me anymore. We haven't had sex in months. He always makes excuses. He did that same thing the last time he was having an affair. We stopped having sex then just like now."

"What's his full name and what does he do for a living?"

"Scott Alexander Kimball. He goes by Scott. He is a financial advisor. He's employed by a fairly large firm. He helps people figure out how to invest their money to make more money. He has his own investments, of course. Also he is a consultant and gives advice to people in other countries who want to invest in the U.S."

Letty nodded. She thought to herself that financial advice was a problem she had never had and probably would never have because there never had been any extra money to invest. Her large Mexican-American family on her father's side and her Native American Tohono O'odham family on her mother's side never had enough left over at the end of each month to even save, much less to invest. Keeping all the kids in the family fed three times a day, or at least twice a day, had always been the number one goal.

"What kind of investments do you and your husband have?"

"Real estate. Stocks and bonds. I'm not really sure. He's always handled all the financial affairs. My job was to take care of the kids and keep our home."

"Where does he consult internationally?"

"He's been to a couple of countries in eastern Europe, Brazil, the Philippines, and Australia. He's done it for years so he's been to a lot of places. Usually he deals with really affluent and politically well-connected people in the countries where he consults."

"Is he in business with anyone?"

"No. He's an employee of the financial company. The consulting he does is independent on the side. He has no other business partners."

"What makes you think he's contemplating divorce and hiding assets?"

"I think he may be hiding assets because of an extra bank account that appeared for only one month in our bank statements. We've always had three accounts: savings, a business account where he deposited his paycheck and also any income he received from other sources such as consulting, and a third household account to use for paying bills like the mortgage, utilities and groceries. The household account was also for home repairs, car repairs and things like that. If I wanted to buy something personal for myself like clothing or for our home like furniture or something for the kids, I went to the business account and transferred those funds to the household account. Then recently a fourth account appeared in the statements but only for one month. Then it was closed."

"You discovered this when reviewing statements?"

"That's right. Normally I don't review the bank statements. My husband has always handled anything having to do with managing money and getting the taxes done. But I've been concerned lately about his behavior so I started checking everything and anything I could think of. That's when I found notice of this fourth account. Mind you, we have other money in other places, too, in investments. I have no idea what this fourth bank account was for."

"Was the amount of money in it substantial?"

"Nearly five hundred thousand dollars. I don't know where the money came from, and I don't know where it went. Normally income would have been deposited in our business account. But Scott hid this new account and the money from me. I went to the file folder where he keeps print-outs of current-year statements. That statement with the fourth account was not in the folder. I'm just afraid he's fallen in love with someone else, and he has divorce on his mind. Why else would he hide money?"

Jen Kimbal's voice became shaky. "I've stood by him for years. I'm the mother of his children. I don't understand this. I mean, if he's fallen in love with some other women, I get that. I don't like it, but I can understand. I'm getting old and frumpy, and I'm not as attractive as I used to be. But cutting me out of assets means I'll be dirt poor for the rest of my life. I have no college degree and no work experience. I married him when I was really young. I was a stay-at-home mom. I have no way to make a real living. I'll end up at a fast food restaurant or one of the big box stores for $10 an hour. He knows that. Why would he do that to me?"

Frumpy? Letty thought Jen Kimball looked great. She was in good shape, had an expensive haircut, streaked blond hair, and well-done makeup and nails. Her clothing was obviously expensive as were her shoes and purse. Also she had the slender, toned look of someone who spent time working out at a health club. She was anything but frumpy.

"Have you discussed any of this with him or asked him any questions?"

"No. I'm afraid to bring it up. If I'm wrong, then it will really make him angry with me. If I'm right, that will make him angry, too, and then he'll know I'm on to him. That's why I came to see you."

"You are right to not confront him in any way or let him know of your suspicions."

"So you'll take this on? I want to know if he's seeing some other woman."

"Yes, consider me hired. We'll surveil him and see if we can catch him with someone else. And we'll try to find out who the other woman is if there is indeed another woman. Meanwhile, you can help me by bringing me information that you already have access to. Let's start with that statement for the account that was only there for one month. Go to your bank and see if they'll print out a statement from that month that shows the account number, the amount, where the deposits came from and where they went. I don't know how much your bank will tell you, but you should at least be able to get a copy of that statement."

Jen pulled a notebook from her purse and began writing down what Letty said.

"There's other information you can compile and give to me that will help me a lot. I need to know your full name, Scott's full name, Social Security numbers for both of you, credit card numbers, cell phone numbers, any social media accounts you have, and past tax returns. Don't bring the originals. Make copies or photocopies and send me the copies in an email. In other words, the more information you can give me, especially financial information, the better it will be for this investigation. Also it would be helpful to have a photo of Scott."

"Okay. It will be good for me to have something to do," Jen said. "But I can't get the bank statements to you immediately. I'm flying out tomorrow to go to a wedding. My big sister's oldest daughter is getting married in Portland. I'll go to the bank when I get back to Tucson next week."

"Fine. Just don't let Scott know you are collecting all this data."

"I'll be careful."

"Miss Valdez?"

"Call me Letty."

"What do you think? Is there any chance something else might be going on? Could I be wrong about an affair and hiding money?"

"It's possible," Letty said. "His behavior is suspicious, but it's just too soon to say what is behind it."

"I guess I'll go home and get started collecting some of this information. Call me if you learn anything. Here's my mobile number," Jen handed Letty a small piece of paper with a phone number on it.

Jen Kimball stood and thrust out her hand.

Letty took it, and they shook hands.

"I'll do my best to find out as much as possible," Letty said.

"That's good. That will help me decide what to do next."

"Do you have an attorney?"

"We have a family attorney. He's a friend of Scott's. They've been pals for years."

"Then consider hiring an attorney to represent only you and your interests. You need someone who will prioritize you, not Scott. I can recommend a good attorney."

Letty was thinking of Jessica Cameron, smart as a whip, blonde, and very attractive. Jessica with her power suits, her pearls, and her high heels had a cheerful and very competitive nature. Jessica had the instincts of a tiger. Go for the throat was Jessica's idea of how to play the game. Letty was glad that Jessica had always been on her side. Jessica would be on Jen Kimball's side, too, and get the best deal for Jen if a divorce was in Jen's future.

"Actually I have a personal friend who is an attorney. I've already called him."

Letty nodded. "Good. Someone you trust is good."

Jen Kimball said her goodbyes and left the office. She wasn't crying, and she seemed more resolute and ready to take on whatever came next.

Letty turned back to her computer and opened a new screen. She googled the Arizona Secretary of State Trade Names and Trade Marks website. She clicked on Trade Names and Trade Marks and then on Entity Search. She typed in Scott Kimball and nothing came up. She tried various forms of Kimball's name and hit pay dirt when she searched under the S. Alex Kimball. There she found a registration for a company registered to Kimball along with Gordon Miller. They were owners of a company registered as SG Enterprises. The nature of the business listed with the state Trade Names site was rather vague. But it seemed to be in the ballpark of financial management, the same line of work that Scott Kimball was in. Letty googled the company name. She found only a one-page website associated with the business name. The website mentioned "investments management." The nature of those investments was not explained. The term "under construction" seemed to well describe this sketchy website.

Hmmm, Letty thought. So Jen's husband Scott Kimball was business partners with someone named Gordon Miller. Letty guessed that Jen Kimball didn't know about the state Trade Names site and didn't know to search to see if her husband had a business partner. No doubt Scott Kimball was counting on her not knowing about the site and not knowing what he was up to, just as he counted on her not looking too closely at their joint bank statements.

She needed to know more about Gordon Miller. She googled his name and found that he was a Tucson real estate developer who had moved to Tucson about twenty years ago from the Chicago area. He was married to a working real estate agent named Kellie Miller, but she worked for a different company, not Gordon's. Could Kellie be the one that Scott Kimball was seeing? Letty sighed. It seemed risky to the point of stupidity to be having an affair with your business partner's wife. But that kind of thing happened all the time. She needed to know more.

Letty picked up her phone and called Marv Iverson. Letty considered Marv one of the few angels in her life. When she returned from Iraq, she spent an extended time period with her grandmother on the O'odham reservation. When Letty thought she was ready to go back into the world and to make a living for her younger brothers and sister, she answered an ad placed by Marv. "Private Investigator seeks assistant. Will train. Veterans preferred." Letty answered, Marv hired her and trained her and eventually, she became a licensed private investigator. A couple of years after she became licensed, she took over Marv's firm so he could retire. He was Letty's gruff, grumpy, foul-mouthed angel. She owed him everything.

Retirement didn't suit Marv well. Occasionally he would get sick and tired of watching sports on cable TV for hours on end: baseball, soccer, basketball, football, hockey, even cricket which he complained about bitterly as a game that made absolutely no sense. If it was a sport, Marv watched it. When he got too tired of watching television sports, Letty would give him a job to do. He told her once that her jobs kept him from dying of boredom.

"Hi, Letty," Marv answered on the second ring.

"How are you?"

"My arthritis is killing me. My blood pressure is too high. My blood sugar is too high. My doctor expects me to go to the gym and exercise eighteen hours every day."

Letty laughed. "You need to get out more. Have you considered getting a dog and taking it for walks?"

"Oh, please. I don't need a dog. I had a dog, and the fucker died on me."

"When was this? How old was the dog?"

"He died maybe ten years ago. He was only sixteen years old."

"Sixteen is really old for a dog, Marv."

"Whatever. I'm not going to go through that again. Why are you calling me anyway?"

"How about doing a job for me?"

"What is it? Finding dead bodies?"

"No. Live bodies, probably naked, engaged in some extramarital hanky-panky of a sexual nature."

He laughed. "Do I get to watch?"

"First you have to catch them at it."

"Sounds like fun. I'll bring my camera. Give me the details."

Letty told him about her meeting with Jen Kimball and then later, finding that her husband Scott had a business partner.

"Keep in mind, Marv, that Kimball may be quick to suspect that he's being watched. If he actually is having an affair, he's probably a little paranoid and will be wary. I don't have any good ideas at this point for potential lovers. The couple has a lot of friends, there's the secretary in the office where Kimball works, and there's a woman named Kellie Miller. She's the wife of Scott Kimball's business partner, Gordon Miller. Scott Kimball's wife did not suggest any names though she did mention a former secretary as a possibility. Interestingly, she didn't know about her husband's business relationship with Gordon Miller either. I'll let you know if I dig up a decent prospect for the hanky panky partner. Meanwhile, you watch Scott and see if he's up to anything. You may be able to identify his lover before I do."

"Okay, Letty, I'll get started right away."

"I'll email you photos of everyone so you'll be able to recognize them."

"Okay."

"You need a dog."

"Mind your own business."

Letty was chuckling when Marv disconnected.

CHAPTER 5

After talking to Marv, Letty thought about her interaction with Jennifer Kimball. It seemed that Jen Kimball was more interested in protecting her financial future than the prospect of losing a husband. That told Letty something about where Jen's real concern lay. She wanted to maintain a lifestyle, if not a marriage. Letty wondered what it would be like to be married to someone for twenty-six years. She couldn't imagine that. In fact, she couldn't imagine being married at all. She couldn't even imagine having a lover. Not after Iraq. Not after losing Chava in Iraq. Letty figured that part of her life was over. She figured she'd lost her chance at ever having that kind of happiness.

Not that she hadn't had an opportunity recently for a little fun on the side. When Interpol director Jean-Pierre Laurent came to Tucson to visit Letty's colleague Zhou LiangWei, Laurent invited Letty to dinner and to bed. He made it clear that he wanted to spend the night with her and make love to her. Letty found him attractive, but he was married. She didn't care to get mixed up in a family drama — assuming there would be one. The French were said to be more tolerant of wayward spouses. Laurent's wife could very well be spending time with another man while her husband was traveling. Not for Letty, though. She wouldn't settle for one night with a visiting and very married Frenchman, no matter how attractive she found him.

There was another reason, too. She had this impression that Laurent, like so many Europeans, was enamored with Native Americans. She didn't want to be just a notch on his belt so he could go home and say he'd made it with an American Indian. Kissing Laurent, though, make her realize that she missed the physical as well as the emotional aspect of male companionship. She hadn't allowed herself to think about that until Laurent appeared a few months ago.

Dan Ennis came into her thoughts. Again. Letty's brother Will and Clarice called him Dr. Dan when they talked about him. But when they spoke directly to him, they always called him Dan because that's what he asked them to do. He was the doctor that had taken care of Letty after she had been attacked, beaten and injured so badly on her last case. Three months later when she was out jogging, Letty's dog Teddy found Dan up in a tree trying to rescue a cat. Teddy alerted her to his presence. Dan came down from the tree, and their conversation led to Dan coming over for breakfast that morning. He had been back to her home several times since then.

Much to her consternation, Letty had to admit to herself that she liked Dan Ennis. She liked him a lot. He was smart and interesting and really funny. He made her laugh. That was a strange experience for Letty. Most of her life she hadn't laughed much, especially since Iraq. Letty didn't know what to think about the fact that she noticed his looks. He was tall like Letty, he had wavy dark hair, and these beautiful blue-green eyes. Best of all, Dan had this lopsided grin that was really....she couldn't think of a word. She felt warm when she thought of him. Oh dear. She felt uncomfortable that she felt warm when she thought of him.

Letty remembered that first breakfast at her home. The four of them, including her brother Will and Clarice, shared a meal together on Letty's back porch.

Clarice and Will kept up a steady stream of questions, and Dan answered cheerfully. Letty sat and listened.

"So we haven't heard of you for a while, Dan," Will said, "What have you been doing?"

Dan turned to Letty and said, "I'm normally in the Emergency Department at Tucson Medical. That's when I was your attending physician." Letty knew this because he had told her as much when he first came down from the tree where Teddy found him. Dan turned back to Will and said, "But I've been in Puerto Rico for a gig the past six weeks or so."

"What do you mean 'gig?'" Clarice asked.

"I do volunteer doctoring for different groups. I had already arranged to go to Puerto Rico when I was hired at TMC so they let me fulfill my promise. I was there to provide care for people in places on the island hit especially hard by Hurricane Maria. We had a mobile unit. An EMT named Herman and I traveled around, mostly in the interior mountainous regions. I treated some injuries. Also we dealt a lot with chronic problems that weren't getting treated. You know, like heart disease and diabetes. I also vaccinated a lot of kids and adults, too, mainly for tetanus. I delivered a couple of babies, too."

Letty noticed two things. Dan said 'Herman' with the correct Spanish pronunciation. Also she noticed that Dan had taken the eggs and fruit and biscuits but passed up the bacon. Later she would learn that he was a vegetarian. "I don't want to eat anything that has a mom," Dan explained to her. He grinned when he said it as if he were joking, but Letty knew he was serious. He smiled a lot even when serious. She noticed a third thing. Dan Ennis was a really attractive man.

"I learned some Spanish in Puerto Rico," Dan looked at Letty again. "I have you to thank for getting me started. When you were in the ER, you taught me my first two Spanish words."

"I did? What did I teach you?" Letty asked. She still had trouble remembering her trip to the emergency room.

"'Pendejo' and 'pinche,'" he said with a grin.

"Oh, no! Did I call you a pendejo?" She was appalled and embarrassed.

"No," Dan laughed. "You called that guy who beat you up a pendejo."

"Well, he *is* a pendejo. He's in prison now."

"Where else have you been?" Clarice asked.

"I worked for Doctors Without Borders off and on for about four years. I went to several countries." He listed off Asian and African countries: Thailand, Bangladesh, India, Tajikistan, Uganda, Nigeria, South Africa. "I haven't made it to South America yet."

"Was this after you were in the Army?" Clarice asked.

"You were in the Army?" Letty broke in. She was intrigued but at the same time, hesitant to hear more. She frowned.

"Yes, ma'am. I did a tour in Iraq, and then I went to Afghanistan next. I was a battalion surgeon. I did a lot of emergency trauma work and regular general practice, too."

Letty didn't ask any more questions. Visions of field hospitals in Iraq came unwanted into her head. She could hear the sound MEDI-VAC helicopters approaching and leaving. Then came the unwanted visions of horribly wounded soldiers, some with amputated limbs and or a skull smashed in. Doctors with masks on their faces and blood all over their scrubs and on the floor seemed the norm. She squeezed her eyes shut and tried to forget.

"Dan came here when you were hurt," Will explained. "He told us then that he outranked you."

"Hey," Dan said. "You asked me." There was that lop-sided grin again.

"You came here to the house?" Letty was really uncomfortable now. She couldn't remember him at all. And why did he call her 'ma'am'? He was a doctor. She knew for a fact that his rank was way higher than hers.

Dan noticed her discomfort. "Don't worry. You remembered me at the river and in the ambulance. Someday you'll remember everything."

She could tell he was trying to reassure her.

Later when he was gone, Letty asked Will and Clarice about him. She found out that Dan intended on keeping her one night in the hospital for observation, but she had begged him to allow her to go home.

"You *really* didn't want to stay overnight in the hospital. You said 'please' three times." Will said.

"Doctor Dan came here to our house for a brief time, examined you, listened to your heart and lungs, and he looked in your eyes.

He asked you some questions. And he gave you an injection so you could sleep. He gave me some pills for pain to give you the next day."

"Ah," Letty said. "So he's the one who made you Pill Queen." She felt vaguely uncomfortable that Dan had been in her bedroom. It seemed so intimate. Or was it just him that made her feel intimate. Or something. She frowned. Dan made her feel confused.

"Right," Clarice grinned. "I was responsible for your pain medication. He gave us instructions on how to take care of you, what to feed you and all that."

"When you complained to him about the injection," Will added, "Dr. Dan told you to go to sleep. He said, 'That's an order, Corporal.' And you said, "Yes, sir. Thank you, sir.'"

It was clear to Letty that Will and Clarice were enjoying their memories of this event.

"I asked him his rank, and he said he was a captain," Clarice added. "That's when he said he outranked you."

Letty sighed. "I don't remember any of this."

It was clear that Will and Clarice liked him a lot.

The next time she went to her office, she did a background check on Dan Ennis. She found that he was born and grew up in Minneapolis, he played on winning soccer teams in both high school and college, and he went to college and medical school at the University of Minnesota. He joined the U.S. Army and, just as he'd said, he had served in both Iraq and Afghanistan. There were no outstanding warrants for his arrest, no criminal record at all, just commendations from the Army for his service. If he'd stayed in, he would have been promoted to a higher rank, probably a major.

After that, she couldn't find much about him. There were occasional hometown news stories about his different trips with Doctors Without Borders. She couldn't find him on any of the major social media venues. She did find that Dan and three other doctors moderated a blog in which they wrote exclusively about experiences in Doctors Without Borders. The readers who commented all seemed to be volunteers and workers for the same organization, and most of them seemed to know Dan personally. The on-line conversations were often about how to treat different medical issues, especially when equipment and medicines were in short supply. Then she found a notice on the Tucson Medical Center's website announcing that he had been hired as an emergency physician. He started his job there late last September, only a couple of weeks before he came upon Letty and Zhou on the Rillito River Trail.

More than anything, Letty was very curious about Dan Ennis. Most of all, she wanted to know after all he had seen and done as an Army doctor, how could he be so cheerful? Letty found cheerfulness to be a mysterious state that was rather unattainable. And yet Dan always seemed upbeat and happy. She wanted to ask him about it.

Just a couple of mornings earlier, Letty had followed Dan out after breakfast.

"Want a ride? You can put your bicycle in the back of my pickup."

"Sure," Dan said. He hoisted the bike into Letty's little Nissan pickup and got into the cab of the truck. Letty was already behind the wheel.

"I want to thank you, Letty," Dan said.

"For what?"

"For inviting me to eat breakfast with your family," Dan hesitated. "I had to eat alone a lot when I was young, especially breakfast. I was often lonely. I had a best friend, and I went to his house frequently for supper. His mom kind of took me in. Then when I went off to college and after that, I got used to eating in dorm cafeterias and then later, the Army's chow halls, and also with the Doctors Without Borders group. I actually liked the noise and camaraderie even though the food wasn't all that great most of the time. When I came to Tucson, I only knew a couple of people, and so I've been eating alone again. Now it seems strange for me to be alone, especially at breakfast. It reminds me too much of when I was a kid. So I really enjoy eating with you and Will and Clarice and with your dogs, too."

"Yes," Letty nodded. "Teddy and Millie love eating with you, too. I notice how bits of your food somehow end up falling off your plate and directly into their mouths."

Dan grinned. "They are hard to resist. They look at me with those big, soft eyes."

"And they are trying to tell you that they are starving and no one ever feeds them? Looks to me like they have you pegged as an easy mark."

"You want me to stop giving them anything?"

"No, it's okay. Just not too much, especially for Millie. She can't run because of her damaged front leg so she doesn't get the exercise she needs. She could turn into a little gordita if she gets too many treats."

"Gordita? That means chubby?"

"Right. Gordita is a chubby little girl."

"What happened to her leg?"

"She was stolen from a family in El Paso, Texas, and used for bait in a dog-fighting operation. Getting chewed up caused major damage to her tendons and ligaments."

"Pobrecita."

"Very good, Dan," Letty smiled. "You said 'poor, little girl.' So anyway, about breakfast, you have a standing invitation then. Come anytime."

Dan looked pleased. "Thank you so much."

"By the way, we're planning a surprise birthday party for Will on Saturday. He's going to be nineteen. Want to come?"

"Oh, I'd be delighted. What should I bring?"

"Whatever you want. Maybe something to eat? Just don't bring any booze. There will be a bunch of minors here, and we don't want to be giving them alcohol. Show up around seven."

At that, they fell into a comfortable silence. Letty dropped Dan off at the Tucson Medical Center.

Remembering this interaction, Letty liked it that Dan seemed very open about himself. She felt that familiar warm feeling she had come to associate with him. She wondered why he had been alone so often when growing up. Eating in a noisy cafeteria probably did seem like a relief for a kid who ate alone and in silence when he was young. There's probably a story there, she thought to herself.

* * *

The end of the work day had come, and the sun was lowering in the west. The sky had turned those gorgeous colors that photographers and painters so loved about the Sonoran Desert. She could see palm trees standing tall against the gold and pink sky. Letty decided to head home.

Twenty minutes later, she found her little brother Will at the kitchen stove. Will wasn't really "little." He was six feet three inches tall, taller than Letty, and a classic example of an O'odham man. He'd grown his hair out and wore it in a short pony tail. His skin, like Letty's, was a rich reddish brown. He was a good-looking kid, Letty thought. No matter how old he got, though, Letty would always think of him as her baby brother. She loved him a lot. And she had to admit to herself that Will was transforming into quite a good cook under his girlfriend Clarice's tutelage.

"Where's Clarice?"

"Taking a shower. I think that girl loves to be in the water." He paused, "That's okay. She tries not to use too much since I gave her the 'we live in a desert' talk. And she smells good all the time so I'm not complaining." He laughed.

The two dogs appeared at that moment, both wagging their tails enthusiastically at the sight of their beloved alpha who had been gone all day.

Letty leaned down to pet them: Millie the runt pit bull first, and then Teddy the black Labrador. Millie wiggled joyously in a little circle at Letty's feet. Teddy stood alert, tail wagging slowly back and forth. She reached for a dog biscuit for both of them.

"Sit," she said firmly.

Both dogs sat promptly, and both dogs received a dog biscuit.

"So, Will, what do you want to do to celebrate your birthday?"

"Not sure. My boss is making me work late. I won't be home until after seven."

Letty tried her best to not grin. She had asked his boss at the bicycle shop to delay Will at work so she and Clarice could finish hanging lights in the back yard, set up tables for food and drinks, and to start receiving visitors.

"Well, maybe we can go out to eat or something."

Will nodded and put his attention back to the stir-fry on the kitchen stove.

Again Letty thought about Dan and his cheerfulness. Will had always been a cheerful kid like Dan despite the Ramone family poverty, his father's death in a car accident, and his mother's abandonment of him and his older twin brother and sister, Eduardo and Elena. Will seemed to be just cheerful by nature. Maybe Dan was like that, too. All that blood and those severed limbs couldn't get a cheerful person down. She'd read once that psychologists call that a "resilient personality." She shook her head. She just didn't understand how that was even possible.

Her thoughts wandered back to the encounter she'd had at the homeless camp with Kenny Wilson and Rigo. Some people were cheerful, and many others were angry all the time. Rigo fell in the angry category. There were plenty of vets like him. And then there was sadness. Even more vets fell in the sad category. That was Al, Frankie's big brother. Letty saw herself that way, too. Vulnerable always to sadness. Now Al had Lil to keep him happy, to make love to him, and to drive away the war demons. Lucky bastard. I wonder what it would be like to have that kind of comfort and love, she thought.

Dan Ennis appeared in her thoughts. Again. Oh god. She turned to the dogs to distract herself.

"Let's go outside, you two. Call me when supper is ready. I'm starving."

"Won't be long," Will said.

CHAPTER 6

On Saturday morning, Dan Ennis appeared early at Letty's house to eat breakfast. Letty opened the door and welcomed him in.

"I brought some melon. It's cut up and ready to eat."

"Thanks. We all love melon."

The four of them ate breakfast. As usual, Millie and Teddy managed to position themselves as close to Dan as possible in case he "accidentally" dropped something.

As soon as they'd finished, Letty said, "I have to go to my office for a while. Dan, are you on your bike again? Want a ride?"

"Sure. Take me home, though. I don't have to work today."

He loaded his bike into her truck and Letty took off toward his home.

After a couple of blocks, Letty said, "Dan, I was wondering if you could help Clarice and me hang some lights this afternoon. We're putting up lights in the backyard for the party."

Dan's eyes blue-green eyes sparkled. "You bet. Do you need any tools?"

Beautiful blue-green eyes, Letty thought to herself. She tried not to notice.

"Nope, just show up mid-afternoon. Will has to work until seven. I asked his boss to keep him late."

Dan grinned. "Count me in."

Letty dropped him off and headed for her office. She turned on her computer and checked the local news and police reports.

She sat in her chair for a while and thought about Jen Kimball and her problem. It was Letty's task to find, first, if her husband had a lover, and second, if he had hidden financial resources. Finding a lover was the easiest task. If Letty could prove that, then Jen would have a strong case in divorce court to get a good settlement.

The second task was much more difficult. There was a multitude of ways to hide money, and not that difficult for people to successfully hide money and other kinds of assets. Often records had to be subpoenaed and even then, that didn't always turn up everything. Money could be hidden offshore. Scott Kimball could have a bank account in a foreign country where he'd done consulting.

That brought Letty's lawyer friend, Jessica Cameron, to mind again. She and Letty had worked together on several cases now. Jessica was smart and clever and knew how to make things happen. She was determined and stubborn, too, and she didn't let go easily. Jessica kept Letty on retainer for the occasional job. This meant Letty had a regular source of income though not large. Usually her job was serving papers to people Jessica was suing. This had made Letty rather unpopular in certain circles because it meant those persons had to show up in court and face Jessica's questioning. But Letty's effectiveness made her very well-regarded by Jessica. Letty believed that if there were assets or money hidden, Jessica could find them.

Too bad Jen Kimball had a lawyer in mind already. Letty wondered who the lawyer might be. Thinking about Jen Kimball brought her back to the problem at hand.

This moving of five hundred thousand dollars in and out of a Kimball bank account was intriguing. What was Scott Kimball doing? Moving money to the U.S. from abroad and then transferring it quickly to a new project? That brought Gordon Miller to mind.

Letty made a note to call Gordon Miller's office on Monday morning and try to get an appointment with him. She'd probably have to pretend to be interested in real estate. But once in his presence, she could feel him out about this new company he'd formed with Scott Kimball. She'd have to be careful to not set off alarms that might lead to hiding money more effectively.

Letty headed home just in time to eat a quick lunch with Clarice. Will had already gone to work. Dan showed up not long after. The day was warm for January, in the low-seventies, and a cloudless and intensely blue sky made it a great day for being outside and for having a party.

Letty and Clarice put Dan to work helping them string lights along the perimeter of Letty's back yard. They set up a fire ring of galvanized metal on one side of the yard and a couple of long tables for food on the other. They sent Dan to haul in mesquite logs from the back of Clarice's car.

Finished with that, they assigned him to help them string more lights across an open area for dancing. He worked on that for a little while then he pulled off his long-sleeve t-shirt. He had on a dark blue tank top underneath.

Letty and Clarice were resting now on a bench watching Dan.

Clarice turned to Letty. "Whoa. He's cute, isn't he, Letty?"

"Yeah."

"He's in good shape."

"Yeah."

Dan turned and looked at them with a question on his face. Why are you looking at me?

Letty decided to distract him. She looked up at him and said, "Aren't you going to get cold, white man?" She smiled.

"White man?" Dan teased back, mock shock in his voice. "Well, Indian woman, no, I'm not cold."

"It's late January. I bet the temperature is just in the low seventies. And you're in a tank top."

"It's downright hot compared to Januarys where I grew up."

"Oh, yeah. I forgot," Letty said. "You're from Minnesota."

Dan paused, cocked his head, and said, "And how do you know that, Ms. Private Investigator Valdez? I never told you that."

Oh damn. Caught. Letty felt her face growing warm. She shrugged her shoulders innocently.

"You did a background check on me, didn't you?" He was grinning ear-to-ear now.

"Maybe."

"Maybe?" he chuckled. "Yes, definitely. Not maybe. Well, I'm honored."

"Honored?"

Clarice was trying to smother her giggles.

"It shows you're interested in me, Ms. Valdez." He had that lopsided grin on his face.

Letty didn't know what to say to that so she said nothing. She looked down at her boots.

Clarice rescued her. "Okay, Dan. I think we're done now. Stop embarrassing Letty and go home. Come back around seven. Be prepared to dance."

Dan came and knelt in front of Letty. "I'm sorry, Letty. I didn't mean to embarrass you. Will you forgive me? Please."

If anything, this left Letty even more embarrassed.

She nodded. "I forgive you." She avoided looking at him directly.

Dan leaned forward and kissed Letty on her cheek.

"See you this evening."

Dan left with a smile on his face. They could hear him singing as he went off on his bicycle.

"He's flirting with you, Letty," Clarice grinned.

Letty grimaced.

"Dan is so perfect for you."

Letty groaned. "I'm going to stop talking. I just get into trouble when I talk."

* * *

Party guests began arriving before seven. Clarice and Letty had already filled the tables with food, soft drinks, punch and juice. The guests started eating immediately. Clarice put on some music, and a couple of people began to dance. Letty built a small fire in the metal fire ring. A few guests gathered around the ring and chatted. Millie and Teddy wandered happily among the guests. The two dogs received pets, ear rubs, baby talk, and a few treats everywhere they went.

Probably three quarters of the party goers were friends of Will and Clarice's from college classes, from work and from their bicycle club. Letty invited her friends Seri, Zhou and Jade, and a handful of other people, including Frankie Miranda, his brother Al and his girlfriend Lil. Dan arrived, too. Letty also made a point of inviting Elena, her little sister and twin of brother Eduardo. Elena was very involved in her studies at the University of Arizona and her job in a lab there. They didn't see Elena often. But she promised to make time to be there for Will. Elena's twin brother Eduardo was staying out on the reservation with his girl Esperanza. Eduardo worried constantly about Esperanza's undocumented status so they didn't come to town unless there was an emergency. If Esperanza were caught by Border Patrol, she'd be deported. Eduardo couldn't bear the thought of that. Esperanza was a young woman from southern Mexico whom he'd rescued when she was crossing the desert hoping to find a job in America. They fell in love. They were planning on a big wedding as soon as they could get legal status for her.

Clarice went to fetch Will. When he walked in the backyard, everyone cheered and yelled, "Happy Birthday!" Will was caught off guard. Shock on his face was quickly replaced with complete delight. Clarice disappeared and returned with an expensive racing bike.

"We all chipped in and got this for you. You can ride it in the Tour de France someday," she said.

Will kissed Clarice, thanked everyone, shook hands and gave hugs, and then spent a long time with his bicycling friends inspecting the beautiful, high-tech new bike. They took turns riding it slowly around the backyard.

"Wow, wow, wow!" was all he could say. "This is so awesome."

Dan approached and said, "Here's a little something for you." He handed Will an envelope. Inside were season tickets to University of Arizona basketball games for the current year and the next year's season.

"Dan, this is great. I have never been able to afford these tickets so…well…thanks, Dan." Will gave Dan a hug.

Dan went up on the porch and sat with Zhou and Jade and their baby Ben Ben who was wrapped up warmly against the chilly evening.

Not long after, Elena showed up. She made the rounds hugging and kissing everyone she knew and even some she didn't know. Elena had always been a lot more self-confident than any of her siblings. She was a pretty girl, not as tall as Letty, but with the same black hair and rusty red-brown skin. Her face was a little rounder than Letty's angular features, giving Elena a softer, sweet look. She gave Letty a big hug.

"Letty, I've missed you. I'm sorry about being so scarce. I've had so much to do with school and all." She pulled Letty aside. "I have a message for you."

"What's the message? And from whom?

"My professor, the man who runs our lab, would like to talk with you," she said in a low voice. "His name is Dr. Steven Anselm. His area of expertise is water quality. He's in the chemistry department. Recently a friend of his was murdered up in the Rincon Mountains somewhere. The murdered guy was a volunteer who hiked up to the springs there to determine flow and quality issues. He was found shot to death."

"I think I heard about this."

"Dr. Anselm says the police aren't making any progress on the case. They seem to think it was a random shooting, maybe even an accident when some moron was shooting off his gun for fun. Dr. Anselm doesn't agree. He wants to see if you'd be interested in looking into this. He said he has money to hire you."

"Okay, want me to come to your lab?"

"No, he wants to meet somewhere where he won't be recognized easily. He doesn't want anyone to know he's hiring a private investigator."

"Okay, I'll call him on Monday, and we'll set up an appointment. Maybe we can meet in south Tucson at a Mexican restaurant or something? His faculty colleagues and students are less likely to go there, especially on a week day."

"Okay. Thanks, Letty." Elena moved toward a chair and plopped down. Dan was sitting nearby as was Frankie Miranda.

"Letty," Frankie said. "I'd like to come by your office for a few minutes before I go back to Nogales. Would that be okay?"

"Of course. Call first and make sure I'm there."

Frankie nodded.

The music changed to a slow ballad. Zhou and Jade rose.

"I want to dance with my wife, Letty. Will you hold Baby Ben Ben?

"Sure." Letty took the baby who was fast asleep. He settled into Letty's arms.

Letty turned back to Elena.

"How are you doing these days?"

"School's going well. Other than that, I have a broken heart." She stuck out her lower lip.

"Something happen to your boyfriend?"

"Yeah, I had to dump him. I went off for one week to a conference in Washington, D.C. with our lab team. One week. When I came home, I found he's taken up with this Goth girl groupie. I confronted him about it, and you know what he said?"

"No. No idea."

"If you can't be with the one you love, then love the one you're with."

Dan frowned. He'd been listening. "I know that song. That was mean of him to say that to you."

Elena turned to Dan. "Yeah, that's what I thought."

"Elena, this is Dan. My sister Elena, Dan. And that's Frankie. He's in our family through marriage by way of Uncle Miguel."

"I had to break up with my girlfriend, too. She was cheating on me," Frankie said. "I sympathize."

"So he and I parted company," Elena continued. "I've had it with men."

Letty said, "Elena, you're only twenty. It's too soon to give up on men." She glanced up and saw that Dan was looking at her, his head cocked and a little smile on his face.

Just at that moment, someone put on some music, Aretha Franklin singing "Freeway of Love."

Letty's close friend, university librarian Seri Durand, and Clarice came over and pulled Dan out to the clear area in the yard to dance.

"Watch me. Watch my feet," Clarice said to Dan and Seri. "Single step, single step, double double steps," Letty could hear Clarice guiding them. Seri and Dan both caught on quickly. They formed into a three-person line and began dancing the Dougie together. Everyone stopped to watch and cheer when they finished at the close of Aretha's song.

Letty didn't have the nerve to try anything like that. She'd rather someone try to break her arm. She would know what to do with that kind of aggression. She'd use her martial arts skills and fight back. Yet she did enjoy watching them dance. Or more accurately, she enjoyed watching Dan. Tall, lanky, and with smooth moves, he was grinning the entire time they were dancing. Again, that question came to her mind. Why did he seem so happy?

Seri sat down next to Letty. Seri was Letty's closest friend in the world. She had hired Letty on an earlier case, and Letty ended up saving Seri's life.

"Dan's good, isn't he?" Seri's face was pink from the exertion of dancing.

"Yes."

"And he's smart and fun and really good-looking, too."

Letty said nothing.

"I have a friend who works at Tucson Medical Center. She says all the women there — the nurses, surgical techs, doctors, women in administration — all of them are dying of curiosity about Dan. Finally, she told me that one of the male doctors asked him if he's seeing anyone. Dan told the other doctor that he has a woman he's interested in, and he's working hard to get her interested in him, too. Now, who do you supposed that woman might be?" Seri poked Letty.

Letty frowned. "I have no idea."

Seri sighed impatiently. "Come on, Letty."

"What?" Letty frowned.

"Seems to me you've constructed your life so that you know how to break a man's neck with your gong fu skills, but you don't know what to do if you like a man and you want to get to know him."

"Seri, I don't know if I like him or not."

"Liar. Yes, you do, too, know if you like him or not. I can see the way you look at him."

"Oh, gosh. Is it that obvious?"

"Uh-huh. That's what I thought. And do you see how he looks at *you*?"

"No. What do you mean?"

"He looks like you've bewitched him. He can't keep his eyes off you."

Letty waved her hand dismissively.

"If he's so bewitched, then why hasn't he asked me out?"

"Letty, you can be intimidating. Dan probably can't tell if you are interested in him or not. Show him some interest, girl. Don't be so old-fashioned. This is the twenty-first century. You ask *him* out."

"Seri, stop. You're embarrassing me."

"Oh, get over yourself. You are twenty-nine years old. You're still young. But you are trying so hard to turn yourself into a miserable, lonely celibate who works all the time and never has any fun. Dan looks like he'd be fun and good for a cuddle, too."

Letty hung her head. Why did she suddenly feel like she was fifteen-years old suffering from her first crush. A cuddle? Oh my god.

"I have to go home now. Busy day tomorrow. Go ask him out." Seri snickered mischievously.

"Stop teasing me, Seri." Letty had a pained look on her face.

Seri leaned over and whispered, "Give yourself the gift of a little happiness, Letty. After all you've been through, you deserve it. Dan could be that gift." Before Letty could respond, Seri turned away. She called out and waved goodbye to everyone.

Letty sat alone. Zhou and Jade returned and took little Ben Ben back into their care.

The music changed to a new track. This time it was Beyoncé singing a slow ballad, "At Last."

Dan approached Letty. He smiled and held out his hand, "May I have this dance, Investigator Valdez?"

"I'm sorry, Dr. Ennis, I don't know how to dance."

"I'll show you. Come on. Please."

Please? Letty couldn't say no to his "please." She gave him her hand, and he led her to an open space near where the others were dancing. He pulled her close and whispered, "Just follow me."

She did as he said, and she found suddenly that dancing wasn't so difficult after all. She was acutely aware of how close Dan was to her as they danced. He smelled good.

Yikes, she thought to herself. How did I get into this? And how do I get out? She had this sudden urge to run away. Dan pulled her closer. After the music stopped, Dan led her back to her chair. He thanked her then he went off again to stand around the fire and chat with Will's friends.

The party was winding down when her brother Will approached Letty and pulled her to her feet.

"Go ask him out," he whispered. Clarice stepped forward to stand next to Will.

"What? Ask who out? Out? What do you mean?"

"Come on, Letty," Will said. "You can't fool us. You like him. Dan Ennis is totally cool."

"And he's fun. And he was kind to you when you were hurt," added Clarice.

"We can tell you really like him. It's obvious that he likes you. We think you should ask him out," Will added.

Letty sighed. "I wouldn't know what to say."

"We'll help you. Come on."

Okay. Okay. Okay. Letty wanted to, but she felt very nervous. She had so little experience with men. Letty reluctantly approached Dan. Clarice and Will followed and stood close behind her.

"Dan," Letty said.

Dan smiled, "Yes."

"Uh….well…uh….uh," she looked down at her feet.

Dan looked at Will and Clarice. He shrugged in confusion.

"Letty wants to ask you something," Will said. He poked Letty in her back.

"Stop it, Will." Letty looked into Dan's eyes, silently pleading for help.

"Come on with me. Let's go over there by ourselves." Dan took Letty's hand and led her away from the party to stand together under the big mesquite tree.

"You want to ask me something?"

"Yes…uh…hmmm….Dan… well….uh," Letty radiated distress. She squared her shoulders, put her hands on her hips and looked directly at him. She quickly dropped her hands to her side, realizing that she probably looked like she was going to chew him out rather than ask him out.

"All I know is how to patch up wounded soldiers and how to be a private investigator, and I have to deal with those two," she gestured behind her to Will and Clarice. "I don't know anything about dating or male-female stuff. The only boyfriend I ever had got blown up by an IED. Anyway, he was nothing like you. I mean you are so different from any man I've ever known." She frowned, clearly annoyed with herself. "I'm not making any sense."

Dan smiled and nodded. "Take your time."

"Okay. I'll just spit it out. I want to spend time with you because I like you, but I don't know how to make that happen."

"I like you, Letty, and I want to spend time with you, too," Dan said. "Here's what we'll do. I'll help you to ask me out this time. Then the next time, it will be my turn, and I'll ask you out. Then it will be your turn, and it will be easier the second time. Then it will be my turn. Then after a while, we'll just stop taking turns and decide together. Okay?"

"Okay." She liked the idea of several times together.

"Here's what you say to me. 'Dan, I like you, and I want to spend time with you.' Oh, but you already said that so you are half way there, aren't you?"

"Yes, halfway there."

"Now you say to me, 'How about if we go to the basketball game Tuesday evening with Will and Clarice?'"

Letty repeated what he said.

"That's a great idea, Letty," Dan said. "I already have season tickets. I'll bring the tickets, and you get the popcorn."

"Okay." Letty breathed a sigh of relief.

"I'll tell Will and Clarice that we're suggesting a double date."

"Okay."

"Now that wasn't so hard, was it?"

Letty was smiling now. "You made it easy, Dan."

He took her hand. "Okay, let's go tell your two helicopter-hovering, nosey teenagers that you have a date with me."

They rejoined the group. Dan didn't let go of Letty's hand.

Dan looked at Will in the eyes and said, "You love your big sister, don't you?"

"Yes, I love her a lot. I owe her a lot, too."

"Then you aren't going to tease her when I tell you that she has asked me out on a date for next Tuesday evening. Right?"

Will and Clarice glanced at each other.

"No, I won't tease her." Will looked seriously at Letty. "Big Sister, I do love you a lot. I'd do anything for you. I guess I've been teasing you too much."

"Letty and I would like to know if you and Clarice want to make it a double date. We're going to the Arizona Wildcats basketball game Tuesday. You have your own season tickets now. Want to join us?"

Will whooped, and Clarice started jumping up and down and clapping her hands.

"Okay then. It's settled. Next Tuesday. Basketball. I have to go now because I need some sleep. I have to be in the ER early tomorrow. Happy birthday, Will."

Will gave Dan a hug. Clarice gave Dan a hug.

Dan turned to Letty, put his arm around her shoulders and kissed her on the cheek. "Good job, Letty. See you Tuesday."

Good job? Letty thought. He did everything and made it easy for her. Also he shut down Will's teasing before it got started, and he did so in a really nice way.

Al, Lil and Frankie came to say good-bye.

"Thank you for everything, Letty," Al said, "Life is better today than a week ago, and that's because you made it so. If there's anything I can do for you, let me know."

"I'm so glad things are getting better for you, Al."

"See you next week, Letty," Frankie reminded her.

Lil bent her head toward Letty and said in a low voice, "I need to tell you something."

They waited until Al and Frankie moved toward their car.

"This guy named Rigo came by our house. He's friends with another vet named Kenny Wilson. Al met them when he spent the night at the homeless camp."

"I met Rigo when we were looking for Al. What did he want?"

"He wanted to know how to find you. He said Kenny Wilson has disappeared, and it's your fault. He wants you to find Kenny. He seemed really pissed off."

"I think Rigo is always really pissed off about something or other. What did you say?"

"I said you brought Al's brother here for them to reconnect and then you left. I told him that I didn't know where you were, and that I hadn't seen you since. I don't really think he believed me."

"Thanks for letting me know this. If he shows up again, give me a call. Okay?"

"I'll do that. That guy Rigo made me nervous."

Letty nodded.

The party was over. Everyone was gone. Nothing left but cleanup.

"Let's clean up tomorrow," Letty said.

"Happy birthday, Little Brother." Letty gave Will a hug. She took the dogs with her to her bedroom. Time to sleep. She hoped there would be no Iraq dreams tonight. She fell asleep thinking of Dan Ennis.

CHAPTER 7

After spending Sunday morning cleaning up and putting things away, Clarice went off with Will on a bike ride. Will was so excited to try out his fancy new bike, and Clarice was just as excited to see him so happy.

Letty decided to take the day off. She wanted to go jogging with Teddy, but Millie looked really sad at being left alone. So Letty put leashes on both of them. The two dogs and Letty sauntered slowly down the street, Millie limping along on three legs with Teddy patiently at her side. Letty spent the rest of the day in a comfortable chair in her room reading a science fiction book recommended by Clarice. She tried not to think of Dan, but she did anyway. She wondered several times what he was doing.

Monday morning back in her office, Letty reviewed what she had on her plate.

First, get an interview with Gordon Miller and try to learn as much as she could about his business relationship with Jen Kimball's husband Scott.

Next, spend time searching databases available to her to learn as much as she could about the Kimballs and, if it looks promising, Miller and his real estate agent wife Kellie.

Meet with Elena's professor to discuss the murder of his friend.

Meet with Frankie. She had a feeling he wanted something. What could that be?

Letty thought about what Lil had told her about Rigo showing up at Lil and Al's house looking for Letty. What could have happened to Kenny Wilson? She decided to call Wilson's family to see if he had contacted them. Perhaps he decided to go home to his family and just didn't tell Rigo.

But first, she called Marv Iverson.

"Hey, Marv. How's it going?"

"The Saints lost. I'm pissed."

"Sorry, Marv. Who are the Saints?"

"Letty, you're hopeless. Don't you read the news?"

"I read about murders and break-ins, not about sports."

"Your loss."

"Any news about tracking down a lover for Mr. Kimball?"

"Yes and no. I managed to keep an eye on him both at work and at home. No sign at all that he's meeting someone on the sly. His wife, however, has been quite busy."

"Busy? What do you mean?"

"On Saturday, Kimball played tennis all morning. He met a male friend at a public court so there was no option for a shower like at a private club. I figured he wouldn't be meeting a lover after getting all hot and sweaty. So I decided to beat him back to his house. My plan was to watch his house and see if he left home again after cleaning up. I parked on a street higher than their house up in the foothills. I had a clear sight of the back of the house, the pool, a wall around the property, landscaping, and a big picture window into the back of the house. My vehicle was difficult for anyone to see from that distance. I had binoculars so I could see close up."

"And you saw something interesting?"

"Did I ever," Marv laughed.

"Okay. Stop teasing. What did you see?"

"About five minutes after I got there, this workman in a truck pulled up to the front of the house. He was a young guy in his twenties, Mexican-American dude. He was driving an old beat up dirty dark-blue pickup with yard tools in the back. You know, a rake, a shovel, and shears and all that, a mower, too."

"Yeah. And then what happened?"

"I couldn't see the front door, but apparently Mrs. Kimball opened the door and told him to go around to the side. She came out the back, went around to the side gate and let him in. She immediately started taking her clothes off."

"What?"

"Yep. She was stark naked in a jiffy. She stretched out onto the poolside lounge chair, put her hands back behind her head, and spread her legs. She had no clothes on, you know, so I had quite the view of her lady parts."

"Whoa."

"The Mexican dude, I'm going to guess he was mid-to late-twenties and in good shape, seemed to know what was up. Like he'd been there before doing 'yard work,' if you get my drift. He had his shirt off and his pants halfway down in about three seconds. He was on his knees over her. I could tell she was blowing him. Then he moved on top of her and started pumping away. She was writhing around like she was really enjoying herself."

"Goodness, Marv. So I'm paying you to watch a live porn show?"

"Yeah. And it was a damn good show. Any more jobs like this? I'm available anytime."

"Well, who knew? Jen Kimball claimed to be worried about her husband stepping out on her, and you discover she's got her own thing going on."

"From what you told me, I'm guessing that she's not so upset about her husband having a girlfriend. She's way more concerned about getting her share of the money in a divorce settlement."

"I think you're likely correct about that. So what happened next?"

"The guy slapped Mrs. Kimball around a little. Not really hard. Some women like that, I hear. Seems strange, but anyway. Then he screwed her a second time. The guy has stamina. I'll give him that. Also, note that he never kissed her once. Not once. After banging her twice, he got his pants back on and left. She went inside. Hubby showed up about fifteen minutes later. I bet that he was coming home soon was part of their excitement. You know, the possibility of getting caught adds a little spice to some people's sex lives."

"I'm so glad you saw all that, Marv."

"Me, too."

"I mean for the investigation, not for entertainment, but I'm okay with you having a little fun."

"I got a photo of the man, too, though he never turned toward the camera so you don't really see his face full-on. But it's a start. Oh yeah. When his shirt was off, I could see a lot of tattoos on his back and arms, and on his butt, too. I got a good view of his butt." He laughed again.

"If you get a chance, follow him and see if you can find out who he is. Did his truck have a groundskeepers' logo on it?"

"No. I'm not even sure he's a groundskeeper. I think it maybe just some kind of role-play. A young Mexican laborer shows up and screws the brains out of the affluent, middle-aged white woman. Like that old novel. Lady Chatter something."

"You could be right about the role play. All the same, this is very useful information."

"Also I kept track of Scott the rest of the weekend. He was a homebody. Watched a lot of TV. No sign of a girlfriend at all."

"Okay, take a rest for today. I'm going to try to talk with Scott Kimball's business partner. After that, I'll call you, and we'll figure out what to do next."

"Fine. I'll go watch a game and think fondly of my surveillance job today."

"You need a dog."

"Shut up, Letty." He disconnected.

*　*　*

Following up on Lil's warning about Rigo looking for her, Letty's first call was to Kenny Wilson's family. They had heard nothing from him at all. Letty promised to see if she could find him again to make sure he was safe, and to ask him again to contact his family.

Next she called the office of Gordon Miller. A secretary answered, and Letty suggested vaguely that she was interested in investing in real estate. She wasn't surprised to be given an appointment for Wednesday morning.

Her sister Elena was next on the list.

"Hey, Elena, I'm calling about setting up a meeting with your professor."

"Hi, Letty. I'm in the lab now, and he's here. Hang on a minute. I'll hand my phone to him."

"Miss Valdez, my name is Steve Anselm. Elena tells me that you are willing to talk with me. Could we meet this week?"

"Sure, I'm available. How about this afternoon?"

"That works for me. There's a small restaurant in South Tucson, El Torito. I doubt that I will be recognized there. I don't want my colleagues or students to know what I'm doing."

"Yes, I know El Torito. How about four this afternoon?"

"Great. How will I know you?"

"Elena and I look a lot alike. I'm a little taller, and she's a lot prettier. How will I know you?"

"Oh, ordinary-looking middle-age white guy. I look like a typical chemistry professor."

"Okay. See you at four." She disconnected. Letty wasn't sure what a typical chemistry professor might look like, except maybe for some comedy stereotypes in movies. She figured she could count on few people being in the restaurant at that time of day. The professor should be easy to spot.

Letty turned on her computer. It was time to do some research and see what she could find out about Gordon Miller. Specifically, she wanted to see if Miller had any other relationship with Scott Kimball in addition to the business they had registered together with the Arizona Secretary of State. And while she was at it, she would try to find out more about Miller's real estate agent wife, and a lot more about Jen Kimball. Apparently Jen thought of herself as something of a "cougar." And who was that young man that Marv had seen? Maybe he really was a day laborer doing yard work. If not, if this was all some elaborate role play, where had Jen met this guy? And what was her plan for him once she divorced her husband and won a good financial settlement? Keep him around or dump him?

Letty's phone rang. Frankie.

"Come this morning, Frankie. I have to go to a meeting later."

Frankie showed up a half-hour later.

"Have a seat, Frankie. Is everything okay? I mean with Al?"

"Yes, everything is good. Better than good really. Lil has a very positive effect on Al."

Frankie hesitated. Letty thought he looked nervous.

"Letty, I was impressed at how quickly you found Al, and how you dealt with that asshole Rigo at the homeless camp. So after I saw you, I went to the library and looked up some stuff about private investigation."

Letty's eyebrows went up. So that's what this meeting is about.

"I told you that I really like computers, designing software, and I'm especially interested in ethical hacking."

"Ethical hacking? What does that mean?"

"It means you get hired by a company to find any software vulnerabilities. It means hacking into their system to see where the weaknesses are, and then fixing them. There are a lot of different kinds of systems and vulnerabilities and ways of hacking. There are even hacking contests. All legal. Another term for this work is 'computer forensics.'"

Letty nodded. She knew that for most businesses, large and small, computer system security was a constant worry.

"So at the library, I looked into private investigation. It seems that there are some private investigators who specialize in computer forensics." Frankie squirmed in his chair. He looked worried.

"Frankie, are you interested in becoming a private investigator and specializing in this field?"

"Yeah." He sighed with relief. "You're so smart, Letty."

"It was pretty easy to figure out from what you just told me."

"To get the point, is there any chance you would be willing to hire me part-time at a low rate of pay and train me as a private investigator? I'm honest, trustworthy, and smart. I'll be taking more computer classes so my skills will increase as I go along. Also, I think I could be an asset to your business. You could take on jobs that are in this area of computer forensics and increase your income."

Letty smiled, "You make a good argument, Frankie. Give me a little time to think about this. I hadn't even thought of hiring anyone, most especially not in an area having to do with computer security. I have only the basic skills that most computer-users have. It never occurred to include this field in my investigations. I'd like to talk to Marv Iverson and get his advice. He was the man who trained me, and I took over from him when he retired. Tell me what your schedule is."

Frankie looked more than relieved. Apparently he really wanted to work for Letty and learn the business and the thought of asking her had terrified him. Letty's response made him relax a little.

"I'm going home to Nogales this afternoon on the bus. I'll go visit my mom across the border and let her know how well Al is doing. She'll be really relieved. I'll go back to work, too, at the grocery store. I've already talked to my boss about this. He's a really fine dude. He told me that he'd really miss me, but he agreed that working for you would be a great move toward a real career in computer forensics. He said he had confidence in me, and he thought I'd be a good investigator in this area. He said if you go for it, I can be back here in a couple of days. My friends here in Tucson will let me stay with them until I get a job and find a place of my own. I'm here in time to sign up for a couple of computer classes at the community college. I figure if you hire me, I can work for you maybe three mornings a week. I'll get another job, maybe at a grocery store at night since I have experience in that. Like I said, I can be back to Tucson by Wednesday if you agree."

"Okay. Stay in touch. We've got each other's numbers. I'll text you."

Frankie left Letty's office looking a lot more hopeful than when he first arrived. Letty felt pretty good about his request for a job. It had never occurred to her to expand her investigations into anything having to do with computer security. But potentially it could have a good financial payoff. And she could get Frankie to help her search all these databases for information relevant to her regular cases, like the ones she was working on today. "Computer forensics." Something to think about for sure.

Also Letty wondered about the danger factor. In the cases she'd had recently, she had to deal with some really violent criminals, especially that last one who tried kill her. And also he tried to kill her friend Seri. Would shifting to computer investigations be safer? She was thinking of Frankie, too. He was young and small and had no martial arts training. She didn't want him to be a target if he worked for Valdez Investigations.

Gotta talk to Marv about this, she thought.

CHAPTER 8

The drive to the little restaurant and cantina in South Tucson took Letty only a few minutes. South Tucson was a separate municipality south of downtown and completely surrounded by the larger city of Tucson. South Tucson was culturally Mexican and blessed with a number of great restaurants. The little restaurant where she was to meet the professor was empty except for a couple of workers, a cook and a waitress. The cook was doing prep work for the evening meal, and the waitress was straightening everything, adding napkins to dispensers and related work.

At Letty's request, the waitress brought her a cup of coffee.

Professor Anselm showed up five minutes later.

Letty stood up and smiled. "Hello, I'm Letty Valdez." She reached out and shook the professor's hand. He looked only somewhat like his self-description. Yes, he was a white man and middle-aged. But he was hardly the stereotype of a professor with rumpled clothing, thick glasses, and a general air of having his head in the clouds, or in his case, the periodic table. Anselm was tanned, well-built, and rather good looking. His brown hair was streaked with gray. He looked like a man who spent a lot of time outdoors.

"Thanks for meeting me, Miss Valdez," Professor Anselm said as he approached her table. "This is a good place. It's not like anyone is going to notice us here."

"You can call me Letty."

"You do look a lot like Elena. But you're incorrect to say she's prettier than you."

Letty gestured to the chair on the opposite site of the table. She sat down.

"Why are you so intent on no one finding out that you're interested in hiring a private investigator?"

"Maybe I've watched too many cop shows on TV, but as far as I'm concerned, my friend was murdered. Anyone could have done it. That includes my colleagues, my students, anyone. So I want to remain under the radar. And I'm Steve to you."

Letty nodded. "Tell me about your friend."

"His name is, or I mean was, Edward Becker. He was an older guy, well into his seventies. I met him six years ago when I went on a hike through one of the local hiking clubs. I'd just moved to Tucson. I wanted to get to know new people and to know the Sonoran Desert. I grew up in Missouri, got my doctorate from Stanford in California, worked for a while at Oregon State in Corvallis, then I was hired here at the University of Arizona. I didn't know a soul when I came to Tucson."

Letty nodded. The waitress appeared and Professor Anselm asked for a beer.

"You don't mind if I drink a beer?"

"No. Not at all. So you and Becker became friends?"

"Yes, Edward was a retired high school biology teacher. After retirement, he taught for a while at the local community college. Then he quit teaching all together when his wife became ill. She died about a year later. I think it was some kind of cancer. After she passed away, Edward started volunteering for local environmental groups. He told me he was trying to get out of the house. I think he was trying to deal with his wife's death. They'd been married for forty-something years."

"What kind of volunteering did he do?"

"Oh, he was involved in all sorts of things. Gave talks to school kids, served on the board of local environmental groups, went on outings with seniors and kids, kept track of wildlife like the Audubon's annual Christmas bird count. What is relevant here is that he was out by himself in the southeastern section of the Santa

Catalina Mountains looking for a potential source of pollution that had shown up very briefly in the Agua Caliente spring. Are you familiar with Agua Caliente Park on the east side at the base of the Catalina Foothills?"

"Yes, I've been to the park a few times, but mainly for social events. I went to a wedding reception there a year or so ago. It's a beautiful place with the big ponds and all those trees there."

"It is indeed beautiful. Edward was a member of Agua Caliente Friends group, and he also was a volunteer for another environmental group, Desert Springs Watch. He'd been out there more than once on the mountain side above the park, just to the east, looking for any human-caused pollution that might affect any of the springs in that area. There are a few springs in this region, including in the national forest which is farther east. As far as Agua Caliente spring itself, the flow is irregular and it dries up episodically. The spring seems to be dependent on snowmelt from higher up in the Catalina Mountains."

The waitress brought his beer, and Anselm took a sip.

"Edward told me that one of the Desert Springs Watch student volunteers had taken a sample of the spring water for a class assignment. For a brief time, only about a day, there were traces of the anhydrous ammonia. This is used in fertilizers, among other uses. We figured that someone had been overusing fertilizers on their lawn or something, and somehow some of it made its way into the spring water. But the traces disappeared so quickly that no one thought it was a real problem."

"Where does the water in big ponds come from?"

"Groundwater pumping and from the spring when it's running."

Anselm frowned, looked down at his hands, then back at Letty. "Edward and I had dinner together a few days before he died. This was a week or so after he told me about the student taking a sample of the Agua Caliente spring water. He told me at dinner that he'd found what appeared to be a sinkhole above the park. He said it looked like someone had been pouring something into the sinkhole, maybe chemicals. The sinkhole was in the recharge area of the spring in the park. That means that anything going into the sinkhole, like rainfall, usually ends up in groundwater which feeds the springs."

"Any idea what kind of chemicals?"

"No, he was going out again to take a closer look. Obviously, we thought of the anhydrous ammonia, but this appeared to be something different. There wasn't any chemical residue at the sinkhole, but the space around the sink hole had no vegetation at all. All plant life was dead which suggests something killed everything. He said the smell in the area was strange, definitely something chemical but not the distinctive smell of anhydrous ammonia. He also said there was some trash thrown out around the sink hole that he was going to collect and bring back."

Letty nodded. "You can learn a lot from people's trash. You never saw any of it?"

"No. Edward was killed on that last trip out when he went to investigate. He was shot in the head. The bullet came from a rifle and the shot was long-range, not close up at all. He wasn't near a sinkhole when he was shot. I guess he was killed before he made it to the sinkhole. Or maybe he was on his way back. I just don't know."

"What do the police say about this?"

"They said there was no sign of robbery or direct assault on his body. Because Edward was shot from long-range makes them think it might have been some kind of accident. That would be like if someone was trying to scare off a coyote or something similar. Edward's body probably wouldn't have been found but for the fact that a couple of hikers were passing by and they came across him. He'd been dead at least a day or more at that point."

"What did the police do next?"

"They interviewed a bunch of people. They started with the neighbors who lived in the residential area near the park. It's a pretty affluent area with every house on a small acreage. They also interviewed people who work in the park. Then they went on to interview people that Edward knew, mostly in the different environmental groups he belonged to. But they came up with nothing. He didn't really have any enemies. I contacted the police and told them what Edward had told me about potential pollution at a sink-hole. They listened and took notes. But since I don't know where the sinkhole is or what the chemicals might be....or if there were really any chemicals at all. They didn't follow up. Park officials said they hadn't seen any sign of contamination in the park's pond waters. If there had been any contamination, it had disappeared by that time, too, so there was nothing really to go on."

"The police didn't go up on the mountainside above the park and look for anything?"

"Nah," Anselm shook his head. "Other than when they retrieved the body, I don't think they went back up there again. I kind of get this. The local police are busy all the time with plenty of crime — burglaries, home invasions, murders. My concern about his being killed because of some spring pollution was just too vague and un-substantiated to even follow up."

Letty nodded.

"Oh, yeah. One more thing the cops did was look into his fi-nances. He wasn't wealthy. He was just a retired teacher trying to make the world a better place. Apparently no one had been mon-keying with his bank account, and there hadn't been a break-in at his house either. The shooting looked and still looks like some kind of random event."

Letty watched Anselm closely. He was quiet now, lost in his own thoughts. He seemed sincere. He was convinced his friend had been murdered, and he wanted justice. Also he clearly wanted to protect the natural resources of Agua Caliente Park.

"Do you know the word 'daemon,'" Anselm asked suddenly. He looked at Letty.

"It means 'demon,' doesn't it? And doesn't that word have some-thing to do with software, too? I don't know exactly."

"Yes, that meaning refers to a kind of software program. Unix has a bunch of daemons."

Letty had no idea what Unix might be so she just nodded.

"But I'm referring to an older, lesser-known meaning. Usually people think first of 'demon' which is one meaning, as you said. But it also refers to a special kind of supernatural being somewhere between human and godlike. I often think of water in the desert as a daemon. We humans act as if we were in control of things, but we're not. In fact, if or when the water dries up in the Sonoran Desert, we'll all be forced to move somewhere else. I went once to visit the Atacama Desert in South America. It's between the Andes and the Pacific, and only gets about half an inch of rain a year. Few people live there, and they are mostly in fishing villages along the coast."

Letty's eyebrows went up. "Half an inch? That's not much rain."

Anselm nodded. "You can understand why ancient cultures gave offerings to rain gods asking for enough water in some places, or not too much in other places. That's why it's easy to think of water as a daemon. Water literally means life for those living in a desert. My friend Edward knew this."

Letty nodded her agreement. "I spent my early childhood on the Tohono O'odham Reservation. It's drier out there than in the Tucson area. I learned early to respect water."

"So do you think you can take this on?"

"Yes, though you should keep in mind that the police may be right about it being a random shooting."

"I realize that. But I don't really think it would be random. It seems possible that one of the homeowners just didn't like anyone around too close to their property, and they took a shot at Edward. Maybe they didn't mean to kill him, maybe they wanted to just scare him off, but he ended up dead. But I still think it's linked to the evidence of chemical dumping. That just makes more sense to me than a random shooting. We just need to find evidence."

"Looks like I will be going there and see if I can find what Edward found."

"Good. And if you find signs that someone was dumping chemicals, then I hope I can figure out what the chemicals were. Then you can find out who would be the most likely person or persons to be dumping those chemicals. If they were doing something so obviously illegal, they would probably want Edward out of the way."

"Okay, Steve. I'll get started on this."

"Thank you, Letty. I feel better already just to be taken seriously."
They rose at the same time.

"I'll pay for your coffee," Anselm said. "By the way, I want you to
know that your little sister Elena is doing very well indeed. I think
she'd make a great chemist or maybe go into an environmental field.
She's smart and hard-working."

"That's good to hear. These days she seems to be having boy trouble."

He shrugged his shoulders. "She's young. Hormones, you know."

Anselm stopped just before they were to leave the restaurant.
"Letty, you are very intelligent and attractive. I wonder if you'd like
to go out with me sometime."

This took Letty entirely by surprise. She hesitated and then said,
"Not now. I have a rule about being social with a client. Also there's
this guy I'm ..." Her voice trailed off.

Anselm chuckled. "I get it. Well, maybe later when this is all over.
And if you lose interest in that guy."

They parted with a handshake, and Letty headed back to her office.

Back in her office, Letty checked her email again. Marv sent her
an email with an attached photo of the man he saw at Jen Kimball's
house.

There were four photos of the man, and a fifth of the pickup truck.
The young man's face could not be seen in any of the photos. All
Letty could see clearly was that he was just as Marv had described:
mid-to-late twenties, maybe five feet nine or ten, medium-brown
skin common in Mexican-Americans, dark hair, and a lot of tattoos.
Maybe she could link the tattoos to a specific gang or some other
group. She really wanted to know who this man might be and what
he was to Jen Kimball other than a sexual relationship.

On her drive home, Letty also thought about Anselm's invitation.
She was unsure of why she was getting male attention these days.
Much to her dismay, she realized that when the professor had asked
her out, her first thought was of Dan Ennis.

CHAPTER 9

The next morning Letty arrived early at her office. Her first task was to call Frankie's boss, Gonzalo, at the supermarket in Nogales.

After a brief conversation in which Letty explained what she wanted to know, Gonzolo said, "Here's the bottom line, Miss Valdez. I hate to lose him, but Frankie deserves more than clerking and doing inventory. He's smart, he knows computers backwards and forwards, and he's completely trustworthy. In fact, he reorganized my accounting and inventory records, which ended up saving me money. After he did that, I put him in my office part-time and on the floor the rest of the time. He's a great employee. If I were you, I'd snap him up before someone else gets him."

Letty thanked Gonzalo for the strong recommendation. Her next call was to Marv Iverson.

"Hey, Letty," Marv said when he answered. "Any more juicy surveillance jobs for me?"

"Well, you could try to find that Chicano dude. He may be providing yardwork services for more ladies in the neighborhood. I can't guarantee that they will go outside in the open where you can watch, though."

Marv laughed. "I'm on the lookout for him. He provided a lot of vicarious thrills for this old man."

"I'm calling to ask you what you think about my hiring a young guy to work with me part time. His name is Frankie Miranda. He's in my extended family through marriage. I just talked to his boss in Nogales, and the boss gave him an unqualified, topnotch recommendation. Frankie is into computers. He wants to be a private investigator and specialize in something called "computer forensics."

"What the hell does that mean?"

"You know how businesses get their computer systems hacked? They lose private data and a lot of money in the process. Guys like Frankie are hired to hack into the systems to find vulnerabilities before the business gets hacked, or after its hacked, and then try to fix what went wrong. It's also called "ethical hacking." It's a growing business."

"Well, I don't know shit about that, but it does sound like a good business move for you. I'm getting a little tired of hearing about you getting beat up and shot at. Maybe hiring Frankie would mean some of the jobs might be a little safer for you. If you have the money to hire him, I say go for it. Of course, if I take him out on surveillance with me, he might just change his mind and want to surveil full-time." He laughed again.

"Okay, I'll give Frankie a call. I also want to mention what else has come up. You know about Jen Kimball. I just took on another job." Letty told him about her conversation with Professor Anselm and her agreement to look into Edward Becker's death.

"You're getting busy."

"Yeah, that's one reason why I think hiring Frankie Miranda might be a good idea." She paused. "Thanks for the feedback. One more thing, Marv."

"What?"

"You need a dog."

"Shut up, Letty."

Letty called Frankie next.

Frankie answered on the second ring.

"Hey, Letty, what's up in the big city?"

"Frankie, I talked to your boss. He said he doesn't want to lose you, but he gave you a five-star recommendation. I talked to my old boss Marv, and he thinks hiring you is a good idea. So now I'm inviting you to come in to the office when you get back to Tucson.

That's tomorrow, right? Consider yourself a part-time staff member of Valdez Investigations from here on out. Part-time only. I can't afford full-time."

"Oh my god. Oh my god. *Awesome!* This is *great* news. I'm going to call my mom. This is totally awesome. Thank you so much, Letty. You'll never regret this. I promise."

"Okay, Frankie. I'll see you tomorrow."

Letty turned on her computer and started searching for background information on the murdered environmentalist Edward Becker. While she was at it, she decided to look into Professor Steve Anselm first, just to make sure he was a reliable informant. Anselm had a good record. He was divorced with no children, did not have a police record, was listed by students as a good or excellent teacher, and he had served on several university faculty committees. He had a long list of scholarly publications with titles that, for Letty, might as well be in a foreign language. They were all about chemistry. She knew next to nothing about chemistry.

Not for the first time, Letty regretted that she didn't have more education. Dan Ennis popped into her thoughts again. Dan was very well-educated with a bachelor's degree and a medical degree. Letty couldn't figure out why Seri and Will and Clarice all seemed to think he would be interested in her. She had a sudden thought that the reason he came to breakfast and agreed to a date with her was simply because he didn't know anyone in Tucson, and he was lonely. Maybe later when Dan met more people, she would never see him again. The thought was somewhat distressing.

Back to the computer, Letty went into some depth learning more about Edward Becker. His background was a little more exciting than Professor Anselm's. After a career as a well-loved high school teacher and then time spent caring for his dying wife, Becker became something of an environmental activist. He had attended and organized numerous protests, and he had even been arrested a couple of times. But he was pretty quickly released after paying his fines. He had traveled outside the U.S., too, to participate in conservation projects in Mexico and Chile. Letty checked his Twitter account, which was still up. The tweets were mostly messages about different environmental problems, possible solutions, and strong criticism of polluters at all levels, from international to next-door.

Maybe someone had decided to relieve themselves of an irritant by killing Edward Becker, Letty thought. She needed to hike up into the Santa Catalina Mountains to see if she could find the sink hole that Becker had found. She wanted to see for herself if there were any residual signs of chemical pollution.

Letty called Alejandro Ramirez, head of the Tucson Police Department's Homicide Unit. Alejandro was cousins with Letty's childhood friend Adelita García, a former cop who had married a few months earlier and now was enjoying her first pregnancy. Alejandro and Letty had become friends, too. Alejandro had moved from Robbery to Homicide when the former head, Tony De Luca, had gone back to his hometown, New York City.

"Hey, Alejandro, how's it going? Staying out of trouble?"

"Hi, Letty. Good to hear from you. I've had too much work to do to get into any trouble. We've been really busy lately."

"Yeah, I keep up with the news. It's one of your cases I'm calling about. Remember nearly six months ago there was an older man, Edward Becker, who was out hiking up in the Catalinas? He was shot in the head long-range."

"Yes, we've been cooperating with Pima County Sheriff's Department on that one because it took place just east of the city limits. We haven't really made any progress on that."

"I just want you to know that I've been hired by a friend of Becker's to find the killer."

"So he's convinced you that Becker was murdered?"

"No. But I'm going to look into it. I'm keeping an open mind. The friend thinks Becker found evidence of chemical dumping. Have you had any thoughts on this case?"

"No, Letty. Been too busy with the everyday nutcases shooting their wives or their best friends or fellow drug dealers standing in a circle shooting each other. As far as Becker is concerned, there wasn't any credible evidence that he was murdered. We couldn't find any signs of illegal dumping. It seemed to be a random, perhaps accidental shooting. The case is open, but we haven't made any progress on it. I consider it a cold case. I'm glad you're looking into it so we can put this to rest one way or the other."

"Okay. I'll keep you informed."

"Thanks, Letty. I hope this time you manage to settle this without getting shot at."

"Yeah, me, too."

After her phone call with Alejandro, Letty decided to see if she could find the missing vet Kenny Wilson a second time. She would try to determine if he were still in Tucson. If she could find him, she would ask him again to call his family. She had a lot of sympathy for Wilson. She knew firsthand how many vets came home wounded with what the experts liked to call "combat stress injuries." Too many of them couldn't find a way to return to normal life. We can't forget what we saw in a war zone, Letty said to herself. She hoped she could find Miller and maybe point him toward some help.

* * *

Letty first returned to the mid-town encampment where she and Frankie had found Kenny Wilson a few days earlier. The day was warm and sunny, one of those Sonoran Desert late winter days with an intensely blue sky, no clouds in sight. She would have enjoyed it more, if the task at hand wasn't so unpleasant.

Kenny wasn't there and neither was Rigo. She asked the few men still in the camp if they knew of other camps around town where Kenny and Rigo might have gone. No one knew anything. She left quickly and headed to the next potential location on her list.

On the northwest side of town, Letty easily found a big encampment in a dry wash that had been there for a while. The arroyo was lined with velvet mesquite trees. There must have been thirty or forty individual camp sites along the banks and some in the middle of the wash. The campers would be safe there most of the year. But during summer monsoon, the washes would fill with raging waters within a few minutes. Those caught in the torrent would be carried away to their death. The campers went elsewhere during the monsoon. Now, though, everything was dry.

She left her vehicle in a box store parking lot and approached the wash. Unlike the smaller encampment in mid-town, this large camp had both men and women residents. One of the women came forward.

"Hi," Letty said. "I'm looking for someone. His name is Kenny Wilson. He and I are both Iraq War vets." She held out her phone with Kenny's photo.

The woman, who looked to be in her mid-forties, had obviously spent a lot of time in the sun considering her lined face. Her clothing was worn and mismatched but not dirty like so many of the men. Despite her poverty and marginal status, she had a kind of quiet dignity about her.

"I'm Shannon. I've haven't seen this guy at all, and I've been here for several months. You are not the first to ask about him."

"Oh, yeah? Someone else is looking for him?"

"Yeah, that guy," she gestured to a man coming up behind Letty.

It was Rigo. He was stomping toward her, an angry scowl on his face.

Letty stepped to stand next to Shannon. A couple of the men in the camp had come out to watch.

"What are you doing here, bitch," Rigo growled.

"No need to be so rude, Rigo," Letty said. "I'm looking for Kenny."

"You mean you don't know where he is?"

"No. Why would I know?"

"You're the one who insisted that he call his family."

"I didn't insist anything. I just told him that they wanted to know if he was okay, and to please call them. But he didn't call. He didn't go home. He's disappeared again."

"I know. I know. I've been looking for him everywhere."

"How long has he been gone?"

"At least two days."

Rigo scowled at Letty and took a step forward.

"This is all your fucking fault, bitch."

"I had nothing to do with his disappearance."

"Bullshit. You came waltzing in unasked, and you told him that his family is asking for him."

"That's so bad?"

"Kenny has been on the edge since they discharged him. We were in the same squad, but I was discharged a month before him. He came out here to find me not long after he returned to the States. He kept talking to me about going back to Afghanistan to die. You telling him about his family just sent him over the edge. He said they shouldn't have to put up with him and all his problems. He was so depressed that he almost never talked. I'm afraid he's gone and enlisted again. He said it would be easy to just go back to Afghanistan and get shot and die."

He grimaced and then looked at Letty with disgust. "You started this. Get the fuck away from here, stay out of our business, or I'll beat the shit out of you."

Letty sighed. "Don't threaten me, Rigo. That didn't work out too well for you the last time, did it?"

This last comment sent Rigo over the top. He rushed at her, attempting to smash into Letty's mid-section. She managed to turn just enough to send him flying past her. Rigo stumbled and caught himself. He paused and then he grabbed an iron bar from under a folding table. He turned and went for Letty again.

This time when he came at her, Letty didn't turn aside. She grabbed a nearby folding chair and came forward to meet him. She took a swipe with the chair at his upturned arm and hand holding the iron bar. He stumbled backwards. Before he could get his balance, Letty threw aside the chair. She moved quickly toward Rigo and grabbed his arm holding the bar. She jerked him toward her and as he went past, she kicked him hard in the small of his back. He went down sprawling, face in the dirt. He rose and turned, but this time, two men in the group grabbed him and held him back.

"Leave it, Rigo," one man said.

"Yeah, she knows how to fight. Let it go."

Rigo struggled against them for a moment. Then he gave up.

"I'm going now, Rigo. I will continue to look for Kenny. You stay out of my way."

Letty turned and walked away. She didn't look back.

* * *

The basketball game that evening was a unique experience for Letty. From the moment that she, Will, and Clarice piled into Clarice's car and went to pick up Dan at his place, the air was filled with excitement. Dan slid into the backseat next to Letty. "Hello, Ms. Valdez. Are you ready to show your support for the Wildcats?" He was grinning.

"I've never been to a basketball game at the University," Letty replied. "I'm not sure how to behave." She didn't add that her childhood and young adult poverty made such a sporting event far too expensive for her.

"Just watch the game. You'll see how much fun it can be. It's very exciting."

And fun it was. The four of them walked briskly to the arena from the parking lot. They were surrounded by hundreds of other fans heading the same way. Letty's eyes grew wide when she entered the arena for the first time. The basketball arena was huge with hundreds of seats filling rapidly with fans. A band was playing upbeat music, and cheerleaders already on the floor were doing gymnastic tricks and leading the crowd in cheers. The atmosphere was electric. It became even more exciting when the players from both teams came onto the floor and began warming up.

Clarice and Will were beside themselves. They giggled and chattered nonstop. Letty was happy to see them so happy.

She turned to Dan and said, "Thank you for inviting us to this."

Dan smiled. "Letty, if you remember, you invited me. It's going to be my turn to invite you now."

Oh yeah, Letty thought. Then she frowned. What could he have in mind?

Dan saw her frown. "Don't worry. Everything will be okay."

"Sorry, Dan. I tend to worry too much."

"Yeah, I noticed that." He laughed. "I consider it my task to have fun with you so you can relax a little. Let's start by going to get some popcorn before the game begins." They went back up the steep stairs, bought two big buckets of popcorn and returned to their seats. Letty handed one of the buckets to Will.

The game was exciting and Letty began to relax as she watched. Letty didn't know all the rules so Dan explained the players, what they did, the fouls, and more. He gave her explanations and tips of what to watch for when the players ran up and down the court. If the Wildcats made points, he and Will lost it and began jumping up and down and yelling their approval. The two of them high-fived each other every time the Wildcats moved ahead. Letty and Clarice giggled every time they high-fived.

During halftime, Will and Clarice went off to say hi to some friends.

"Okay, now that we're in halftime, we can talk. It's my turn to invite you out, Letty," Dan said. He was smiling again.

She turned to face him. "Okay, what do you have in mind?"

"I'd like to invite you to come to my house tomorrow evening. Just you. Bring your dogs. We'll take a walk first, and then we'll eat."

"You know how to cook?"

"Of course. I have many talents." He grinned and wiggled his eyebrows.

Somehow Letty thought he wasn't talking about medicine and cooking just then. She felt herself grow warm.

"Don't forget. I know how to climb trees. That's just one of my many talents."

Letty relaxed and smiled. She remembered how Teddy had alerted her to Dan who was sitting on the branch of a eucalyptus tree. He'd gone up the tree to rescue a cat. She knew he had taken care of her in the hospital when she'd been attacked by three thugs. But she had forgotten most of that due to pain and medications. Finding Dan in the tree marked the real beginning of their relationship.

"That you do. You're a good tree climber," she said. "Should I bring something?"

"Just you and Millie and Teddy."

Halftime was over, and they all went back to watching the game. The Wildcats won.

CHAPTER 10

Early the next morning, Letty unlocked her office and turned on her computer. She wanted to know more about Gordon Miller before she went to talk to him. She filled an electric pot with water and plugged it in. A cup of instant coffee soon followed. She grimaced as she sipped. The instant coffee tasted awful, but at least it had caffeine in it. Letty tilted her old office chair backwards a bit and sipped the coffee as she watched the early light move across the ridges and canyons of the Santa Catalina Mountains. This was her favorite time of day.

The front door to her office opened, and Frankie Miranda came in.

"Hi, Letty," he said quietly. He looked hesitant, even nervous.

"Hi, Frankie. You're here early." She got up from her chair and went into the outer office.

"Yes, I got a ride from a friend last night. My mom told me I should show up early so I can leave a good impression." He frowned.

"You already left a good impression. Tell your mom to quit worrying." She smiled.

"Okay." He took a deep breath and sighed.

"I see you have a laptop with you. That's great. Later we'll get you a computer just for here at work. But today, I'd like to fill you in on how all this works and give you a chance to get started. Sit here." She gestured to the front desk.

Frankie sat down and opened his laptop.

"For you to become a licensed private investigator," Letty paused, "and you do want to become licensed, correct?"

"Yes, definitely."

"In Arizona, you have to work for three years full time as an investigator for a government agency or a private firm like mine. I can only afford to hire you part-time now so you'll probably have to put in more than three years to get the license. This is a big commitment."

"I understand, Letty. I always thought I'd go work for some IT company. But when I read about computer forensics, I immediately thought that was the coolest thing ever. I intend to continue taking classes and get at least my associate degree, maybe eventually a bachelor's degree. I'll learn as much as I can and bring it back to Valdez Investigations. I am very grateful for this opportunity."

"Good. You will be learning how to do in-depth on-line searches, and you'll be using some private databases that I have paid to use on a subscription basis, plus some free, public databases. These searches can be for things like due diligence searches for potential investors who want to know about the financial status of an investment. Searches also include looking for missing people, looking into financial records and things like that."

Frankie nodded.

"Everything you do will reflect back on Valdez Investigations. If you do anything illegal or unethical, it could put me out of business and ruin your chances of becoming licensed forever. Understand?"

"Yes."

"Another important thing to always remember: What goes on here is private. You cannot be talking about your job and what you do here to anyone. Understand?"

"Yes, I'll keep everything to myself."

"Also I think you'll need to learn many of the skills private investigators have such as how to do surveillance and not get spotted. You can also learn how to process papers."

"Yes, I want to learn everything. I want to be really good at this."

"Also I think your idea of taking gong fu classes from Zhou Liang Wei is a good idea. Self-defense skills are fundamental. Just yesterday I had to defend myself against an irate homeless vet. Oh, yeah.

You know him. You remember that guy Rigo we met at the homeless camp? I saw him yesterday. He came at me again."

Frankie frowned.

"So you have to be prepared. You never know what's going to happen."

"I'm going to go by Mr. Zhou's school later today and get a class schedule. I'm not very big. I'm five feet six barefooted, and five seven with shoes. I've been picked on my whole life. I would really like knowing how to defend myself."

"Good. Okay. Let's get you started. Here's the Wi-Fi password and the password to my website and email service." She handed Frankie a slip of paper with the passwords. "You can get yourself up and going right now. Set up an email address for yourself at Valdez Investigations so I can pass proprietary info to you. Again, you cannot share or talk about this with anyone. Once you're set up, I'll pass on to you some photos, and you can get started on your first job."

"Awesome." He was grinning now.

"I've been hired by a woman named Jen Kimball. She thinks her husband is having an affair. She wants to make sure that she's covered financially if they get a divorce. But my boss and mentor, Marv Iverson..." Letty paused. "I'll take you to meet Marv sometime soon. He is retired, but he still does some surveillance for me occasionally. You can learn a lot from Marv."

Frankie nodded. He pulled out a notebook and wrote down Jen Kimball's name.

"Jen thinks her husband is hiding funds from her. She's afraid that if they get a divorce, she won't get her fair share of the assets. I found out that Scott Kimball has a business partner that Jen didn't know about. His name is Gordon Miller. Take a look at this."

Letty typed a name into Google and a website popped up. "This is a free database available to anyone. It shows you all the business trade names registered in the state of Arizona. After I leave this morning, I suggest do a little exploring and learn how to use it. It's easy really. You won't have a problem."

Frankie nodded. He had a little smile on his face now. He's enjoying this, Letty thought. Good. If he likes what he's doing, he'll do a good job.

"So you can see here that Jen Kimball's husband is a partner with Gordon Miller in some kind of investment business. That's where I'll start."

Letty continued. "Also Marv was setting up a surveillance of Jen's husband and accidentally found out that Jen is having some kind of sexual relationship with this young Mexican guy, probably only a little older than you. He appeared to be doing yardwork for her and a lot more. They put on quite a pool-side sex show for Marv, which he thoroughly enjoyed."

Frankie grinned. "This job is getting more and more interesting."

"We decided to look into that, too, to see what Jen is up to. Her situation may be more complicated than just a wife who has a cheating husband. Marv and I are thinking maybe she doesn't care so much about the divorce, but she does care about getting a good financial settlement. Beyond that, we don't know what she's up to. So I want you to use your search skills and find out what you can both about Jen Kimball and her husband Scott. For sure do some background on him first, then on her. Jen was supposed to bring some financial records here, bank statements to be exact, but she hasn't shown up yet. Also the other task is to see if you can identify the Mexican laborer. I have to add that I don't know if he actually does yard work or not. The whole thing might be some kind of sexual role-play. I'm going to forward to you some photos that Marv took. He couldn't get the guy's face on camera, but he did take several photos of the guy's tattoos. I know it's a long shot, but I'm hoping you can identify at least one of the tattoos. It may be gang-related. We want to know if he's in a gang, and if so, which one."

"This will be a lot of fun." Frankie was smiling now. "I didn't realize you did so much background stuff, even on the clients."

"We have to because it's not uncommon to discover that the clients are lying about something. Okay, get busy and when you have everything set up, email me with your new email address. I'll respond with the photos."

"Will do."

Letty returned to her inner office desk. Ten minutes later, she received an email from Frankie at Valdez Investigations. She immediately responded and sent the photos attached to her email.

"Got 'em," Frankie called out.

Letty returned to her outer office. "Excellent. We're up and rolling now. I'm going to go visit Gordon Miller and see what I can find out about him and his business dealings with Scott Kimball. I should be back before lunch. I'm not expecting anyone this morning, but if someone shows up, find out what they want and how to reach them."

Frankie nodded. As Letty opened the front door to leave, he called, "Thank you again, Letty. This means everything to me. You opened a door for me."

As she drove to Miller's office, Letty remembered her first encounter with Marv Iverson. Marv opened a door for her, too. She'd come home from the Iraq War and had gone directly to live with her grandmother on the Tohono O'odham Nation. Thank god for that, Letty thought. The quiet and peace of the desert had a much-needed healing effect on the young Army medic. After a few months at her grandmother's, she felt together enough to apply for a job. She could see the dire poverty her grandmother lived in, and how she was taking care of her grandchildren, Letty's brothers and sister, after their dad had died in a car wreck and their mother had abandoned them. Letty wanted to help. Marv Iverson was the Vietnam vet private investigator who gave Letty a job and a new path in life. She could never repay him.

The drive to Miller's office on the northwest side of Tucson took about twenty minutes. She went into the office and checked in with the receptionist. She sat and waited to be called into Miller's office.

* * *

Gordon Miller came out of his office all smiles and approached Letty with his hand extended. "Miss Valdez? So nice to meet you."

Letty smiled and shook his hand. His friendly demeanor gave Letty insight into how he had become so successful. He was the owner of a large real estate firm with nearly fifty employees. Miller made potential investors feel important and wanted.

Miller guided Letty into his office.

"I understand you're considering investing in some real estate. A business or a home?"

"Neither actually. I'm interested in your business, SG Enterprises. Your website doesn't have much on it. That's what I'm looking into now. I'm hoping you'll have some information that can help me."

"SG Enterprises? I'm sorry. My business is all about real estate. I'm not familiar with SG Enterprises."

"You are a partner in SG Enterprises, aren't you?"

"No. What's this about then?"

"Do you know a man named Scott Kimball?"

"Sure. Scott and I have known each other for years. We were in the same fraternity at the University of Arizona. We still meet occasionally to play tennis. He and his wife and my wife see each other frequently at social events."

"What about your business relationship with him?"

Miller shook his head and frowned, "I don't have a business relationship with Scott. He's a financial advisor, and I'm in real estate."

"The Arizona Secretary of State Trade Names and Trade Marks website has an entry that indicates otherwise. It says that you and Kimball are partners in a business called SG Enterprises."

"What?" Miller looked genuinely dumbfounded.

"Yes, SG Enterprises even has its own website although there's not much on it."

Miller turned to his computer and typed in the company URL on his keyboard. He stared at it for a moment. He was frowning and shaking his head no the entire time. He switched his gaze from his computer to Letty.

"I don't have any idea what this is about."

"Have you had any discussions with Kimball about starting a business together?"

"Absolutely not. When I see Scott, we usually talk about tennis. Can he just do that? Register a business claiming that someone is your partner without them even knowing?"

"He'd have to have access to your personal information." Letty felt a little tingle at the back of her neck. Personal information.

Miller was clearly disturbed. His earlier friendly real-estate salesman persona was all gone now.

"What do you suggest I do now? This has major implications for me and my own business. I mean if I'm in a partnership with another person that complicates everything. My tax situation with the IRS, just for one thing."

"I suggest you contact Kimball directly, and find out what he's up to. Then will you call me and inform me as well? I have an ongoing investigation into his business activities."

"Sure. Sure. I'll call you and let you know. I wouldn't have known about this at all if you hadn't come here. This is very disturbing. I feel like I'm being used, and I don't even know why or what for."

Letty nodded. Miller was giving every indication that he had not known anything about the joint business registration. She found his denial very believable.

Miller paused and added, "What do you mean you have an ongoing investigation?"

"I'm a private investigator."

"Ah. So you are investigating Kimball. Who hired you?"

"That's confidential."

Miller stared off into space for a few seconds. Then he turned again to Letty.

"Look. I have a luncheon appointment with a client. I can't miss it because there's a lot of money involved. I'll deal with Scott Kimball this afternoon. In fact, I'll go to his office and ask him directly about this. I want to see his face when I ask him. I want an explanation."

Letty stood. "Please call me when you learn what's going on."

Miller shook his head, clearly distracted. He came out from behind his desk and opened his office door for her. They went out the front door of the building together. Letty began walking toward her pickup which was parked out on the street.

"I'll call you later, Miss Valdez. Thank you for informing me about this."

She turned back toward Miller, nodded and gestured that she'd heard him. Miller headed the other way toward the parking lot at the back of his firm's office building. She saw him approach a Toyota Land Cruiser. As she walked away, she was reminded that she'd been thinking about getting a new vehicle, one with a backseat and maybe a hatchback. With a bigger vehicle, she could take more than one person and the dogs with her plus some supplies when she went out to visit her grandmother on the reservation. But it wouldn't be a Land Cruiser. At nearly $85,000, the Land Cruiser was too expensive for Letty.

Letty continued walking toward her pickup.

Suddenly a huge explosion blasted in every direction from the parking lot at the rear of the building. The shock wave hit Letty a second later and threw her violently forward away from the explosion. Her body twisted in the air, and she hit the pavement simultaneously on her right hip and on her upper back just below her right shoulder. She slid across the concrete, her shirt shredding against the rough pavement. The contact between concrete and her skin caused an instant, severe abrasion high on her back near her shoulder. The abrasion looked and felt like a bad burn. She stayed still for a moment, lying stunned on the pavement. The pain in her hip and back was intense. She was expecting gunfire to break out next. Where were the insurgents? Were they coming for her? Was it her imagination or reality that someone was calling for a medic? She looked around, but she didn't see any soldiers. No insurgents either. No gunfire. She tried to get up then sat back down, slightly dizzy. This isn't Iraq, she told herself. I'm in Tucson. This is not Iraq. This is not Iraq. Her ears rang from the blast noise.

Finally Letty pulled herself up and limped forward toward the explosion. A few people had gathered already. She could hear women crying. Then she saw Miller's SUV. It was completely destroyed, nothing but a blackened, twisted pile of metal. It was just like the Army's light armored vehicles when they hit an IED. Smoke rose from the blast. A small fire burned beneath what had been the engine. The cars on either side were severely damaged. Miller himself was now nothing but a skeleton of blackened bones and a skull halfway in and halfway out of what was left of the driver's side door. Broken glass and chunks of burned metal were everywhere.

She heard sirens. She sat down on the pavement, feeling dizzy again. She didn't know how long she'd been there when a fireman approached her.

"Are you okay, Miss?" he asked. "I can call the EMTs for you."

Letty looked up at him. "I'm okay. I didn't hit my head."

"That's good. Let us know if you need help."

She nodded and waited. She knew the police would come.

Maybe twenty minutes had passed, maybe more. Letty couldn't be sure. Her hearing was starting to return to normal. She could feel the pain of a major bruise on her hip already making itself felt, and there was that scraped off area of skin on her back that stung and burned. She waited and tried to get her bearings.

A police officer approached her. "Sure you don't need any medical attention?"

"No, I'm okay. I think there was a bomb."

"Did you see the explosion?"

"No, I was walking away facing in the opposite direction."

"I need your name and contact information. We'll contact you soon for a statement. Don't leave Tucson. Understand?"

"Okay." She pulled herself to her feet. She found one of her cards in her wallet and handed it to the police officer.

Letty headed for her pickup truck. She did her best to not limp because she suspected the police officer was watching her. To her, he had this big-brother feel about him. She knew she was going to have a big bruise on her hip. Her right back shoulder hurt where the abrasion was located. She would clean that up when she got home and maybe put a bandage on it so it wouldn't bleed on her clothing. She was very grateful that she hadn't hit her head. A concussion would have put her out of action for a while. Concussions could be serious. She got off easy. Gordon Miller did not.

* * *

On the drive back to her office, Letty's thoughts began to clear.

What the hell? That was totally unexpected. Someone obviously wanted Gordon Miller dead. Was there any connection to the case she was working on? Or had he made enemies elsewhere? She had no answer to that. Worse, she still felt a bit muddled, and the scrape on her back was really starting to hurt.

Letty wanted to check on Frankie before she called it quits for the day, but he wasn't there. He had shut everything down, turned off the lights, and locked the door behind him.

I need to get him a key, Letty thought to herself. She turned on her computer to check emails one more time before going home.

There was an email from Frankie using his new ValdezInvestigations.com email address.

It read:

"Hey Letty, I did some surfing, and I found info both about Jen and Scott Kimball. I'm writing up a report. They are quite affluent and socially well-connected. I have a list of his business interests, too. Also I made some progress on that dude's tattoos. I couldn't find a gang connection, but there may be a connection with the military. Most vets have tattoos these days. This dude's particular tattoos are linked to a U.S. Army platoon that served in Afghanistan. I think your Mexican landscaping man is a vet. Do you know how to track down individuals who served with a particular group of soldiers? If so, I bet we can figure out who this guy is. Oh, yeah. I found that the business you showed me in the Secretary of State's database, the SG Enterprises? This business is the owner of a house over on the east side. So that means Kimball and Gordon Miller own a house together, right? See ya' tomorrow. Frankie Miranda, Private Investigator In Training. LOL"

Impressive, Frankie, Letty thought. He's really taking to this.

A house? Why would these two guys own a house? Maybe it's just one of their first investments together. That made sense. Miller, after all, was in the real estate business. Too bad she wouldn't get a chance to ask Miller about it.

Letty sat still, suddenly aware that some idea or sensory impression or a memory was trying to make its way into her consciousness. The car bomb. It had something to do with the car bomb. Something she had seen just before it went off. That was all. She couldn't remember. Her shoulder and hip hurt. It was time to go home and get ready for her date with Dan.

CHAPTER 11

After a quick shower, Letty tended to the wound on her back as best she could. She stood with her back facing her bathroom mirror stretching to the side to see where she was hurt. She'd done her best to clean the wound in the shower, and now she sprayed some antiseptic on it. That was awkward, too. She managed to put a light gauze bandage over it and tape it to her back, not easy given where the wound was. That gauze would keep it from bleeding onto her blouse. She could see a bruise forming under and around the abrasion. Her hip already had a bruise as well. She shook her head in frustration.

Twenty minutes later, Letty arrived at Dan's home with two dogs in tow. He lived in a new house, a big house, squeezed next to several other big new houses that lined Alamo Wash just south of the Rillito River. She took the turn off Swan Road into the housing development, following a street that ended in a circle. She went around the circle and pulled into the driveway of a house with the number Dan had given her. The driveway ended in a garage, and the door into the house was to the left of the garage.

Dan must have been watching because he was there on the sidewalk as Letty opened her car door.

"Hello, hello, hello," Dan said. "You found me."

"Not that hard," Letty said with a smile. "If you remember, I dropped off you and your bike here already."

Dan nodded. "Come inside. This way, doggies."

Letty and dogs piled out of her truck. Both Teddy and Millie jumped around Dan wagging their tails as if they hadn't seen him in forever. Then both dogs relieved themselves. Millie squatted next to Dan's mail box, and Teddy hiked his leg next to a mesquite tree in Dan's front yard.

"I see they are marking territory," Dan said.

"Yes, your house is their house now."

"That's good. I needed some dogs to keep away the coyotes. They show up here sometimes. Come on. I'll give you a quick tour."

"What's in the garage?"

"My bike. I don't have a car. I usually jog or bike to work. Come on inside."

They entered through a short hallway. Off to the left was the living room and to the right, a staircase that went up to the second floor. A kitchen and dining area was beyond that at the back of the house. She could see two doors off the kitchen that led to a laundry room and a small bathroom. The dining area had big windows that led to a covered outdoor patio. The backyard was small and desert landscaped with a velvet mesquite tree near the house, a fifteen-foot tall saguaro and a small orange tree, both near the back wall. Letty approached the wall.

"Here. Step up on this, and you can see." Dan put a small wooden bench next to her.

Letty did as he directed and stepped up. She could see a dirt-packed trail that led off in both directions along the stone wall that lined the backyard of all the houses. Along the trail on the other side were metal railings, then a steep drop-off into a wash.

"Alamo Wash," Letty said.

"Right. We'll go walk there later. Come on, and I'll show you upstairs."

They left the dogs out in the back yard. Dan had left a bowl of water, and both dogs slurped.

They returned to the house, and Letty followed Dan upstairs.

"This is where I sleep." The room had a king-sized bed and a small desk with a computer in the corner. She noticed a bathroom, too. This must be the master bedroom. The king-sized bed was big. It was made up in a very tidy fashion. She wondered if he had ever had overnight guests that shared the bed with him.

Dan led her down the hallway.

"This room is a bedroom whenever I have friends stay over. Some of my Médecins Sans Frontières pals will show up from time to time. Two have already visited. I have an open invitation for them all. My mom and her friend will probably come to visit, too." The room had two twin-sized beds. Dan led her back into the hallway. They passed another bathroom. It was much larger.

"Your dad?"

"He died several years ago. Mom has a guy she sees. But now I'm talking about her friend Kulap. Sometimes they go on vacations together. Kulap is my friend, too. They'll show up here eventually, probably when it's twenty below in Minneapolis." He laughed.

"Kulap. That's an usual name."

"Yeah, she's Thai. Her name means 'beautiful rose.' She was the mother of my best friend when I was growing up. I spent a lot of time at their house. She's really like a second mother to me. It's a long story. I'll tell you later."

Finally Dan reached the last room. The door was closed.

"This is my meditation room." He opened the door, and they both stepped in. The almost-empty room was full of early evening light streaming in from windows with no curtains, only light bamboo shades that were rolled up. There was no furniture. On one wall was a small table with a figure of the Buddha carved from some unknown stone, a candle and a bowl full of oranges. A rug was on the floor in front of the table.

Letty didn't know what to say. She'd never seen anything like this. Dan stood there smiling.

Letty looked at him. "You're a Buddhist?"

"Yeah, I guess so," he shrugged his shoulders.

She looked at him. She really didn't know what to say. She didn't know any Buddhists.

"I know it's a big house. I was going to try to find a roommate, but the idea of having a room for my visiting friends and family, and a meditation room, too, was too much to resist. A lot of my friends are also Buddhists, and they will like this room. So I filled the space myself. After the way I had been living before, I'm living in total luxury now."

Dan closed the door, and they retreated back down the stairs.

"Let's go take these dogs for a walk, and then I'll fix you something to eat."

"I have leashes in my backpack."

They retrieved the dogs, leashed them both and left Dan's house for the street. Dan took Millie, and Letty had Teddy on his leash. They walked north along the street. Then Dan led them off on a dirt path that led down to the wash. They passed through large palo verde trees that lined both sides of the Alamo Wash. They had to go slowly because Millie limped on three legs.

"Do you trust them to come if you take them off the leashes?"

"Yes, they are both well-trained." Letty bent down and took Teddy's leash off. He stood waiting for a command. Same with Millie.

"Good dogs," she waved her hand. "Go play."

They both began sniffing everything in their path. Teddy ran in circles that got larger and larger. He sniffed everything he encountered, and Millie limped along behind him sniffing, too.

Letty and Dan walked together. Letty felt relaxed to be outdoors in such a beautiful place. She was enjoying the view. Facing her were the Santa Catalina Mountains. Her only problem was her hip which was hurting now. Too many sharp moves made the bandage on her shoulder shift as well, and she could feel irritation of skin that had been scraped raw. She tried her best to not limp. She didn't want Dan to see her discomfort.

Ten minutes later the wash opened out onto the Rillito River. The wide river bed was mostly dry, but there was a rivulet of water flowing gently in the middle. The view of the mountains expanded.

"I guess the snow pack in the Catalinas is still melting," Dan said.

"Yes. We should have water for a while. Let's not let them get too muddy. They'll make a mess of your house."

The dogs played in and out of the water as Dan and Letty sauntered along slowly. They were quiet. Peaceful. That's how Letty felt. Peaceful.

After a while, Dan said, "Okay, time to go home. I bet you're hungry."

"Before we go back, I'd like to ask you a question," Letty said.

"Okay. Go ahead."

"I know what you saw and experienced over there in the war zones. So many of us came back depressed and with PTSD and drug and alcohol problems. You're not like that at all. I can't understand it. You seem cheerful all the time. I just don't get it. Why are you so happy?"

Dan was quiet for a few minutes. "Well, it's kind of a long story. I wasn't always like this. I'll tell you everything if you want to know. It gets down to my having to confront some delusional thinking on my part. I had to make an existential choice between misery and contentment. I decided to be content."

Letty had no idea what he was talking about. How could a person choose to be content?

"Come on. I'm getting hungry. I'll tell you all about that later."

They made their way back up Alamo Wash, back along the dirt trail then the street. Dan went inside and came out with a towel. Letty wiped down the dogs and managed to get most of the wet sand off their legs and paws.

"I made a bed for them. It's an old piece of foam with a cover on it." Dan led the dogs to a water bowl, and they drank. He directed them to the dog bed, and they settled down immediately.

He turned and looked at Letty.

"So, Letty, are you going to let me take care of you now?"

Letty looked at Dan sharply. "What do you mean?"

"Come on, Letty. You can't fool me. You're hurt. Something happened, and now you're hurt." His voice had changed. He wasn't Dan anymore. He had become Doctor Ennis.

Letty sighed. "So obvious, huh?"

"You're limping, and you're favoring your back or shoulder. I can't tell which. What happened?"

"A car bomb."

"A car bomb? Good grief."

"I got thrown back against the pavement. There's a bruise on the hip and an abrasion and bruise on the back just below the shoulder. The abrasion was caused by scraping bare skin against the pavement." She thought her voice had changed, too. She had become a medic again describing a soldier's wounds. Some other soldier. Not her.

"Other than you, did anyone get hurt?"

"Yeah, the guy getting into the car got incinerated."

"Is this part of your job as an investigator?"

Letty nodded.

Dan sighed and shook his head.

"I'm going to take care of you now." He went into the small bathroom. She could hear him washing his hands.

"No, Dan, I'll be okay."

"*Letty.*"

"You shouldn't have to work all the time. This is your day off."

"*Sit down!*" Dan led her to one of the dining room chairs against the wall and pushed her down. He sat in the chair nearest her. He took her hands in his.

"Do I interfere with your work as a private investigator?"

"No," she said weakly.

"Then don't interfere with my medical work. Doctoring is what I do. It's my life's work, my duty, my right action, my spiritual path. Get it?"

He sounded annoyed. Letty couldn't ever remember Dan being even slightly annoyed.

"I don't know what that means, but if you say so."

"I say so. You have a bruise on your hip. Is there an abrasion there, too?"

"No, just a bad bruise."

"Sure it's just a bruise? Do you need an x-ray to see if the bone is fractured? Maybe a hairline fracture?"

"No, the pain isn't that bad."

"Okay, so take off your blouse so I can have a look."

Letty froze. She stared into space, and then she scrunched up her shoulders.

Dan sighed. "You are so full of contradictions. You are a martial arts expert who carries a gun in your back pocket, beats up on the bad guys, solves mysteries and brings justice to the world. You are also a very sweet and shy woman who doesn't want to take off her blouse in front of a man. Am I right?"

Letty shook her head yes timidly.

"You know, you don't have anything I haven't already seen."

Letty grimaced.

Dan sighed impatiently. "Wait a minute."

He left the room and went into the nearby living room. He returned with an afghan in his hand.

"I'm going to turn my back now. You take off your blouse and slip your bra strap down off that shoulder. Cover your front with the afghan. When you are ready, let me know."

It only took her a minute to do as he said.

"Ready," she said.

Dan came to stand behind her. He reached above Letty's head to turn on a light. He removed the bandage that she had put on herself. He took a good look at the abrasion on her back.

"Hmmm…" he said.

Letty waited patiently.

"Hmmm…"

Letty frowned.

"Hmmm…"

"*What?*"

"This wound needs to be cleaned. Did you clean it?"

"As best I could. I stood in the shower."

She heard him click his tongue. 'Not acceptable' was the clear message.

He left her and came back with his medical bag.

"Turn your head away. I'm going to spray this with a topical anesthetic so you won't hurt when I clean the wound. Hold your breath for a few seconds." She did as he said. He moved her long braid to the side, and he sprayed the area. The spray was cold.

Dan waited a minute. He began cleaning the wound. She could feel him moving against her, but she felt no pain.

"You know you can get a bad infection if you don't clean wounds properly. You could get *Clostridium perfringens* bacteria from the dirt."

"That sounds lovely."

"Smart ass."

She could feel him working slowly and carefully.

"I'm going to put a heavy towel here and irrigate the wound now."

Letty waited patiently.

"I think I got out all the little bits of sand and tiny rocks. Now for the antibiotic cream. Then I'll put a light bandage on top of this to keep it from bleeding any or weeping on the fabric of your shirt. I'm going to give you some amoxicillin tablets, just to make sure. Will you take them? Yes, you will," Dan answered before she could say anything.

Letty sighed. "Yes." Somehow it felt good to have Dan caring for her.

"What's this?"

She could feel him moving her braid again. He touched her other shoulder. There was a scar there just above her scapula.

"That's a scar."

"I see that. What caused the wound?"

"A bullet."

"A bullet? You were shot?"

"Yes, in Iraq."

"Ah. What happened?" He was sitting in front of her again.

"An IED went off. I went running forward toward the soldiers in the blown-up vehicle. I saw this shadow passing in front of me. I looked up and there was an insurgent on the roof of the nearest building. He was pointing his gun at me. He pulled the trigger. I think he meant to shoot me in the head or throat. He wanted to kill me. But the bullet went all the way through my shoulder. Front to back."

"Does it bother you at all?"

"No, not really."

"They did a good job of treating you. The scar is not easy to see."

"Yeah, the doc said my collar bone was nicked. I didn't even bleed all that much. But it hurt."

"Yeah, getting shot usually hurts. So you have a Purple Heart, Letty Valdez."

"Yes."

"Does your family know?"

"I don't know. I never mentioned it."

He shook his head. "Where is this Purple Heart?"

"In a box in my drawer."

"What else is in the drawer? A big pile of medals that you've never mentioned to anyone?"

"No, just my underwear."

Dan chuckled.

"What's funny?"

"Well, you don't really expect a Purple Heart to be surrounded by a lady's panties."

Letty shrugged. "It's all part of the past now."

"I went out on a couple of ambulance runs, and they shot at me, too. But they missed."

"They shot at *you*?"

"Yes, can you believe that? And I'm such a nice guy."

She looked up at him. He was grinning. Of course.

Dan securely taped the bandage to her back.

"Okay. Finished." He reached into his bag and pulled out a small bottle of pills.

"Take all of them. Follow the directions."

"Okay."

"Promise?"

"Yes, Dr. Ennis. I promise."

Dan smiled. "Then you can see your regular physician if you don't want me looking at you again. Who is your physician?"

Letty frowned.

"Oh my god. You're such a handful. You don't have a regular doctor, do you?"

"Not really."

"When was the last time you had a pap smear or a mammogram? Or any vaccines?"

Letty looked down at her hands.

"Okay. We're going to change that." He got up from his chair and went to a small desk in the front hall. He returned with a card.

"This is a friend of mine. Her name is Nadia Ochoa. She's an ob-gyn doctor here in Tucson. We've worked together. Puerto Rico was the last time we were on the same team. You call her and make an appointment. Tell her I sent you."

"Okay."

"About this abrasion, I'll check you again in a couple of days. I'll change the bandage, too."

"Thank you, Dan."

"My pleasure. I'm going to fix you something to eat now. My back will be turned so you can put your blouse back on safely without any bad boys leering at you." He paused, "You know, I am a doctor. I've delivered babies."

Letty nodded. She felt a little silly.

Dan rose, went to the kitchen and began preparing their meal. Letty put her blouse on again.

"Can I help you?"

"Nah. I'm making easy stuff."

"Will you tell me sometime about your volunteer doctor experiences?"

"Sure. What do you want to know?"

"I don't know. Just tell me what comes into your mind. I've never known anyone who has done that kind of volunteer work."

"Well, conditions are often rough. Usually it's not very luxurious so the ones who volunteer are ones who don't mind living rough for a while. But it's satisfying work."

"What was the best experience?"

"Hard to say. Ouch."

"What happened?"

"I'm just clumsy. I haven't cooked for anyone for a long time. I just pinched my finger. It's okay. So the best experience? I've had several. This last one in Puerto Rico was good. We went into the back country and took care of people in very rural mountainous areas who normally don't get to see a doctor. They were very welcoming. The Puerto Ricans are a lot of fun. They like music and dancing."

"What was the worst?"

"I would say trying to provide care to Rohingya refugees when they fled Myanmar and went to Bangladesh. There were thousands of them there. Living conditions were awful. No clean water, little food and it was often contaminated. There was a lot of disease because of that. Our team members had to be careful not to become sick ourselves. The suffering was tremendous. I had a hard time especially with seeing infants and small children suffer so much."

"Do you think you'll continue doing this kind of work?"

"Maybe. Not any time soon. I have a job here that I like, and I'm meeting some interesting people."

"Oh, yeah. Like who?"

"*You,*" Dan chuckled.

Letty shook her head.

"I'm not interesting."

"I get to decide that, Letty. I think you are very interesting. Here. Put these plates and silverware on the table. And chopsticks, too. Do you know how to eat with chopsticks?"

"Sort of. Clarice showed us."

"Okay. I think we're ready to eat."

CHAPTER 12

The meal was unusual, a first for Letty who had never had Thai food. Dan made several dishes in small amounts so that Letty could try everything. She found all the dishes to be delicious, and she said so. As they tried each dish, he gave her the Thai name.

"This is *tom yum* soup. This is *som tam*. It has papaya in it. Do you like papaya?"

"I don't know. I've never eaten it. It's a fruit, right?"

Dan nodded.

"*Gaeng keow wan gai* is a curry that usually has chicken, but I put fish in it. This is *pad thai* rice noodles with shrimp. Everyone knows *pad thai*."

Letty didn't. She was reminded of just how restricted her knowledge of the world was compared to Dan.

"Try this drink. *Nam manao*. It's limeade, and it's very sweet."

As they finished their meal, Letty said, "Everything is delicious. How did you learn to make all these dishes? Is cooking your hobby?"

"Well, I never had thought of it that way, but maybe so. When I was in the monastery, another monk and I liked to cook, and we tried all these new...."

"Whoa. Wait. What? Time out. Monastery? Monk? You were a *monk*?"

"Yeah, that's part of my story."

"Tell me."

"I'm afraid you'll think I'm weird." Dan seemed shy all of a sudden.

"I already think you're weird." Letty smiled. "Tell me."

Dan frowned. "Really? You think I'm weird."

"Yes. Weird charming. Go ahead."

"You think I'm charming?" He was smiling again.

"Very charming. Interesting, too. You're sort of intriguing. I think about you a lot. It's annoying. You're such a distraction. Now tell me everything."

"Oh. I like that. You think about me? I think about you, too, Letty."

"*Tell me.*"

"Okay. The first part is sad, and then it gets better. But first, let's go sit on the couch in the living room so we can be comfortable."

They went to the living room and sat down next to each other. The dogs followed them into the living room and stretched out on the carpet.

"Okay. I'm ready," Letty said.

"When I was in middle school and high school, we had several deaths in our family."

"Your dad?"

Dan nodded. "He was the last one. My grandparents first, and then my brother, too."

"You had a brother? How old were you when he died?"

"Just turned thirteen."

"How old was your brother?"

"Thirteen. We were twins."

"Twins? What was his name?"

"His name was Dev. We were identical twins. It was hard to tell us apart."

Letty sat dumbfounded. There's was a lot more to Dan Ennis than she ever imagined. A monk? An identical twin?

"We looked alike, but we had different personalities. He was a lot more reckless than I ever was as a kid. He died when he was goofing around with some kids and fell off the back of the football stadium. It was about a sixty-foot drop. He broke his neck."

"That's awful. So sad."

"Then my dad died about eighteen months later. My mom was devastated by my brother's death. When my dad died, it was too much for her. She just lost it and stayed in a bed for a couple of months. She was very depressed."

"Oh, your poor mom."

"Yeah. Then she pulled herself up, and she went to work as a social worker. She worked all the time. I think she was running away from the pain by working so much. Anyway, I didn't see much of her. I don't blame her. She was traumatized."

"That was when you ate alone and were lonely?"

"Yes. So I started going over to my best friend Preed's house. Preed's family is Thai. His parents are immigrants. Kulap is Preed's mom. I mentioned her earlier. I ate supper with them nearly every evening. Preed and I were close friends from the sixth grade on. We played on the same soccer team in high school and college, smoked weed together, drank beer together, talked about girls together, we both loved music and shared CDs, everything. He used to yell at me when we played soccer. He'd yell at me, 'Ennis, you suck big time!' and then he'd laugh like insulting my soccer skills was the funniest thing ever. I laughed, too, but I tried harder and I became a better player because of him. Preed was my best friend in the whole world."

He paused. Letty waited.

"I went to med school then into the Army. Preed went to grad school in engineering. Then he went into the Army, too. The idea there was to get financial aid for school. We reconnected when we were both deployed to Afghanistan. One day a huge bomb exploded in the Kabul market. They brought our soldiers in first. Later we worked on the civilians. They brought Preed to me. He was mortally wounded. The hole in his chest was huge. He had all sorts of organ damage. Blood was everywhere. He knew he wasn't going to make it. The last thing he did was to look me in the eyes, and then he said, 'I love you, Dan.' He died in my arms. My best friend."

Letty's eyes were filled with tears. She'd seen too much death. She knew how Dan felt.

"I'm so sorry, Dan. That's so sad."

Dan hesitated for a moment then continued.

"I started drinking. I mean seriously drinking. After I was discharged and I came home, I stopped working. I went into my mom's basement every evening and drank myself into a stupor. Often I didn't wait until the evening. I was drunk most of the time really. I don't know how many bottles of bourbon or vodka or something alcoholic, anything alcoholic, disappeared down my throat over the next few months. I didn't want to feel anything. The war, all the misery, then Preed dying. I think my drinking was a kind of slow suicide."

Letty shook her head. Her tears spilled over.

"Don't cry, sweetie," he said gently. "It gets better."

Dan took her hand in his.

"My mom tried to get me to go to the VA and get help, but I ignored her. Finally she and Kulap got together and came up with a plan. Remember Kulap is Preed's mom. She thought of me as a second son. Kulap called her brother in Thailand, and he came and got me. He took me back to Thailand with him. I was drunk when I got on the plane. Kulap's brother was a muscled-up guy, and I was no match for him or his friends once we arrived in Bangkok. They took me to the monastery and handed me over the monks. The last thing he said to me was, "You were my nephew's friend. Honor him with your life." I found out later my mom and Kulap paid the monastery to keep me until I stopped drinking and turned my life around. My mom and Kulap and the monks saved me."

"What happened at the monastery?"

"I tried several times to break out. The monks would find me pretty quickly. A drunk, six-foot tall white dude was pretty easy to spot. They would find me and take me back. There was one monk, a big guy who didn't mind a bit whacking me on my backside with a stick like a misbehaving child. It was embarrassing, and it hurt. The other monks giggled when he did that. Once they got me back home to the monastery again, I would go to my teacher with a long string of excuses about why I shouldn't have to stay in his monastery. He always listened. Then he would laugh and walk away."

"So no more booze?" Letty asked.

"No booze in the monastery. The first few times I broke out, I got drunk first thing. Then last time I escaped, I didn't get drunk. I realized right away that I had screwed up. I realized that I really needed to be in the monastery. I needed the monks' help. I needed to learn what my teacher had to teach. I went back, but they wouldn't let me in. I stayed on the front steps of the monastery for two days and two nights. Finally my teacher came out. He took my hand and led me back in."

"Wow."

"For the entire time I lived there, I had to sit in meditation three hours every morning starting at half past three a.m. and three more hours in the evening. I listened to my teacher instruct us every day. In the other waking hours, I worked in the monastery cleaning and also cooking."

"You learned the Thai language?"

"I had to. No one spoke much English."

"And you changed?"

"I did. Eventually. I was stubborn at first. Finally I started really listening to what my teacher had to say. I decided to try to follow the Eight-Fold Path. Developing Right Understanding was my first task. Somewhere along the way, I figured out that my misery was self-inflicted. I had a choice. I realized that I could follow the teachings, choose the right way to live and claim contentment. I thought a lot about how I could honor Preed with my life like his uncle said."

"Then what happened?"

"After a couple of years of this, my teacher started sending me out to provide medical care to orphanages and other monasteries in Bangkok, and eventually to the aid groups I work with now. My teacher told me that it was my path in life to care for people. Then one day, he told me I could leave the monastery, but wherever I chose to live, I was to continue working as a doctor. So I came to Tucson. But that's another story about how I came to be here."

Letty had been listening raptly, bent over staring at him, elbows on knees, her chin on her hands. She sat up and took a deep breath.

Dan smiled at her. "So that's the answer to your question, Letty. That's why I'm content and happy most of the time. I chose this path."

"What an incredible story."

"And I remind you, you think I'm charming, interesting, and intriguing, too. I think the same about you."

She smiled. "But that's not very monkish, is it?"

"I am no longer a monk. I live in the world, and I enjoy the pleasures of the world."

Dan looked directly into her eyes. There was that crooked smile again.

Pleasures of the world? What does that mean? Letty asked herself. She suddenly felt very warm.

"Do you want to listen to some music?" Dan asked.

"Okay."

"What do you like?"

"I don't know. I don't listen to the radio much. My brother Will and Clarice talk about musicians sometimes, but I don't know who they are talking about."

"Tell me the last music you heard that you really liked."

Letty considered this. "Well, I can tell you the musician's name. But there's a story that goes with it. It's not very nice."

"Okay. Do you want to tell the story?"

"Yes. I'll tell you. I don't usually talk about this, but I'll tell you."

"What was the musician's name?"

"Yo Yo Ma."

Dan's eyebrows went up. "Really? You constantly surprise me."

"What did you expect?"

"Honestly, I didn't know what to expect, but not Yo Yo Ma."

"I like when Yo Yo Ma plays Bach. I found it on the internet so I could listen to it."

Dan stood up and went to a case against the wall. He opened the door and pulled out a CD. He slipped it into the CD player.

The sounds of Yo Yo Ma playing "Cello Suite No. 1 in G Major-Prelude" filled the room.

"That's it. That's the one I like."

They listened for a few minutes.

"This is nice listening with you," Letty said. "This is my best experience listening to him play. The first time wasn't so great."

"Tell me the story of your first time to hear Bach played by Ma."

"My commanding officer called me to his quarters one evening. This was playing on his CD when I entered. It was so beautiful. We listened for a while. I couldn't believe what happened next."

"What?"

"He forced himself on me and tried to rape me."

"*Letty, no!*"

"Yeah, the prick. At first he tried to seduce me with the music. He tried kissing me, and I didn't respond. I pushed him away. When the music didn't work for him, he ordered me to take off my clothes. *Ordered me!* He said having sex with him was for the good of the company."

Dan was red in the face now. "That's outrageous. That really pisses me off. Who is this fucker?"

"Calm down, Dan. We never got that far."

"What do you mean?"

"I accidentally broke his nose."

Dan's eyes got wide. Then he guffawed.

"Accidentally?"

"Maybe."

"Maybe accidentally?"

"Yeah, maybe."

"You are so amazing. That fucker deserved a broken nose and a whole lot more."

"I think he realized that he'd gone too far. He decided that he wouldn't discipline me for his nose if I didn't report an attempted rape. Not that it would have done any good if I had reported it."

"Yes, I understand sexual assault is common in all branches of the military."

"Most women don't report, and if they do, too often nothing happens. Guys get raped, too. Things could have turned out badly for me. He could have raped me *and* disciplined me for breaking his nose."

Dan shook his head. "So wrong."

"Let's pretend that never happened," Letty said. "Let's pretend the first time I heard this lovely music was at Dan Ennis's house in Tucson, Arizona, one evening after a Thai dinner and with a couple of dogs snoozing on the carpet in front of us."

Dan leaned back against the couch. He took Letty's hand in his.

"Yes, let's pretend. This is your first time to hear Yo Yo Ma play Bach."

They listened again through the entire piece.

Letty was smiling now.

"Do you have any more stories to tell me about yourself?" she asked Dan. "Time traveling? A visit to another planet maybe?"

"Sorry. I've never been to outer space."

"Do you mind telling me about your brother?"

"No. What do you want to know?"

"What was his name?"

"Devlin Alexander Ennis. His name Devlin means 'fierce bravery' in the original Irish language."

"That's a nice name. What was he like?"

"As I said, he was more reckless than I was. I've always wondered if maybe he was a little hyperactive. He liked to think up new things to do. He'd drag me along with him. We constantly got in trouble together. He was smart and also pretty ornery."

"And people had trouble telling you apart?"

Dan was smiling now, remembering. "Yes, we played tricks on people."

'I think he wasn't the only one who was ornery."

Dan shrugged. He had a very innocent look on his face.

"Is it true that identical twins have a psychic connection?"

"Yes. It was true for us. I knew the instant he died."

"How did you know?"

"It was like a light went out. I felt dark and cold and very lonely in a way I'd never felt before in my life. I think that's why I started going over to Preed's house so much. I was lonely. My parents couldn't cope. My mom just fell apart. I was on my own."

Letty nodded. "Devlin had a very pretty name."

"We both have Irish names. Our family is Irish."

"What is your name?"

"Daniel Aidan Ennis."

"Gosh, that's a beautiful name."

"You think so?"

"Very beautiful."

"What is your name? Tell me one name at a time."

"Leticia."

"Ah, Leticia. That sounds like the name of a Renaissance princess. Nice. And that's where Letty comes from?"

She nodded. "Next name. Fernanda."

"Oh my god. Are you serious?"

"Yes," Letty looked surprised. "What?"

"That's so incredibly sexy. Fernanda," he let name slowly roll off his tongue.

"Why do you think it's sexy?"

"I imagine you in a tight black dress with lots of cleavage and a slit up the side of the skirt. You're wearing black spiked heels and you have a rose in your hair which is stuck in a bun at the back your neck."

"That sounds like a costume for a tango dancer."

"Exactly. Fernanda." Again he rolled the word off his tongue.

Letty laughed. "You're funny. You have quite an imagination."

"Let's go to Buenos Aires sometime and dance the tango. Will you do that with me, Fernanda?"

"Maybe."

"Not maybe. For sure," Dan said. "Okay, keep going. What are your other names?"

"Antone. That's my mother's last name. It's a common name on the O'odham reservation."

"And Valdez?"

"That's my Mexican-American father's name. Valdez is also fairly common."

"Can I meet your O'odham and your Mexican-American families sometime?"

"Sure, but be warned."

"Warned about what?"

"On the Mexican side, the Valdez family is huge. There are a bunch of women in the family from sixteen and fifty who are going to jump all over you."

"Why?" he looked confused.

"Because you're a doctor and because you are a good-looking guy."

"Oh, Letty. You think I'm good-looking? Weird charming and good-looking?"

"Yes. They will like you. But I'll protect you. Don't worry."

Dan laughed. "Sounds like a good deal."

Letty smiled. "I have to go home now. Thank you for dinner. Thank you for taking care of me. And thank you for changing Yo Yo Ma into a good memory."

Dan followed Letty out to her pickup. She gestured to the dogs, and they jumped in.

"Now it's your turn to ask me out. Don't forget," he said.

"I won't forget."

"And don't forget to take your pills."

"I won't forget."

Letty nodded then added, "Dan."

"Yes?"

"My gun is in a holster, not in my back pocket."

Dan threw back his head and laughed.

"Sorry. My bad," he leaned forward and kissed Letty on her cheek.

Letty headed home. That night before she went to bed, Letty turned on her computer and googled Buddhism's Eight-Fold Path. How can a person choose to be happy? Weird.

CHAPTER 13

The next morning, Letty arrived early at her office. She felt well-rested, probably because no Iraq dreams had tormented her in the night. She brought decent coffee with her in a thermos from home and sipped a cup as she watched early sunlight hit the ridges of the Santa Catalina Mountains. She went over everything that happened the evening before.

Dan. Her mind was filled with thoughts of Dan. Funny, sweet, handsome, and with the wildest story she'd ever heard. A Buddhist monk. Who knew? She told herself that she was going to have to show some self-discipline now. She couldn't be thinking about that man all the time, no matter how interesting he seemed to her. Too much work to do. No, she had to stop thinking about Dan. Oh, but those deep blue-green eyes.

Letty forced herself to concentrate. She went back over her conversation with Gordon Miller. She kept coming up with the same conclusion. He did not appear to know anything about the business link with Scott Kimball. And what, if anything, did that have to do with his sudden and horrifying death? The car bombing wasn't really her problem to solve, especially if it had nothing to do with Jen Kimball, her client. But what if it did indeed have something to do with the Kimballs?

Letty called Alejandro Ramirez at Tucson Police Department's Homicide Unit. She and Alejandro had become friends on her last case. She knew she could be more open with him than anyone else at TPD.

"Hey, Letty, I'm glad you called," Alejandro said when he answered his phone. "I was about to call you. You're scheduled to give a statement to one of our officers about that car bombing yesterday. I told them I wanted to talk with you myself."

"That's good to hear. That's exactly why I was calling. How about if I come to your office later this morning? I'll fill you in on what I know."

"It's a deal. See you later."

Frankie came in the front door just as Letty disconnected.

"Hi, Letty, are you okay? You went to see that dude who got bombed. I saw it on the news."

"Yeah, I was about a half a block away when it went off. I got banged up a little but not seriously hurt. I saw Dr. Ennis, and he fixed me up."

"Yeah, I met Doc Ennis at Will's birthday party. He's a nice guy. I'm really glad you're okay."

Letty nodded. "I did get a chance to talk to Gordon Miller. He didn't know anything about his new business relationship with Scott Kimball. I believed him, too. He was surprised and seemed upset to learn that he had a new business partner. He said there were tax implications among other things. He was going to confront Kimball later, after his luncheon date with a client."

"That makes sense. I guess I'd be upset, too, if I found out I was in business with someone, and I didn't even know it."

"So what's this about Miller and Kimball owning a house together?"

"Yeah, that's right. The owner is SG Enterprises with the same address as the one listed on the Secretary of State's database. It's a postal box."

"Too bad I can't ask Miller. How did you discover this? Usually we have to go to the county tax assessor to find out who owns property in Pima County."

"I didn't know that. I just wanted to know if their little company owned anything, and I figured if they did, it would show up in taxes. So I searched Google and found this article that said you could search the tax assessor, just like you said. So I went to the tax assessor's online site and searched. I put in SG Enterprises and got the address of the house they own."

"You're a clever guy, Frankie. You'll make a great detective."

"That stunt you did with the sub sandwiches to find my brother was very informative," he grinned. "You did a great job of acting, and you inspired me to get creative, too."

Letty smiled. "Thank you."

"My next step was to look at Zillow. That's an online real estate site. I found that this property owned by SG Enterprises is currently for sale. It's listed with Mariposa Real Estate. So I called Mariposa and asked about the property. I pretended that I was thinking of buying it. I asked the woman who answered the phone if anyone was living there or if it was empty. She told me that no one was living there. I asked her who owns it now, and she said the property was owned by SG Enterprises. I'm not sure she was supposed to tell me that. I think she was the receptionist. No agent was available at the time. That means she verified what I'd already found."

"Do you know where the house is located, or anything else about it?"

"Yes, it's over on the east side of Tucson just east of Agua Caliente Park. It's uphill a little bit from the park. The house is big, over five thousand square feet. Two stories. It's on a couple of acres. I looked at Zillow's valuation. It's worth over a million dollars. The current asking price is one million two hundred thousand."

Letty's eyebrows went up. "Whoa. Nice place, huh? And that means I've got a possible connection to another case I haven't told you about yet. Monday afternoon after you left here, I went to talk with a chemistry professor from the university. He wants me to look into a murder of a friend of his that happened about six months ago. The guy was shot in the head near where you say this house is located. They found the body uphill from the park. That means the body was also found uphill from this house."

"Is that just a coincidence?"

"Maybe. Maybe not. It's worth checking into. I was going to go over that way this morning to see if I could learn more about where the guy was killed. My contact with TPD tells me the murder has become a cold case. Show me on Google maps where the house is."

Frankie opened his laptop and within a few minutes, he showed Letty the house photographed from the air.

"Hmmm…" Letty said. "Okay. I'm definitely going to check this out. Meanwhile, I'd like to give you my extra key to the office, and you go get a copy made for yourself. Then go to your favorite computer store and pick out a computer that you think will work for you here. You'll leave the new computer here every day. I don't want you to use your own computer and be carrying it around with you. The info would be too sensitive in case someone steals your laptop or a friend decides to do some snooping."

"That sounds great."

"Can you charge it to your credit or debit card and I will repay you before the charges come through?"

"Sure."

"Just don't get the most expensive thing out there. Get something useful for our investigations."

"I'll get something good for business purposes, nothing fancy."

"I want to mention that I'm impressed at how you just jumped right in and came up with some very useful information. Well done."

"Thanks, Letty." Frankie looked very pleased to get this praise. "Working for you is way more fun than stocking shelves in a grocery store."

"Okay. I'm going to be gone most of the day. First, I'll go check out this place on the east side. Next I'm meeting with Alejandro Ramirez at TPD. I have to give a statement about what I saw at the bombing. I may not see you until late today or even tomorrow."

"What would you like for me to do next? After I get the key and a new computer, I mean."

"See if you can find out anything more about Gordon Miller and Scott Kimball. Miller claimed that their relationship was mainly social. See how far back they go, if they had any business dealings together in the past, anything you can find. I'll eventually go talk to Kimball. I want to know as much as possible before I ask him about Gordon Miller and what they've been up to. Look into Miller, too. For example, did he have any past legal troubles?"

Frankie nodded.

"I'm off. Text me if you need to."

"Bye, Letty. Thank you, Letty."

Letty went home to get Teddy, his leash, and her big sunhat. It had a floppy brim that partially hid her face.

"Maybe we need to get you a friend to stay with you when Teddy and I are on the job," she said to Millie. "Maybe a dog with only three legs? Just your style, huh, Millie."

Oh Lordy, Letty said to herself. What was she talking about? That's all she needed. Three dogs.

She felt bad about leaving Millie on her own, but she knew Clarice and Will would be home soon. She left a note for them.

* * *

The drive to the east side of Tucson took Letty nearly thirty minutes. The road narrowed from several lanes to only two as it drew closer to the Santa Catalina Mountains. She turned onto Soldier's Trail then turned again to arrive at the entrance of Agua Caliente Park. The park was a jewel of Tucson and Pima County, but Letty had always been surprised at how it was not well-known, even by locals. She drove past the big trees and into the parking lot. But instead of going into the park, Letty leashed Teddy, and they took off walking east on the road they had come in on. Soon they came to a turn off that led uphill past several large houses on small acreages. At one point, they walked around the side of a metal gate that blocked the narrow road into the area. The narrow road sloped gently upward toward the foothills.

Letty was wearing her floppy hat with Teddy the black lab leading happily. Letty thought they passed quite well as a neighbor and her dog out for a morning walk. They walked past a couple of pedestrians, one of whom had two small dogs. The dogs barked at Teddy in an unfriendly way. Teddy wagged his tail the entire time.

She found the house Frankie had shown her on the map. She and Teddy continued uphill past the house, higher into the foothills of the mountains. The narrow paved road quickly turned into a rough dirt road only passable by a four-wheel drive. She could see that there was a lot of territory to cover on the hillsides above her. Professor Anselm didn't know exactly where Edward Becker had found signs of chemical dumping. But the sinkhole had to be somewhere east of the park.

She turned and looked back. The view was magnificent. She could see the Tucson Mountains on the west side of Tucson. Far beyond that, Baboquivari Peak on the Tohono O'odham Reservation was visible. Her grandmother, her aunt and uncle and her little brother and his girlfriend all lived on the other side of Baboquivari Peak.

Letty looked down at the big house that belonged to SG Enterprises. Behind the house on the uphill side, there was a large RV parked. It wasn't visible from the paved road below because the house was so big. The two stories of the house pretty much hid the RV. Near the RV was a dirty dark-blue pickup truck with groundskeeper's tools in the back, rakes and shovels and a wheel barrow. The pickup looked a lot like the one in that photo that Marv had sent her of the young Mexican-American worker who visited Jen Kimball.

Letty pulled out her phone and took a photo of the pickup. Next she texted Frankie.

"Frankie, keep looking for that tattoo and see if you can figure out which Army platoon it's associated with. There may be a link to the Kimball case."

"Will do."

Letty and Teddy went a little higher on the mountainside and looked around a bit more. Maybe she could set aside several hours for a hike and see what she could find. Maybe Dan could come with her. He seemed open to anything she suggested. She could call it a "working date." Wonder what he'll think about that, she asked herself.

She headed back downhill. Just before the turn onto the main road that led back to Agua Caliente Park, she saw a woman watering a tree in her front yard. A long, curved driveway behind the woman went past a large boulder near the street then led up to a house a short walk away.

"Hello," the woman called out. "Nice dog. What's his name?" She dropped the water hose into the depression at the base of the tree.

Letty looked at the woman. She was older, maybe in her sixties, fit and trim with short-cut gray hair. She was smiling at Letty.

"Teddy. He's a black lab."

"I like those big dogs. I inherited my mom's Chihuahua when she died. He's an annoying little shit, but I love him anyway."

"I'm out for a walk. Do you know anything about that big house up there? Does anyone live there?"

"No. It belonged to someone, but they sold it recently. It doesn't look like anyone lives there, but there's this young groundskeeper guy who comes and goes all the time in his pickup. He's the only one I've seen up there. Maybe he lives in the RV in the back."

Letty nodded. "So you haven't seen any middle-aged white guys here?"

"No." She paused for a moment. "My name is Agnes Olsen. You're Letty Valdez, right?"

"Yes. How do you know my name?"

"I'm an ex-police officer. I was on the force in Milwaukee for thirty-one years. I was in charge of the Canine Unit. That's why I like the big dogs. My service ended when I was shot, and my dog was killed. My wound did me in for any more service so I decided to retire. Since I moved here, I just naturally have been following the local city cops, the sheriff's department, and the private detectives, too. The crimes in this region are really very interesting. As for you, Miss Valdez, I know you worked on a case about a real estate deal over on the west side. And Teddy is a trained detection canine. Or some people call them sniffer dogs."

"That's right. He found my friend Seri down in a secret compartment in a barn. He's a good boy and a good detection dog, too. Nice to meet you, Agnes. Call me Letty. So you've probably figured out that I'm here in your neighborhood on business."

"I thought maybe so, and with good reason. I have a gut feeling that something's not right about that property or the people who own it. The guy in the pickup is trying to look like a caretaker or a groundskeeper, but I don't know about that. Something doesn't seem right. I'm keeping an eye on the place."

"Have you seen anyone other than him up there?"

"No, no one at all."

Letty reached into her pocket and retrieved a business card.

"Agnes, please take my card and call me if you see anything interesting going on."

"I'll do that, Letty. Want my phone number?"

"Sure."

They traded cell phone numbers.

"Agnes, I have to go now. I'm meeting with TPD's head of the Homicide Unit. But I'd like to talk to you sometime. I bet your work was really interesting. I'm sorry to hear about your dog."

"My work was definitely interesting, although it broke my heart when my dog was shot and killed. He was my best friend. His name was Moto. The name comes from an Italian musical phrase, 'andante con moto,' which means to move faster. He was a big Belgian Malinois. Very fast dog. And very smart."

Letty nodded.

"I've been playing with the idea of become a dog trainer," Agnes added.

"You certainly know the business."

"Well, I'll let you go. Come by sometime for coffee. Meanwhile, I'll keep an eye on that place. If anything interesting happens, I'll contact you."

"Thank you so much."

They waved goodbye to each other. Teddy and Letty walked back down the road to her truck at Agua Caliente Park.

CHAPTER 14

Letty headed directly to the main Tucson Police Department's office near Reid Park to see Alejandro Ramirez. Alejandro came out and led Letty back to his office. She still had Teddy with her.

"Thanks for letting me come in with this dog."

"I've heard about this big boy. He's the sniffer that found your friend Seri Durand when that nutcase was holding her."

"Yes, this is Teddy."

At the sound of his name, Teddy looked at Letty and wagged his tail.

"Well, a good tracker-sniffer dog is worth his weight in gold. That's how they find almost all of the smuggled drugs at the border ports-of-entry. We can thank those sniffer dog noses." He leaned down to pet Teddy.

Alejandro offered Letty a seat. "It's good to see you, Letty. I heard from cousin Adelita last week. She says she's doing well, but she says she feels big as an elephant."

Letty smiled. "She's in her ninth month, right? Won't be long before she's a mother."

"Yeah, she'll be a good one, too."

"I think so, too. Adelita is a sweetheart."

"How about that bombing? We need a statement from you. I wanted to be the one to take the statement because I figured I would get a better picture than someone who doesn't know you. Why were you there?"

Letty filled him in on the case for Jen Kimball. "When I discovered that Jen's husband Scott had this side-business that she said she didn't know about, I decided to talk to his partner Gordon Miller before talking to Scott Kimball. I went to Miller's office and learned that he knew nothing about his new partnership with Kimball either. He seemed genuinely in the dark. After we spoke, I followed him out to the parking lot because Miller said he had a lunch date. My plan was to go find Kimball and ask him what he was up to. I was trying to find out if he was hiding assets. I was on the other end of the parking lot when the bomb went off."

"So he hadn't had a chance to get in and turn on the car?"

"No. Miller had just opened the driver's side door of his car. He was just starting to get in when it blew. I think the bomb must have been remote controlled, probably by a mobile phone, because Miller never got a chance to turn on the ignition key. So it couldn't have been triggered by the ignition."

"That's an important observation. I'll add that last bit to your statement. My officer said you seemed to be hurt."

"Just bruised. I have a friend who is a doctor. He patched me up. I'm okay."

Alejandro nodded. "I bet you want to make some guesses about the explosive. I can't really tell you details of the investigation, you know."

"Based on some unhappy events I experienced in Iraq, I'm guessing C-4 was the explosive."

"You're smart, Letty. Such a good guesser." Alejandro was grinning now.

"Anything else I should be guessing about?"

"Well, you know it would be a good guess to think that the forensic team was looking for DNA or fingerprints of the perpetrator. But it's too soon for any results."

"Alejandro, I have another case I'm working on. It's a cold case, the murder of Edward Becker up in the Catalina Mountains about six months ago. Do I need to go talk to someone in the sheriff's department?"

"No. We're cooperating with them. You can tell me anything you think is important. You think it's a murder?"

"I should say 'death' because I don't know at this point if it was just a random shooting as law enforcement seems to think or was it an assassination or what. Anyway, I'd like to know the exact location where the body was found. I'd like to go take a look for myself."

"I can provide you with GPS coordinates. We had a news reporter up there, and he's the one who came up with the GPS location first. It's public knowledge. I'll email that to you."

"There are a couple of tenuous things that seem to be coincidences. My new assistant found that there's a house near where Becker's death occurred. The house is owned by a partnership that included the guy killed in the bombing, Gordon Miller, and another local man, Scott Kimball. I'll let you know if there's any relationship there. As I said, it seems to be just a coincidence."

"Yeah, maybe. But just as likely that the connection hasn't been discovered yet."

"We'll keep looking into it."

"What's this about a new assistant?"

"He's a young guy from Nogales. His name is Frankie Miranda, and he's into computers. He wants to be a private investigator doing computer forensics."

"Oh, man. Everything is changing so fast. If I had to solve a computer crime, I'd be in real trouble."

"Yes, same here. Frankie is working out really well. You'll meet him sometime." Letty rose. "I'll let you get back to work now."

"Thank you, Letty."

Letty took Teddy home and grabbed a quick sandwich. She took one of the pills that Dan had given her. The bruise on her hip hurt a little less. Now the abrasion on her back was itching a little. That means it's getting better, she thought.

Back at her office, Letty called Marv.

"Marv, you heard about the car bomb that went off?"

"Yeah, you okay?"

"Yes, I got knocked down but not really hurt. I gave a statement to the cops and found out indirectly that the explosive was C-4. It appeared to have been detonated remotely. The man who died was in a business partnership with Jen Kimball's husband. His name was Gordon Miller."

"Interesting."

"I interviewed him to see if he and Kimball might be hiding assets from Jen Kimball if they go through a divorce. But Miller claimed he knew nothing about his so-called partnership with Kimball. He told me he was going to go see Kimball to find out what was going on. But he ended up a charred skeleton in the explosion."

"Coincidence?"

"What do you think?"

"In our business, what appears to be a coincidence often isn't that at all," Marv said.

"That's what Ramirez at Tucson Police says, too. I have another maybe coincidence to tell you about. I'm going to send you a photo of a pickup with yardwork tools in the back. The pickup looks a lot like that one belonging to the stud you watched performing with Jen Kimball. Take a look and see if you think it's the same pickup."

"Where did you see this pickup? Do you suppose he has more lady customers?"

"Here's the interesting thing. The pickup and a big RV were parked behind this big house over on the east side part of the way up in the foothills just east of Agua Caliente Park. The house is owned by SG Enterprises, the partnership of Scott Kimball and car-bombed Gordon Miller."

Marv whistled. "*Not* a coincidence. Something is going on. Do you suppose the Mexican dude is being pimped out by Kimball and Miller?" He paused. "Do you suppose a man would pimp out a younger man to his own wife?"

"Possibly. People are strange, and they do strange things all the time. The RV might be some kind of hide-away where this dude hosts his lady guests."

Marv laughed. "Ah, some real entrepreneurial activity could be going on. Maybe a prostitution enterprise servicing affluent middle-aged women rather than men?"

"Yep. Entrepreneurial activity. So watch for my photo and confirm it's the same pickup truck you saw. I'm going to try to find out more. I'll keep you informed. Talk to you later."

"Aren't you going to say anything about a dog?"

"You need a dog."

Marv laughed and disconnected.

Five minutes later, the phone buzzed again. Letty looked at her caller ID. The call was coming from her Uncle Mando out on the reservation.

"Hey, Uncle Mando. I'm glad to hear from you. How's everything going?"

"Our family is fine. Here at my house, Valerina's meals are too good, and I'm getting chubby. My horse groans when he sees me coming."

"Cut back on seconds. Or get a really big horse."

"Good advice."

"How about Grandma and my little brother Eduardo and his girl?"

"All good. Mama is getting old, but she still seems pretty spry. I think she really likes having Eduardo and Esperanza living there with her. They take a lot of the work load off her. She gets to relax some for the first time in her life."

"So anything new?"

"Yes, that's why I called. Nobody is listening to our conversation, right?"

"No, just me. Go ahead."

"I found this family, a mom and two kids, out in the desert southwest of our place. The mom paid a coyote to bring them across the line in the night, but then the coyote dumped them out there. They were out of water already when I found them so I brought them home with me. The coyote went off and left them because the little kid is hurt, and he couldn't keep up. I'm calling to see if you'd like to bring back your old skills as a medic and help this child."

"Give me a detailed description. About how old is he and what's wrong with him?"

"He's eight years old. He apparently cut his leg on barbed wire in Mexico when they were coming north before they even crossed the border. He's got this jagged cut from the barbed wire down the back of his leg. It appears to be slightly infected. His calf is a little swollen and red. The infection can only get worse so I figure he needs some help pretty quickly."

"You're right. We need to stop the infection. It could go septic and end up killing him. How about the mother and the other kid?"

"The other one is a girl. She's thirteen. She and the mother are okay but really scared. The mother says her husband works in Tucson for a landscaping company. Do you think you could call him, and let him know that his family is here?"

"Sure. I have a friend that I think will be interested in this. He knows way more about medicine than I do. I'll ask him. I'll let you know." She disconnected.

Letty took a deep breath, then she dialed Dan's number.

"Letty, how nice to hear from you. Are you taking your pills? And are you calling me to ask me out on a date?"

Letty was relieved that Dan sounded so cheerful.

"Actually, yes and yes."

"Awesome. What are we going to do?"

"Did you mean what you said about how taking care of people is what you really like to do?"

"Yes, it's my thing. It's my life's work."

"Well then, how about a working date? We go out to the reservation and visit my family, and you take care of a little boy who got hurt." Her words all poured out at once. Letty felt nervous. She had no idea how he would react.

"Wow. That's the best date offer I've ever had. Yes. Count me in."

Letty smiled. "Oh, what a relief. I was afraid you'd be offended."

"You're crazy, Letty. Why would I be offended? This sounds really special. I've never been on an Indian reservation. And getting to meet your family is a real plus. Having an opportunity to take care of an injured child is perfect for me. And going on a date with you is the best thing ever. Give me details so I can get my medical bag ready."

Letty told him what her Uncle Mando had said about the family and the little boy's hurt leg.

"One more thing, Dan. This family is....well...uh...if I tell you, then you'll know. If I don't give you specifics, you can always tell the Border Patrol that you didn't know anything."

"No problem, Letty. My Hippocratic Oath comes first. The Border Patrol will just have to deal with that. I don't care if they have papers or not. That little boy deserves good care. Every child deserves good care."

"Thank you, Dan, for being so understanding and for agreeing to go on this date with me."

"Best date ever. I can be ready in half an hour. Pick me up at my house."

"See you very soon."

Letty called her Uncle Mando back. "We'll be at your place in a couple of hours."

CHAPTER 15

Letty found Dan waiting for her outside his front door. He had a couple of leather bags, one fairly large and ready to go. He put both in the bed of her pickup. He was grinning the entire time, that lopsided grin that she found so attractive.

"Wow. Thank you so much for inviting me on a working date. I'd have never thought of such a thing myself. So much better than a movie or going out to eat," Dan said as he jumped into the cab and strapped himself in.

"You're easily pleased, Dr. Ennis."

"You're doing everything right, Ms. Valdez."

Letty took major streets west out of Tucson and soon they were out of the city on their way to the tiny town of Three Points. Neither of them spoke, but Letty could not help but notice that Dan was smiling the entire time.

"We'll cross over into the reservation in a just a few miles, once we get past Three Points."

"I've never been on an Indian reservation."

"Really? Why not? Don't you have Native Americans in Minnesota?"

"Yes, mainly Chippewa and Ojibway north of Minneapolis, and some small Dakota locations, too. I never visited any of the reservations. I had no reason to go because I didn't know anyone there. The Minnesota Native American reservations are a lot smaller than yours."

"Yes, the Tohono O'odham Reservation in Arizona is nearly three million acres in the U.S. It would be a lot more acres if we could count ancestral lands across the border in Mexico."

Dan was looking out the window. "There. Look. There's a sign. We just crossed over into the reservation."

"You're in Indian territory now, white man."

Dan laughed, delighted. "Cool. Are you going take me back to your tipi?"

Letty rolled her eyes. "Not today. I have other plans for you. And we O'odham don't have tipis anyway."

Everything seemed to please Dan. After that, he kept up a running commentary. "There's the turn-off to Kitt Peak. That's the astronomy place, right?" He didn't wait for an answer. "Oh, look, there's a ranch. Horses. Oh, nice. Look at the landscape. Beautiful. Oh, boy. We're coming to a little town."

"This is Sells. Actually this is our capital and the biggest town on the rez." She turned south, and in a few miles, they passed the community of Topawa.

"Will went to school over there," Letty pointed to Baboquivari High School. "I brought him to live with me in Tucson so he would stay out of trouble. He needed some adult supervision."

Dan nodded. "I get that. I was a teenage boy once."

Letty wondered what he was like as a teen.

"What kind of trouble did you get into?"

"Nothing serious. I never got arrested or anything."

"I know."

"Yeah," he grinned. "Your background check told you that."

"Did you have a lot of girlfriends when you were a teen?"

Dan suddenly looked embarrassed. "Maybe."

"That means you had a lot. And even more in college?"

"Maybe." He shrugged and looked out of the window.

"Maybe, huh? I bet more like definitely." She figured Dan deserved to be teased a little.

"Oh, nice. Look! There are more horses. And a big longhorn steer. Look at those horns. And they're all running around loose?"

"Open range. You haven't ever seen a longhorn or a horse before?"

"Of course. I have seen both. I know how to ride a horse. I spent a summer on a ranch in North Dakota. I'll tell you about that later."

Goodness, Letty thought. First a monk in a Thai monastery then an identical twin who died in an accident. Now a ranch in North Dakota. She wondered what he'd been up to on a ranch. Dan had lots of stories.

"Well, since you're not going to tell me about all the women in your life…," she smiled at him.

"That's all in the past. I'm a lot more mature now. I want more than just…," he fell silent.

More than just sex, Letty thought to herself. His life had been so different than hers.

"I'm turning west here. We're going past the turnoff to my grandmother's place. We'll be driving into the northern part of Chukut Kuk district to where my uncle and aunt live. We'll come back to Grandma's place later."

It wasn't long at all before Letty arrived at her Uncle Mando's house. Dan unloaded his bags and followed Letty. Uncle Mando and Aunt Valerina came out to greet them.

"Come on inside. You'll want to meet the family. None of them speaks English, by the way. We'll have to translate everything," Uncle Mando said.

Letty looked back at Dan. He looked different now, still smiling but with an air of seriousness that had not existed earlier. He had transformed himself into Dr. Ennis, ready to meet a patient. His stethoscope was already around his neck.

The mother and her daughter sat on the edge of a large bed Uncle Mando had arranged for them in the extra bedroom. The girl clung to her mother. The little boy was sitting on a second smaller bed against the wall. He looked like he wanted to cling to his mother, too.

Mando introduced Letty and Dan to the family. Their family name was Jimenez. Lupita was the mother and the daughter, Susana. The injured little boy was Juanito.

"Please tell them I'm sorry that I cannot speak Spanish well at all. I'm still learning," Dan said.

Letty repeated everything in Spanish.

"I'll need a light here, please," Dan said to Mando.

Mando returned with a lamp, plugged in it and turned it on.

"Letty, assist me, please."

She came closer. "I'm ready."

Dan first listened to the boy's heart and lungs with his stethoscope. Next he and Letty moved little Juanito onto his stomach on the bed so they could look at his calf. Dan put on his latex gloves. Letty handed him what he needed from his bag as he requested it.

Dan looked closely at the wound. "Letty, this is a jagged wound that is slightly infected. We want to stop the infection before it gets any worse. I'm going to anesthetize locally, clean it, then stitch it up. Then I'll give him an antibiotic injection and a bottle of pills. He'll need a tetanus shot, too. Please explain to Mom."

Letty translated to the mother.

Letty spoke to the little boy as Dan began working. Their conversation was in Spanish.

"Do you know the song 'Este Torito?'"

"Yes," Juan whispered. He looked scared.

"Sing with me." The song was a traditional Mexican folk tune known by most children and adults, too.

Letty started singing softly. Dan looked at her and grinned.

"Este torito que traigo lo traigo desde Tenango,"

Juan listened then he began singing along. His sister joined, too.

"Lo traigo desde Tapango, este torito que traigo,"

His mom added her voice, and now Valerina came in from the kitchen and sang along. Valerina had come from Mexico to the U.S. many years earlier, but she still remembered those childhood songs. She was smiling.

"Y lo vengo manteniendo con cascaritas de mango."

Soon enough, Juanito was smiling, too. The local anesthetic meant that he felt no pain as Dan stitched him up.

"The wound needed eight stitches. Now I have to give him two injections. Tell him to be brave. It will hurt for just a second." Letty explained to Juanito. He nodded and scrunched his eyes closed.

Dan gave him the injections.

"Tell him that his leg will hurt today and tomorrow but after that, it will get better day-by-day. Tell him to take one pill every day." Letty said this to Juanito, and he nodded his head.

"Now I have a surprise," Dan said.

"Una sorpresa," Letty repeated.

He reached into his bag and pulled out a package of five Hot Wheel toy cars with movable wheels. They were in different colors and looked like little race cars.

Juanito's eyes grew big. His little face broke out into a huge smile as he took the cars into his outstretched hands.

"¿Qué dices?" Lupita said to her son.

Juanito looked at Dan and said, "Muchas gracias, Señor."

"De nada." Dan turned to Juanito's little sister.

"Una sorpresa," he repeated Letty's Spanish, and he handed Susana a small package with a necklace visible through the plastic wrap. It was a delicate chain with a gold cross attached.

Susana took it and whispered, "Gracias, Señor."

Dan smiled and turned his attention to Letty.

"Letty, here's the bottle of antibiotic tablets. Please explain to the mother that he must take *all* of them, one each day. It's very important to take every single one."

Letty translated, and Lupita shook her head in agreement.

"You're next, Letty. Want me to look at your back?"

Letty frowned. Time to stop being so shy, she said to herself.

"Okay," she said. She turned her back to everyone and pulled up her t-shirt over her head to the front.

"I got hurt, and Dan is taking care of me," Letty said to everyone in Spanish.

"What are you telling them?"

"That you are taking care of me because I got hurt and that you are a brilliant physician and tremendously kind."

"That's so right." He laughed.

Dan removed the bandage and inspected the wound.

"Looks good, Letty. I'm putting on a little antibiotic cream and a small bandage. Tonight before you go to bed, you can take it off so the wound can breathe."

"Okay."

"Unless you want me to take it off for you and then tuck you in," he whispered in her ear.

Letty looked at Dan. There was that lop-sided grin again. She rolled her eyes at him. She pulled her shirt down.

"You're flirting with me."

"I can't help myself. You're very flirtable."

"Flirtable is not even a word."

"It is now."

Lupita spoke next, again in Spanish. "Senorita, could you please help us? My husband is in Tucson. He doesn't know we are here. We need to reach him." She reached into her bag and pulled out a business card. She handed it to Letty.

Letty took it. It read, "Count On Us Landscaping" in bold letters, then in smaller letters, "No job too big or too small." Contact information had three names and phone numbers. One was for Luis Jimenez.

"My husband does not know that we were forced to cross the border."

"What happened?" Letty asked.

"Two of the cartel gang members came to our house ten days past. One told me that he would return in one month to take Susana with him." Tears were in Lupita's eyes. "He said he could make a lot of money from a young girl like my daughter. You understand what they want."

Letty frowned and nodded. The gangsters would traffic the thirteen-year-old and turn her into an unwilling prostitute, but only after she'd been gang-raped by cartel members. Thirteen years old.

"I understand. I will do my best to find your husband and let him know you are here."

Lupita nodded and smiled.

"Dan, time to go. We're supposed to show up for dinner at my grandmother's house."

Letty turned to Valerina and Mando to give them goodbye hugs.

"Thanks to both of you for helping this family. I think it won't take me long at all to find Lupita's husband. He should be able to come and pick them up soon."

Back in Letty's pickup and back on the dirt road, Letty explained to Dan why the family had come across the border.

"I think they were hoping to come in legally once the father got his papers in order. But circumstances changed so they crossed at night. They paid a smuggler to bring them in. I'm just glad Mando found them. They had already run out of water."

"Given what you told me about the daughter, they didn't have much choice, did they?"

"No, I would have done the same thing."

"That little boy will need some follow-up to check on the infection," Dan added.

"We can check on the family once they get settled in Tucson. I bet it will only take a couple of days for the dad to pick them up."

Dan nodded.

"What was that song about?" he asked.

"A little bull. It's about getting the bull to come with you by giving him mango peelings."

"You have a nice voice."

"I don't sing much."

"Let's change that."

"You say that now. You may regret it later if you have to listen to me."

Dan just smiled. "I doubt that."

Ten minutes later, they arrived at the home where Letty's grandmother had lived for nearly sixty years after she married into the

Antone family. Letty spent her early childhood years here, too, as well as those months after she returned from Iraq.

Her grandmother, brother Eduardo, and his girl Esperanza came out to meet them. Letty got and gave hugs and happy greetings. Dan hung back until they grabbed his hand and gave him hugs, too. Letty brought a box of supplies in from the back of her pickup which included nonperishable foods and laundry soap.

Eduardo put his arm around Letty, "You don't have to bring this. I have a job now."

"I know. I just want Grandma to know how grateful I am and how much I love her. I brought her some figs and dates, too. She really likes those."

At supper around the table, Eduardo and Letty did most of the talking, catching up with each other and talking about other members of the family. Esperanza ate quietly. She looked at Dan frequently.

Esperanza finally spoke to Letty in Spanish and asked if Dan could speak her language.

"Not really. Just a few words," Letty answered in Spanish.

"Es muy guapo." He's really handsome, Esperanza said. Eduardo looked at her, surprise on his face. He grinned.

"Es tu novio?" Is he your boyfriend? she asked Letty.

Letty hesitated. "Pues, no sé," she said. I don't know. She looked down at her plate.

That made Eduardo laugh.

"What are they talking about?" Dan asked.

"They are talking about you and how handsome you are. Esperanza wants to know if you're Letty's boyfriend."

Letty threw half of a rolled-up tortilla at Eduardo. "Shut up!"

"What did Letty say?" Dan asked. He looked at Letty, a big grin on his face.

"Oh, my poor big sister. She's really clueless. She says she doesn't know."

"I think we're embarrassing her," Dan said. "I seem to do that a lot. Maybe we'd better just shut up."

"Yeah," Eduardo said. "Give it a rest or we'll have all the women mad at us."

Throughout the meal, Letty's grandmother said nothing at all, just stared at each of them smiling, as if she were trying to memorize their faces forever.

* * *

After dinner and cleanup, Dan and Letty left the others inside Grandma's little house. She led him to a bench near the big open-air ramada. The night sky was inky black and full of a million stars.

"I've never seen so many stars," Dan. His voice was subdued. "It's so beautiful here."

"You've been living in places that had too many lights. We're dark sky all the way here. Also there's not much moisture in the desert air. It's easier to see because the air is very clear. That's why astronomers like it out here so much."

Letty pointed out several stars one at a time and told him the names of the stars in the O'odham language.

"See that one? That's ceşoñ, the mountain sheep star, in Orion's Belt."

"Ceşoñ," Dan repeated.

"And there's kakaicu, the mountain quail star."

She pointed to the Kitt Peak Observatory several miles to the northeast.

"Can you see the lights on the domes of the observatories? There are several on the mountain."

"Yes. I see them."

"We'll go there sometime. They have evening programs. They let you look through the big telescopes. You can see stars really, really far away. Will and Clarice told me about it. I've never been there."

He nodded in agreement. "We'll go together. We'll make it a date."

She smiled and nodded.

They sat together in silence for a while listening to the sounds of the desert night. From a distance, a coyote howled. A series of coyote yips and howls could be heard in response.

Dan threw his head back and howled. Far away, one coyote howled in response.

"Better watch out, Dan. That lady coyote may come looking for some lovin.'"

He laughed. "You're so funny, Letty."

Dan Ennis has to be the only person in the world who thinks of her as sometimes amusing, Letty thought. She thought of herself as always serious, and everyone else did, too. Not Dan.

Suddenly they heard a gunshot.

"What was that?" Dan asked.

Letty shook her head. "Somebody shooting at something — maybe a skunk or a coyote. Or just playing around. Drunk maybe. I don't know."

She rose.

"Time to go to sleep. We have an early start tomorrow. You have to work tomorrow and so do I."

They went back under the ramada.

"Let me take off that bandage," Dan said. He pulled out a flashlight.

Letty pulled her shirt up, and he removed the bandage.

"Looks good, Letty. You're healing fast."

They each lay down on cots that were placed at ninety degree angles from each other. Their heads were close to each other.

"Good night, Dan," Letty whispered after a few minutes. She could hear his breathing, slow and deep. Dan was already asleep.

Sometime in the night, Letty began tossing and turning. She threw the blanket aside. Her breathing became ragged, and she shivered in the cold air of the desert night. She cried out, "I'm coming! Where's my ... It's a chest wound. Oh no! Oh no!....Sniper! Oh, god. He's bleeding out," she whimpered. "I can't find him. There's blood everywhere." She panted and cried softly.

Then there was a warm body next to hers, stretched out her entire length. The blanket was pulled up to cover them both. Arms were close around her, holding her, stroking her hair, whispering,

"I have you. You're safe now. We're both safe. I'll take care of you. Everything is okay. I have you now."

Letty stopped crying, she relaxed and her ragged breathing turned slowly into soft, even breaths. She went back to sleep after a few minutes. Now it was a deep, peaceful sleep.

Morning came. The sun wasn't up yet, but the sky was becoming lighter by the minute. Letty rose and pulled on a sweatshirt. Dan wasn't there.

She looked around and didn't see him. The house was dark and silent. Everyone was still asleep inside. She went around to the back of Grandma's house. That's where she found them.

Dan and Grandma were seated next to each other in rough, hand-built wooden chairs with grass-stuffed pillows. They were both looking out into the desert to the east watching the light change in the sky. Baboquivari Mountain was still in shadows. Both Dan and her grandmother were sitting silently, eyes half-closed, breathing slowly. No words passed between them. They looked like a couple of monks meditating together, Letty thought. So peaceful.

Letty watched them for a few minutes. Nothing changed. Dan and her Grandma sat together in silence with eyes half closed.

Letty went inside and started coffee. Esperanza was awake now, and Letty could hear Eduardo moving around in the old storeroom that had become his and Esperanza's bedroom. Coffee made, Letty started breakfast.

* * *

Later on the drive home, they were quiet. Dan broke the silence.

"Letty, did your grandmother say anything about me?"

"Not much. She doesn't talk much."

Dan turned his head away and looked out the window. There was slight frown on his face. He said nothing.

They were quiet for a few minutes.

Letty sighed. "You're not going to let me get away with anything, are you?"

"Probably not." He was smiling again.

"Okay. Grandma pulled me down close to her, looked me in the eyes, and she said to me in a firm voice, 'He is a good man. You keep him.'"

Dan grinned. "Awesome."

He was silent again for a few miles. Then he said, "So, Letty, will you follow your grandmother's advice?"

Letty smiled. "We O'odham respect our elders and, yes, we try our best to follow their advice."

She glanced at Dan. He had a big smile on his face.

"I know why your life got better after Iraq. Living with your grandmother was the best thing you could have done. She's like my teacher in the monastery. They are kindred spirits."

Letty nodded. She had never thought of her grandmother as a Buddhist monk, but she could see what Dan was saying. She could never love her grandmother enough.

CHAPTER 16

Back in Tucson, Letty dropped Dan off at his house.

"I'm working in the ER today and tomorrow, Letty, so I can't ask you out. I'll try to think of something fun to do next. But I don't think I can top today. This date was superior. I really enjoyed meeting your family, seeing the reservation, and getting to take care of that little boy. Any time you want to go on a working date, count me in."

"You have an unusual view of what fun is, Dan. If you want to work, I can find you plenty of work. Maybe next time I'll take you along with me when I'm the one working."

"Sounds exciting," Dan reached over and kissed her on her cheek. "I'll call you. Or you call me."

Another kiss on the cheek. She sighed.

Letty headed back to her office. She found Frankie at the front desk staring intently at his new computer.

"Hey, Frankie. What's up? How are things going?"

Frankie looked up at Letty. "You're not going to believe this."

"What?" Letty suddenly felt apprehensive.

"I was checking the local news. There's a breaking story. You know that guy Scott Kimball who has a business and a house with Gordon Miller? Miller, he's the one who got bombed."

"Yeah?"

"Kimball was shot dead yesterday evening."

Letty's mouth fell open. "No."

"Yeah, he was shot long-distance like from a sniper kind of shot."

"The news is reporting that was how he was killed?"

"Yeah. Apparently the cops could see right away that it wasn't some close up with a regular handgun kind of murder. They reported that they've already checked all the security cameras in the area. No one else was on the street at the time. He was shot in the head, assassination-style."

Letty was quiet for a moment then said, "Now who would want to assassinate Kimball? Have you found any evidence of Kimball being involved in any criminal activity in the past? Or connections to any organized crime? He's done financial work overseas. He may have pissed off someone."

"No, I haven't found anything at all that suggests that kind of connection."

"Of course a connection might take time to find. Those criminal gangs are pretty good at hiding their tracks."

"True. I'll keep looking."

"Frankie, it's bothering me that this is the second long-range shooting that's happened in recent months, not to mention that his business partner Miller was just killed in that car bombing."

"Yeah, you told me about that old dude who was killed." As he spoke, Frankie was typing on his keyboard.

"Yes, Edward Becker."

"Here," he said. "Wikipedia says that the longest recorded sniper kill was 3,540 meters. That's 3,871 yards which is over two miles. It was a Canadian special forces soldier in Iraq who did that."

"So the killer theoretically could have been far from the scene. Does the article say anything about the firearm used by snipers?" Letty asked.

"Yeah, it says this kind of shooting requires a special weapon, special ammunition, and special technology like rangefinders and ballistic calculators. I don't know much about guns so I don't really understand all that. Also it says special training and practice is required. In fact, it says 'intense training.'"

"This also means that we could be dealing with a professional assassin. And my guess is that he's former military. Where else would you get that kind of intense training?"

"Right."

"And you think the Mexican groundskeeper might be former military based on tattoos?"

"Yes, I think that that's who he is."

"We've got to track him down and see what's he's doing other than screwing Jen Kimball. Your idea about the tattoos is the best so far since we have no idea what his name is or when he served," Letty added.

"I'll keep looking."

"You told me earlier that SG Enterprises listed the property above Agua Caliente Park with Mariposa Real Estate. The house is still currently listed for sale?"

"That's right."

"Kimball wouldn't list the property with Gordon Miller's agency because Miller didn't know about SG Enterprises. Kimball wouldn't want Miller to know that he was using Miller's name. But why choose Mariposa to handle the sale?" Letty wondered.

"Could be just a random choice?"

"Maybe. I don't know. It's also possible that he knows someone there. I'll look into that right away."

"Okay. And I'll keep looking for a tattoo connection that might lead to this groundskeeper guy. Considering that Marv saw him with Jen Kimball, could she be involved?" Frankie asked.

"Yes, possible. If this Mexican dude is an assassin, we'll have to find out if he was hired to kill Miller or Kimball, or both. Or one or both killings might be something personal between the Mexican man and the husbands. And a car bomb is a different method of killing. Our gunman may not be connected to the bombing at all. Jen Kimball seemed mainly worried that her husband Scott was going to divorce her and cheat her out of jointly-owned property. There was no indication that she was interested in hiring a hit man to take her husband out. Of course, she could have been lying about his philandering and lying about the possibility of divorce."

"Yes, unfortunately I've learned recently that some females are hopeless liars, and you can't believe a thing they say." He frowned.

Letty knew he was talking about his former girlfriend.

"Hey, Frankie."

"What?"

"Not all girls are liars. And there are a lot of girls in Tucson."

"Then maybe I can find one who doesn't lie all the time."

"Yep. Or even some of the time. Okay, well, this looks like I need to find out more about Gordon Miller's wife, Kellie, and you try to find the tattoo man. I'm going to call Marv and see if he can start watching Kellie Miller. There could very well be a connection there as well. But I don't know what the environmentalist Becker has to do with all this. I need to look into that, too. And talk to Jen Kimball again."

Letty sat thinking. She shook her head finally.

"Also, Frankie, I want to settle up with you about this new computer. Do you have a bank account? I can wire the money to you."

"Yes, I just opened one at a local credit union. I also rented a small apartment. It's furnished but just barely. I'll move in this weekend. My sister is coming up with boxes of stuff for me like dishes, some pans to cook with, and a shower curtain and basic things. The apartment is sort of mid-way between Valdez Investigations and Pima Community College downtown where I'll be taking classes. Both are on the city bus line. Here's the account info."

Frankie handed Letty a piece of paper.

Letty went into her inner office.

"Good. Very good," she said to herself.

"Are the investigations always like this? So much fun?" Frankie said from the other room.

Letty looked back at Frankie and smiled.

"Figuring out how everything fits together is the fun part. Not so much fun is dealing with the bad guys. They don't like it when you find out what they are up to. Personally I prefer it when the cops take over at that point. I don't like getting beat up or shot at. I hope if we move in a new direction, like that cybercrimes idea you told me about, maybe we'll find it less personally dangerous. Another area is due diligence we can focus on. That's where we determine if an investor can trust what he's being told about the potential investment."

Frankie grinned. "So many directions to go."

"As for me, I've always had a preference for finding missing persons."

That made Letty think of Kenny Wilson again. Perhaps there were a couple of more homeless camps she could visit. Strange that he just disappeared like that. Maybe he was trying to get away from Rigo.

Letty turned on her computer and did a search for Mariposa Real Estate.

Five minutes later, she called out to Frankie, "Guess who's the owner of Mariposa? Kellie Miller."

"Interesting. So she's going to be the agent who sells the house that the two murdered husbands owned together?"

"Yes. How convenient."

Letty turned on her computer, transferred money to Frankie's account and retrieved her email. About twenty minutes later, Frankie came to the door of her office.

She looked up. "Find something?"

"Yes, something important. I searched the tax assessor's website again, and I found the name of the former owner of the property before SG Enterprises bought it. I emailed him and asked for a contact to the real estate company which handled the sale of his house to SG Enterprises. He responded and said the real estate agent was Mariposa. He also said the agent told him that she would be buying the house for herself."

"Whoa. So Kellie Miller claimed to the original owner of the house that SG Enterprises was her business, and SG would be buying the house?"

"That's right. He told me that when he signed the deed, the ownership went to SG Enterprises. He thought that SG was a business name that Kellie Miller was using to purchase the property. He assumed that she was buying it for herself, and her real estate company, Mariposa, was just handling all the paperwork."

"This means that Gordon Miller and Scott Kimball may not have known about the house at all. Your contact said that Kellie bought it for herself, and she was using Gordon and Scott's business name."

Letty thought for a moment.

"It also means that Gordon and Scott may not have known about SG Enterprises either. Scott may not have been the one who registered SG with the state. Maybe Kellie did."

"We could find that out. Every computer has an IP address. It's short for 'internet protocol.' We can get the IP address for Mariposa Real Estate from one of their emails. If we can get an email from the person that registered SG Enterprises with the Arizona Secretary of State, then we can get that IP address, too. If they are the same, that means that Kellie definitely created that business. She would know her husband's personal data to put in."

"And Jen would know Scott's personal data. Those two could be in this together."

"Can we get that info about emails from the state?"

"I don't know. But I know a really good lawyer who could subpoena that information. Her name is Jessica Cameron. You'll meet her."

"Maybe the pieces are falling together."

"Yes, I think we might be dealing with a couple of dangerous bad girls, not to mention a trained assassin. See if you can find any connection between these two women other than the social stuff you've already found. Something in the past maybe. I'm going try to find out how the environmentalist Becker got mixed up in all this. And what the Mexican groundskeeper is up to."

* * *

Letty called Marv.

"Hey, Marv."

"Hey, Letty. I heard about Kimball getting shot in the head yesterday. This case is getting more and more interesting."

"Yes, Frankie's been on his computer finding some interesting connections. He's trying to track down that groundskeeper..."

Marv snorted. "Groundskeeper, my ass."

"Whatever he's up to, he could be our assassin. We're trying to find out if he has been in the military and if he received any training to be a sniper or handling explosives."

"So maybe he's being pimped out as an assassin, not a ....what do you call a male whore?"

"I don't really know. He could be both an assassin, and I think the word you're looking for is 'stud.' Guys get off easy when it comes to multiple sexual encounters. I do know that we need to find out who he is. It's meaningful that he's staying at that house owned by two murdered men, or the two women as the case may be. And that the house is so close to where the murdered environmentalist was killed in the same manner as Scott Kimball seems meaningful, too. I'm going to be spending some time trying to find out if Becker, the environmentalist, had any connection to Miller or Kimball."

"Meanwhile, I'm guessing you want me to start watching Kellie Miller."

"Right."

"Well, I'm ahead of you, Letty. When I heard about Gordon Miller getting shot in the head, I started following Kellie around. Guess what? Jen Kimball isn't the only one getting serviced by the groundskeeper dude. He showed up at Kellie's house just about dusk. I recognized his pickup. He knocked on her front door. It's in sort of an alcove so it's not easy to see the front door unless you're at an angle. I had already positioned myself at that angle. She opened the door and stepped out. He didn't say a word to her as far as I can tell. He just ripped the front of her blouse open, pulled down her bra, and grabbed her tits. She was into it the whole time. Her hands were on his butt pulling him closer. He pushed her into the house and kicked the door closed with his foot."

"Goodness. That groundskeeper is a busy man. But I'm sorry to hear, Marv, that they didn't do the deed outside where you could see them. That would have been entertaining for you."

"Yeah, that part was definitely a disappointment. However, we can conclude that our stud likely has a sexual relationship with both Jen Kimball and Kellie Miller."

"Yes, and it's even more complicated than that. That big house on the east side is for sale right now. Kellie is not only the agent who is trying to sell it. She's also the current owner. We're trying to prove now that she and very possibly Jen Kimball may have been the ones who registered SG Enterprises as a business. It's looking more likely that the two husbands didn't know anything about the new business or the house. Maybe the wives decided that their husbands had become expendable. It's very possible that Kellie and Jen are using the groundskeeper dude to do their dirty work."

"Why do you suppose they went to the trouble to buy a house, hide that from their husbands, and now they are trying to sell it?"

"I think that will come out as we proceed. But I'm guessing that they were siphoning off financial resources, hiding the money in a house which they would reclaim later just for themselves. Maybe it recently occurred to them that each woman stands to get everything from their husbands' estates if the husbands are dead, not just divorced. What I don't know yet is if there's a connection to the murdered environmentalist Becker. His body was found somewhat close to that house. He'd already told a colleague about chemical dumping. Those three may be up to something else, too, that we haven't discovered yet."

"Letty, this sounds potentially dangerous. You better watch your back. Carry your gun with you. Okay?"

"Okay, Marv. I'll be careful."

* * *

Before the day was over, Letty tracked down Luis Jimenez just heading out for a landscaping job. He and another man were in a truck and just pulling away from Luis's apartment.

"Señor Jimenez?"

"Sí?" Jimenez looked at her suspiciously.

"My name is Letty Valdez. I have news about your family." She continued in Spanish.

Jimenez's face changed when Letty mentioned his family. He looked concerned now.

"Just a moment. I'm going to make a call and you can talk to them."

Letty pulled out her smart phone and called her Uncle Mando. His house was not close to the fiber optic cable that brought internet service to the reservation. Most of the time, it worked, but sometimes not. Using WhatsApp, she made a voice call.

Uncle Mando answered. She could see him grinning at her.

"Hey, Letty."

"Uncle Mando, can you please bring Señora Jimenez to the phone? I have someone here who wants to talk to her."

"Sure. Just a minute."

Letty handed the phone to Señor Jimenez.

Suddenly his wife's face appeared on Letty's phone. When she saw her husband, she began to cry and babble in Spanish.

"Mi amor," he said repeatedly. His eyes were full of tears.

The two had a brief conversation in which Señora Jimenez explained recent events. Then she gave the phone back to Uncle Mando.

"I will give you some backroads to use for your return to Tucson. You'll be less likely to encounter La Migra." Mando used the Mexican slang term La Migra for the immigration authorities, the Border Patrol. He explained to Jimenez how to find his home. Jimenez said that he would go to Uncle Mando's on the following morning to pick up his family.

Jimenez returned the phone to Letty. She said goodbye to Mando and disconnected.

"Señorita, I am forever in your debt. Thank you so very much for helping me to join my family again. I have missed them so much. Now we will all be together again. Thank you."

"My pleasure."

"Que Dios te bendiga. How can I repay you?"

"No payment, but I could use some help finding someone."

"Yes?"

Letty showed him the photo Marv had taken of the Mexican groundskeeper's dirty dark-blue pickup with tools in the back.

"If you see this pickup, write down the license plate number. Okay?"

"Yes, of course."

"But most important, Señor Jimenez, do not approach this man. Do not allow him to see you writing his license plate number. You must stay away from him. He is very dangerous."

Jimenez nodded his head somberly. "I will do as you say. I will look for him, and I will be careful."

"Good. Here's my phone number. I'm going now. Enjoy your family."

"Thank you again, Miss Valdez. Thank you."

CHAPTER 17

Letty decided to spend the rest of the day trying to learn more about Edward Becker's death and if it had anything to do with the SG Enterprises case. She hoped to find time as well to visit another homeless camp before the day was over. Maybe she could find Kenny Wilson at a place Rigo had not yet discovered.

She drove to Fourth Avenue near the University of Arizona to visit the office of Desert Springs Watch. Professor Anselm told her that Edward Becker was a volunteer for this independent environmental group which studied desert springs ecology. The nonprofit was known for its fierce protection of Sonoran Desert water quality, especially the desert springs.

Letty entered the small office. Two people, a young man and a young woman, were at desks in the front office. She could see an older woman, maybe late thirties, through an open door into a second office. All three were working on their computers. Letty looked around. The walls were covered with big maps of the southern Arizona mountain ranges, often referred to as sky islands. The maps had markings indicating the location of springs. Any space between maps was for color photographs of springs throughout the Sonoran Desert region.

"Hi. I'm Letty Valdez. I'm looking for some information."

The young man looked up and smiled. He had dark curly hair and a beard and looked to be in his early twenties. He was wearing a flannel shirt and jeans.

"I'm Forest. What can I do for you?"

The young woman said, "Hi. I'm Meadow." She, too, wore a flannel shirt and jeans.

Letty smiled to herself at their names. Would the woman in the inner office be an Ocean or a River or some other nature-oriented name?

"I'm an investigator looking into the death of one of your volunteers, Edward Becker. I'm looking for some background information."

The woman from the inner office appeared at the door. More flannel and denim.

"Are you with the police?"

"No, I'm a private investigator. The person who hired me thinks perhaps Mr. Becker was murdered. And you are?"

"Katherine Ames. I'm the manager of Desert Springs Watch." So much for the nature names. "For the record, we agree. We think he was murdered, too."

"Why is that?"

"We don't buy the idea that this was just some random shooting like the police are trying to tell us."

Letty noticed that both Forest and Meadow were nodding their head in agreement.

"Did Mr. Becker have any enemies or had he been in any conflicts with anyone lately?"

"No, Edward was a valued volunteer. He was very well liked," Katherine said.

"Yes, we all loved Edward. We went to his memorial service." Meadow added.

"I went out with him a couple of times to visit springs," Forest said. "He knew a lot about water resources. I learned so much from him. We really miss him."

"I understand that Edward may have found some evidence of contamination in the area above Agua Caliente Park."

"That's right," Katherine Ames said. "Edward thought someone was dumping something, and we think that someone killed Edward to keep him quiet."

"Can you give me any idea of what Edward may have found and where?"

Katherine gestured to Forest.

"I was alone here in the office one day," Forest said. "Edward arrived in the late afternoon. He told me he found a sinkhole east of the park. He was pretty sure chemicals were being dumped because all the vegetation around the sinkhole was dead. He was worried that chemicals could enter the groundwater and end up in Agua Caliente Spring or the big pond at the park. He was going back up there and to find some samples that he could get tested. He said there was trash, too. He didn't stay long because he was going to meet a chemistry professor friend of his."

So far everything Letty was being told mirrored what Professor Anselm had said.

"I think it would be a good idea for me to try to find this sinkhole. Can you give me any idea at all where he might have been hiking when he found it?"

Forest walked to a map on the opposite wall. "I don't know for sure, but he had to have been fairly high above Agua Caliente from his description. Based on what Edward told me, I think it's got to be in this area." He pointed to a place on the map well above the park and the residential area. There was no way to know if the sinkhole was in the privately-owned areas or within the Coronado National Forest. The forest boundary was farther east.

"Do you know where his body was found?"

Again, Forest pointed to the map. The two locations were close to each other.

Letty studied the map. She turned and handed her business card to all three.

"If you think of anything Edward said that would help me, please contact me. Especially any more details about what he found. As for me, I think I'll be taking a hike up there. I'd like to find what Edward found."

Katherine Ames nodded as she took the card. "Thank you, Ms. Valdez. I really hope you can find the truth. If Edward was murdered, he deserves justice."

*　*　*

Letty called the city of Tucson's Natural Resources, Parks and Recreation Department. She spoke to an employee there who was glad to share information. He repeated what Letty had already learned, that the spring was dry most of the time. When the park opened the big pond to public fishing, he told her that the staff at the park tested fish tissue in the pond to make sure the fish were safe to eat. There had been no signs of toxic pollution or contaminated fish in the spring or the pond.

Letty headed east to visit Agua Caliente Park again. After parking her little pickup in the park's parking lot, she walked west into the park instead of heading east up the road toward the residential area in the foothills. She first visited the Ranch House. The park had originally been a privately owned ranch, and the family had lived in the sprawling ranch house. Now it was the home to a tourist shop, an art gallery, and administrative offices.

She walked around the perimeter of a large grassy area surrounded by big fan palm and date trees. Native mesquite and palo verde trees were common, too. She'd been out to the park on weekends several times and had seen many families enjoying picnics. Today there were a couple of teens kicking a soccer ball around in the central grassy area.

Letty returned to the location marked as Agua Caliente Spring. There was a sign posted with an explanation of "sources and pathways" of water for the spring. The sign made clear that how the springs were fed was not fully understood. The spring itself, according to the sign, flowed "infrequently." On the diagram, Letty could see where water, presumably rain water, seeped from the surface through sediments into the groundwater below the surface. That's what was referred to as "recharge."

Down lower on the mountain side, a spring might break through to the surface. The source of the water for the spring was the groundwater and also what the sign called "thermal artesian water" that came from much deeper underground. No doubt the level of winter snowfall higher up in the mountains had an effect on groundwater levels, Letty thought. It was the groundwater that interested her, not so much artisanal water from deep below the surface. If Edward Becker had come upon a source of pollution affecting the groundwater, he would know that the pollution was a potential threat to the Agua Caliente Spring. Knowing that could provide a clue to his death.

Professor Anselm had already told her that the water in the big ponds in the park was primarily replenished by groundwater pumped from below the earth's surface. Park officials had been working diligently in recent years to reduce evaporation from the ponds, and most of all, to reduce the need to pump so much groundwater.

The remaining text on the sign Letty was reading had an historical note that left Letty shaking her head. "The flow rate from the spring has varied over time reportedly as high as 500 gallons per minute to an unmeasurable seep in recent years." The sign explained that originally there had been two springs back when the park land was owned by individual families. The first spring was cool. It was fed by groundwater. The second was hot water, about one hundred degrees. The sign continued, "In the 1940s owner Gib Hazard dynamited between two springs that were present at that time resulting in a single spring and reduced flow."

People always seemed so willing to jump in and make changes without considering consequences. Human recklessness never failed to amaze Letty.

Now with a general idea of the geology above the park and how the spring in the park was impacted by what went on up in the Catalina foothills, Letty continued her exploration. This time, she walked close to the water's edge of the big pond. Letty quickly came upon an artist sitting in front of an easel working on a painting of the scene in front of him. Letty agreed that the pond, the trees on the other side, the mountains beyond, and the clear blue sky were worthy of any artist's attention. She said nothing to the artist, not wanting to disturb.

Letty continued walking around the park. She came upon several birders with binoculars and cameras. She chatted with each one. They were all quite willing to share information about birds. But when she asked about any problems in the park with pollution, no one knew anything.

She approached a man who appeared to be providing maintenance of the big pond. He was using a long pole to retrieve unwanted items from the water. A child's plastic ball was in his sights.

"Hi," Letty said.

The older man with white hair turned toward her. He had a little lapel sign that gave his name and identified him as "Volunteer."

"Hi," he said. "Are you a birder or just enjoying a walk around the park?"

"I'm looking for some information. My name is Letty Valdez, and I'm investigating the death of a man named Edward Becker."

"Yeah, I knew Edward. He was a great guy. He did a lot of volunteer work for park. He took kids out and showed them around."

"I understand that he thought maybe someone was dumping trash or something up above the park. Have you heard about anything contaminating either the spring or the pond here?"

"No, sometimes the kids throw stuff in the water. That's what I'm doing now, trying to retrieve toys and plastic bottles and stuff like that."

He looked out at the pond again. "We try to keep everything clean and natural."

"Yes, it's lovely here."

"Of course, we had a huge contamination problem earlier this week." The man frowned.

"What do you mean?"

"This guy drowned himself here." The volunteer looked like he'd like to forget what he'd seen. "We're trying to figure out how he did it." He pointed to a spot out in the middle of the pond. "It's about ten feet deep out there. He managed to get out there in the deep part with a concrete block tied to one of his feet. We found an old

170

mesquite log in the cattails, and we think maybe he floated himself out there, rolled off, and the concrete block pulled him under. The log could have come from the old orchard on the grounds. The bottom is really soft so it would have been hard for the man to pull himself out even if he wanted to. But the cops are still investigating."

"How did you know he was out there? Didn't the concrete block hold his body under the surface of the water?"

"Yes, you're right about that. But the park administrator had given this tourism agency permission to use a drone to photograph the park from above. At one point, the drone went in low over the water. The water is pretty clear out there. You could see the guy's body just below the surface. The cops brought a boat with them to retrieve his body. I saw them bring him out."

Letty had this uncomfortable feeling. Chills went up her spine. She knew it was nothing rational, but she'd learned from past experience to pay attention to her intuition.

"What can you tell me about him?"

"Young man, maybe late twenties. Tall white guy with dark hair. He had on an Army jacket."

"I'm sorry you had to see that."

"Yeah, you gotta wonder what goes on in people's heads that they want to kill themselves, especially when they're young like that. I survived colon cancer. I want to live as long as I can."

Letty stood with him quietly for a few minutes, then said goodbye.

Back at her truck, she called Alejandro Ramirez.

"Alejandro, I understand you had a death here at Agua Caliente Park. Maybe a suicide."

"Yes, we haven't let news out about this until we figure out who he is and then contact his next-of-kin."

"I'm going to send you a photo by email, and you see if it's your guy."

Five minutes later, she received a text from Alejandro. "Yes, that's the man. Know who he is?"

Letty felt this pain in her shoulder where she had been shot in Iraq. A feeling of great sadness came over her. She called Alejandro again. "His name is Kenny Wilson. He's a vet who was living in a homeless camp here. I've been looking for him, trying to connect him to his family. When I get back to my office, I'll send you his family's contact information. Did he leave a note?"

"Yes. It just says that he was tired and wanted to rest. He asked everyone to forgive him."

"Oh, that's so sad."

"Yeah." He sounded sad, too.

"Talk to you later, Alejandro."

"Later."

* * *

Letty called her friend Zhou.

"Hi, Zhou. How would you like to put on your Detective Inspector hat? I'd like to visit with you and get your ideas about a case I'm working on."

Zhou LiangWei had been a Detective Inspector for the Chinese Ministry of Public Security earlier in his life. He'd been sent by Interpol all the way from Beijing to Tucson to investigate Hong Kong triad gangsters operating smuggling and trafficking operations in southern Arizona. He and Letty became fast friends and colleagues, working together to bring down the smugglers and to free three abducted young women. One of those women was Letty's friend Jade, an elementary school teacher in Tucson. Zhou and Jade fell in love and married. Now Zhou ran a martial arts school in Tucson.

"Of course. Please come here. Your cases are interesting for me."

Thirty minutes later, Letty was sitting on Zhou and Jade's back patio.

"Are you enjoying being a dad?" Letty asked her friend.

Zhou smiled. "Baby Ben Ben is the funniest little fellow I know. Yes, I think being a parent is very entertaining. I laugh often, especially when he laughs. He is funny when he laughs."

"Ben Ben is a real cutie. He may not be so much fun when he's a teenager."

Zhou smiled. "I put him in gong fu class. He will learn discipline."

"Uh-oh. That sounds serious." Letty chuckled.

"I mention to you that I have a new student. He works for you."

"Frankie? I told him to go see you and sign up for classes at your school."

"He is small, but he is strong and flexible. Most important, he has good self-discipline and good attitude. I think he will do well following the gong fu path."

"If he needs any help with the tuition, let me know. I'll chip in."

Zhou nodded.

"Okay. I'm working on two cases that may be related." Letty proceeded to tell Zhou everything she knew about Edward Becker's death and also the murders of Scott Kimball and Gordon Miller.

"Letty, I agree that Becker's death is possibly related to the other case. If you can find the sinkhole he described, you can find evidence."

"Becker was concerned about a chemical dump that might affect water resources. Can you think of any other possibility?"

"If not dumping, perhaps Becker saw something he should not have seen. Perhaps there is some illegal activity at this house. Perhaps smuggling drugs or people."

"Not people," Letty said. "That would attract too much attention in a quiet residential area. Maybe drugs. But there's really not that much traffic to and from the house. There could be something else we haven't thought of. There's a woman who lives down the hill, Agnes Olsen. She's a retired cop. She told me she has a feeling that something is going on at that house. She's keeping an eye on it."

"I think you cannot say more until you know more about what Becker found and where he was killed, and then see if there is a connection to that house."

"About the other matter, the two men who were killed."

"A professional assassin would have sniper and bombing skills."

"Yes. But I'm especially curious about the two women, the wives of the murdered men. Obviously, if their husbands are dead, they both inherit everything, unless there's something in the men's wills that give assets to someone else. That seems unlikely, though. And I don't understand why Jen Kimball hired me to investigate her husband if she was planning on killing him anyway."

Zhou sat quietly for a few minutes.

"Look at this over a larger time period. Criminals sometimes start with one idea and then the idea changes as events develop. Perhaps the two women started with the idea of divorce. Jen comes to you hoping to get evidence of husband's infidelity. Then in divorce, she will have advantage. But she, too, is guilty of infidelity. Perhaps she thinks hiring a private investigator to collect information on her husband will take attention away from her behaviors. Then maybe later, the two women change the idea. Instead of divorcing the husbands, they consider murder. The advantage of murder is that they receive all assets. It is impossible to know the time sequence of their thinking."

"So why create this fake business in their husbands' names?"

"Again, when first idea is divorce, the women drain assets from husbands to buy big house. They plan to sell house then send sale funds to their own personal accounts. Husbands lose money. Wives gain. Divorce comes. Wife still gets half of whatever he owns but what he owns is less now because wife has removed a large amount of the money to her own bank account. He gets less. She gets more."

"That all makes sense."

"It will be helpful to learn more about this Mexican groundskeeper who is the lover of both women. Did they first give him sex, or sex and money, or perhaps some other benefit for assisting them? Did they decide later to use him, to make him be the killer of their husbands?"

"We're trying to find out something about him now. Frankie tracked down his tattoos to a specific platoon in the U.S. Army. But we need to know his name before we can find out when he served, where he served, and what exactly he did while he was in the Army."

Zhou nodded. "Letty, I think perhaps this is more dangerous than your typical case. You must be careful."

"I will, Zhou. Thanks for knocking ideas around with me."

They sat together in easy silence.

"Zhou, I have another question for you."

He nodded.

"What do you think about that man Dan Ennis who was at Will's birthday party? I saw you talking to him."

Zhou looked at Letty and smiled. "He is a good man. He has served as medical doctor in many difficult places in the world. He does good work."

Letty stayed silent.

Zhou added, "I was curious about his martial arts practice as well."

"What martial arts practice?" Letty asked. Even to herself, she sounded a little shocked.

"Thai kick boxing. They call this Muay Thai."

"He does Thai kick boxing? How do you know that?"

"I asked him. He told me."

"How did you know to ask?"

"The way he moves. Often I can tell who has a martial arts practice from body movement. When I was Detective Inspector, I watched to see if opponent had training. This is important to know before fighting someone, Letty. I learned early to watch body movement. Dan showed training."

Letty frowned. How could she have missed this? Dan never mentioned it. Of course, he did live in Thailand for several years. It had never occurred to her to ask.

"Dan told me he enjoys the exercise," Zhou continued. "But he does not enjoy using the skills against another person."

"He doesn't want to hurt anyone, right?"

"That is correct. He is a doctor and caring for people is his first concern, not hurting them."

Letty sighed. Maybe her brother Eduardo was right about her being clueless.

"Letty, remember when Monsieur Laurent was here? I warned you about him. He is what Jade calls 'a player.'" Jean Pierre Laurent was an Interpol agent who had come to Tucson to visit Zhou on business. He was a very attractive man who had asked Letty to spend the night with him so he could, in his words, "make passionate love" to her. Letty declined the offer.

"Yes, I remember. I took your advice."

"I give more advice now."

"Okay. What?"

"Dan Ennis is a good man. I see the way he looks at you. He likes you. I think you like him. I suggest you respond to him. I think he will make you content."

Letty nodded. Everyone seemed to really like Dan.

Jade came in at that moment, all happy smiles, with a big shopping bag in her hand.

"Hi Letty. Zhou, our baby boy is still asleep."

"I play with him. I make him tired," Zhou said, smiling.

"Jade, what do you think of Dan Ennis?" Letty asked.

"That friend of yours at Will's birthday? He's adorable. You'd better jump on him."

Zhou laughed at that, and Letty felt herself growing warm. Again.

Letty said goodbye to them both. She went home and called Dan Ennis.

CHAPTER 18

Dan answered on the second ring.

"Hey, Letty."

"Hi, Dan, want to go with me on a working date?"

"You bet. Should I bring my medical bag?"

"Nope. This is a working date, and I'm the one who's working. Do you like to hike?"

"Yes."

"Then dress for a hike, boots, a backpack, water, all that. I'll pick up you up tomorrow morning around eight."

"I'll be ready."

Letty disconnected before she said something stupid. She didn't know why Dan got her so rattled.

Will came into the kitchen.

"Hey, Big Sister. I haven't seen much of you lately. What have you been up to?"

Letty mentioned that she had a couple of cases she was working on. She also told him about her trip out to the reservation with Dan.

"That's awesome, Letty."

"What do you think of Dan Ennis, Little Brother?"

Clarice came into the kitchen and stood next to Will.

"He's the right man for you, Big Sister."

Clarice nodded her head in agreement.

"Oh god," Letty groaned.

"Go for it, Letty," Will said. "You need a boyfriend."

* * *

The next morning, Letty picked Dan up at his house and they headed east toward Agua Caliente Park. She drove past the park. They continued past the turnoff that led to Agnes Olsen's house, and to the big house owned by SG Enterprises higher up the hill. She drove to the next winding road and turned into the residential area. She found a place to leave her pickup under a big mesquite tree.

Letty and Dan made their way on foot upward into the foothills, moving to the northeast. Letty was keeping her eye on the ground around her and also on the homes down the hill.

"I'm not supposed to talk about my on-going investigations. I'll just tell you that the big house you can see down there is under observation. There's also a big RV there."

"I see it."

"Sometimes there's a dirty, beat-up old dark-blue pickup there, too. The pickup isn't there right now, and that's a good thing. We're going on farther up where he won't be able to see us if he shows up. We're going to look for a sinkhole that shows signs of chemical dumping. The man who found this sinkhole was murdered. The murder may be connected to the man with the dark-blue pickup who has been seen at that big house."

Dan nodded.

"We're going to stay behind this low ridge for most of our hike. We don't want anyone to see us. If we do see someone, just act like you're out for a hike."

"A hike with my novia."

Letty turned her head to look at him.

"That's a Spanish word."

"Yes. Esperanza helped me learn that new word, 'novia.' It means girlfriend."

"I know."

"You told Esperanza that you didn't know if you are my girlfriend or not. So just to clarify, you *are* my girlfriend."

"Gosh." Letty didn't know what else to say. Dan was grinning.

They walked around up above the house in a more-or-less systematic fashion. Letty continued to look around her for signs of a sinkhole with no vegetation growing around it.

"If you see any bare spots, let me know," Letty said.

"Okay. Is that what we're looking for? Bare spots with no plants?"

"That's right." She led Dan forward for a while, then slightly uphill and back the way they came. They repeated this pattern for about an hour, going north and south, east and west up the hillside, being careful to stay out of sight of the house and RV.

Letty looked over at Dan. He was looking at the desert landscape, the mountains and the sky, not at the ground like Letty.

"What's that really far over there?" he pointed to the west.

"First you see the Tucson Mountains just over on the west side of the city. The other mountains, much farther to west, are the Baboquivari Mountains. You saw them from the other side when we went to visit my family."

"Can we go hiking there sometime?"

"Sure, that would be fun. The terrain is much rougher. It's pretty wild country over there. Maybe we could borrow a couple of horses from my uncle and go riding. You said you know how to ride, right?"

"Yes. I learned to ride when I was younger. This Sonoran Desert is so much different from what I expected. I thought it would be a desert with sand dunes like the Sahara or something. But, really, there are all these interesting plants and animals, and it's much greener than I expected. I especially like the saguaros."

Dan backed up, opened his arms up, and thrust his left arm directly into a large cholla cactus.

"Ouch." He held one arm up, bent at the elbow. His shirt sleeve was rolled up, and his forearm was bare. Fuzzy little spines from the cholla were clearly visible in the sunlight all along the length of his forearm.

"Don't touch them. They'll just go in deeper," Letty said.

"They look like little hairs." Dan reached out and touched a cluster with his finger.

"Dan, seriously. Do not touch. You'll just push them in deeper and get them in your fingers too. They're not hairs. There little spine thingies called glochids. They can cause a skin inflammation or an infection."

"Ouch! It itches and stings."

"Sit down, and we'll try to get some of them out with duct tape. This is just a temporary remedy. Later when we get home, we'll put some Elmer's glue on the area, let it dry and peel it off. Glue works wonders. That usually gets them all."

He reached out and tried to touch them again.

"*Dan, don't touch.*"

He looked at Letty, frowning. "It stings."

"Sit down. Let me help you."

She noticed his lower lip was sticking out.

"You're acting like a two-year old, Dan."

"It hurts." Dan sat down.

Letty sighed, exasperated. She retrieved a roll of duct tape and some small scissors from her backpack.

"Why do you carry duct tape in your backpack?" he asked.

"So I can rescue newbies from Minnesota who don't have the good sense to stay out of a cactus."

"Okay, okay," he said. "It's just that duct tape and glue don't sound like good medicine to me."

"Wait a minute. You'll see."

Letty cut off a couple of strips of duct tape and applied them to Dan's arm. She very lightly pressed the tape then began peeling it away. She could see a thick layer of hair-thin spines stuck to the duct tape.

Dan was quiet as she worked. Finally he said, "Okay. I'm acting like a two-year old. But you were a tyrant when I took care of you in the emergency room. So we're even."

He was referring to the time when Letty was attacked and beat up on the Rillito River Trail. He was jogging there at the time, and he helped Letty when she was in trouble. He called for an ambulance, and not long after, he treated her in the hospital emergency room.

"A tyrant? What do you mean?"

"You were giving me orders. 'Don't give me any opioids,' you demanded. And then you made it clear you were absolutely opposed to staying in the hospital overnight. When I came over to your house later to check on you, you told me, 'don't be so pinche demanding.'"

Letty was grinning now. "Did I say that?"

"Yes, ma'am. You seemed to have forgotten that I'm the doctor, not you." He looked at her sternly, frowning, trying not to smile.

"That's when you pulled rank on me?"

"Right. I ordered you to go to sleep, and you did. You said, 'Yes, sir. Thank you, sir.' Then you dropped right off."

Letty nodded.

Dan chuckled, remembering. "What would it take for you to say that again? 'Yes, sir. Thank you, sir.'"

"Don't press your luck, Captain. We're not in the Army anymore."

Letty continued to pull spines from his arm. "Thank you for taking such good care of me, Dr. Ennis."

"And thank you for taking care of me now. I can feel the difference already. That's amazing."

"It looks like they weren't in too deep yet. We're getting a lot of them. We'll still need to do the glue thing later to make sure we got them all. Glue is the best. And we'll need to wash your arm really well to get rid of bacteria."

After she finished with a second layer of tape, Dan rubbed his arm. "That feels so much better. Thank you, Letty. How did you learn this?"

"I'm a desert rat. We know stuff like this. For example, we know better than to back into a cholla cactus." She smiled at him.

"I want to be a desert rat, too."

Letty was quiet for a moment. He teased her a lot. Maybe she'd just turn the tables.

"You can be a desert rat, Dan. You have to apply online, pay a fee, and take an exam. If you pass, you get a certificate." Letty avoided looking at him.

"*Take an exam?*"

"Yes, I'll tutor you."

She glanced over at Dan. He had a look on his face somewhere between dismay and consternation. He looked at her, and suddenly his face changed. He relaxed, cocked his head and smiled.

"Letty Valdez, there is no test is there?"

Letty shrugged her shoulders.

"In fact, there is no on-line application, no exam, and no certificate, is there, Letty Valdez?"

"Maybe not." She couldn't help herself. She laughed out loud.

"Well, if bullshitting me makes you laugh, then that's okay with me."

"Here's how you become a desert rat. You hang out with desert rats and learn what you need to know."

"Like today."

"Yes, like today. You just learned a new use for duct tape, and later you'll learn a new use for glue. So you are well on your way to becoming a desert rat yourself."

There was that lopsided grin again.

"Thank you, Letty."

Dan pulled a liter bottle of water from his backpack and took a drink. He stretched out flat. He put his head on his backpack and his hands on his stomach. He closed his eyes and sighed.

Letty sat next to him. They were quiet for several minutes. She thought that maybe this was a good time to see if she could find out what was up with him, especially after he'd declared her to be his novia. She was aware that she felt very nervous.

"Dan."

"Letty," he matched her serious tone. She could see a slight smile on his face.

"Dan, we've known each other for a while, but I don't feel like I really know you very well. I want to ask you some questions."

"Okay," his eyes were still closed but his smile remained.

"Dan, do you really like me? You said you did. Remember?"

Dan's eyes opened in surprise.

"Of course. You know I do, although I wouldn't say that 'like' is the right word. Rather it would be correct to say that I'm bat-shit crazy about you."

"Oh," Letty said. She didn't really know what to say to that. She hesitated.

"Well, uh, do you like me in the way that a man likes a woman?" There. She'd said it.

"Yes, definitely. Do you want details?"

Details? What could that mean?

"Okay, give me some details."

"I desperately want to kiss you. I'm aroused the entire time I'm around you. I frequently ….."

Letty's arms rested on her knees. She lowered her face in her arms to hide her embarrassment and also her pleased smile.

"Uh oh. Too many details?"

Letty lifted her head. She couldn't look at him.

"No, that's okay." She hesitated again. "If you feel that way, why haven't you ever tried to kiss me? I mean really kiss me."

There was what seemed like a long pause to Letty.

Dan breathed in. "One summer my dad sent me out to work on a horse ranch in western North Dakota. I didn't know it at the time, but my dad was dying. I think he didn't want me to see him go through chemo. He died a few months after I came home."

His eyes were closed, remembering.

"The ranch hands found this wild horse out on the prairie, a little filly. She had been separated from her herd somehow, and she was alone. They brought her in and put her in the corral. It was our job to get her to trust us and eventually, to accept a saddle. Do you know what a filly is?"

"Yes, Uncle Mando always had horses when I was growing up. Still does. A filly is a young female horse."

"That's right. Only one or two years old, never bred."

Dan fell silent. Eventually he spoke.

"That summer was my first sexual experience. With Julia." He was smiling now, remembering.

"Who's Julia?"

"She was Mr. Walker's daughter. He was the owner of the ranch and my dad's friend. Julia was fifteen that summer. Julia wanted to give herself a birthday gift. She asked me if I would be her gift to herself. I said yes."

"You had sex with a fifteen-year old?" Letty was aghast.

Dan looked at her and shrugged. "I was fourteen, almost fifteen."

"*Fourteen!*" Letty gasped. "That's so young."

"Hey, I was up for it." He collapsed in laughter. "No pun intended," he gasped.

Letty rolled her eyes. Men. Finally she spoke.

"I'm confused. What does that filly have to do with never kissing me."

Dan sat up and looked directly into her eyes. His voice was serious now.

"You are like that filly. Intelligent, high-spirited, exceedingly beautiful, and very, very skittish. I am being very patient with you just like I was with the filly. Julia and I didn't push her. We encouraged her to come to us. Most of all we wanted her to trust us. Eventually she came to us, and she nuzzled us. We knew then that she trusted us."

"And you want me to trust you?"

"That's right. Like that filly, if I push you too soon or too hard, I'm afraid I'll lose you. I really don't want to lose you. So I'm waiting."

"Waiting for me to show my trust?"

"That's right. And I am a patient man."

He leaned back again and rested his head on his backpack. He closed his eyes again.

Letty noticed his breathing had become regular. She wondered if he might be falling asleep. Damn! she thought to herself. She had managed to get herself stuck in a corner. The ball was in her court now. It was almost as if he were playing hard to get. She would have to take the initiative. Just like when she had to ask him out that first time. She bit her lower lip. Well, why not? There was no law that said the man had to go first.

"You are a clever man, Dan Ennis."

He smiled, but he didn't open his eyes.

Letty leaned toward him and pushed her nose and mouth against his cheek a couple of times.

"Ah, my little filly is coming in for a nuzzle." His voice was soft.

Letty kissed him. Not just once but several times. Dan put his hand on her neck, pulled her closer and kissed her in return, long, slow kisses.

Letty became aware that the wind had picked up. The breeze was ruffling Dan's hair. She looked around. A twenty-foot tall saguaro was close by.

"Listen, Dan. Can you hear that?"

He was quiet. "Yeah, I hear this kind of whistling sound. Comes and goes, high and then lower. I think the word 'ethereal' is a good description of that sound. What is it?"

"See that saguaro over there? It's singing to you."

Dan looked at the saguaro. "What do you mean, 'singing'?"

"The wind is passing over thousands of spines on the body of the saguaro and making them vibrate. The vibration makes the ethereal sounds. We call that a 'singing saguaro.'"

He smiled. "That makes me happy to know that."

They both fell into silence. Suddenly the wind brought more than sounds. Another gust brought a strong, ugly smell coming from the west, from down the hill.

"Yuck." Dan wrinkled his nose.

Letty frowned.

"Smells like urine. Like ammonia," he said.

"Yeah," Letty said. "That's not good."

"What do you mean? Is there a big mountain lion on the other side this rock taking a piss?"

She crept up and looked over the rock on the ridge above them. Down below at the big house, the dark-blue pickup was parked next to the RV. The door to the RV was open.

"There's a couple of other smells I'm detecting, too. The ammonia is a give-away. I think we just figured out what's going on down there."

"What?"

"Meth production. That smell is common when people are cooking meth."

Letty rose and put her backpack on again. Dan rose, too.

"Let's be careful going back. We don't want to be seen."

She started hiking back in the direction that they'd come earlier that morning.

Dan reached out grabbed her hand and pulled her toward him.

"One for the road?" he asked.

Before Letty could say anything, Dan pulled her close up against his body and kissed her with considerable enthusiasm.

"Goodness," Letty said breathlessly when he finally let her go. "I guess I got what I asked for."

"You can have more, too. You can have as much of me as you want."

Letty knew exactly what he meant by that. She felt herself getting warm again.

They hardly spoke all the way back down the mountain.

When they arrived at Letty's pickup, she said, "Some women would be offended at being compared to a horse."

"You're not *some women*. Are you offended?"

"No, not really. I like horses. I like dogs, too."

Dan smiled. "And I think you like kissing me, but I bet you'll never admit it."

That made Letty laugh again. "Maybe."

"Yeah, maybe." He was grinning now.

"I'm taking you home now, Dan. Do you have any glue or rubber cement at your house?"

"I have Elmer's glue."

As they were driving past the entrance to Agua Caliente Park, Letty noticed an unfamiliar movement along the side of the road in some tall grass. She pulled over. She and Dan got out and walked toward the movement. It was an injured dog.

"Oh, no. Look. It's hurt," Dan said.

The dog, a female Golden Retriever, was whining and trying to get up onto all fours. It was clear that one of its hind legs was broken or dislocated at the joint. The dog looked up at Letty with a scared and yet hopeful look. Her eyelashes were really long, and her eyes were really big.

"We can't leave her here," Dan said. He started talking to the dog in a low, calm, reassuring manner.

"No, we're not leaving her. Just a minute." She went to her pickup and returned with a dog muzzle in her hand.

"Since she's hurt, she might bite. Let's see if we can get this on her." Dan continued to talk to the dog. Letty reached out and slipped the muzzle onto the dog.

"Okay. We don't have much room in the pickup for her, and I'm afraid she may try to jump out if I put her in the back."

"I can hold her." And he did. They lifted the dog together. Dan slipped into the passenger seat with the dog in his arms, and Letty helped arrange her body in the most comfortable position without putting pressure on the dog's leg. She struggled slightly and whined. Dan held her firmly and continued to talk to her.

"We'll take her to the vet who takes care of my dogs."

"She doesn't have any license tags, but she does have a name tag on her collar. Her name is Maizie."

"Maizie," Letty repeated.

The dog looked at each of them in turn. Her tail wagged weakly. Off they went to the veterinarian's office.

An hour later, Letty and Dan were back at his house.

"What will happen to Maizie? She needs someone to take care of her," Dan asked.

"Don't worry. I have a plan. I know just the man for the job. He needs a dog to take care of him, and Maizie needs a man to take care of her. Meanwhile, let's look at your arm again."

Letty treated Dan one more time at his kitchen table. She smeared a thick layer of glue on Dan's arm. Dan was watching her and smiling the entire time.

"While we're waiting.....,"Dan pulled her close and kissed her again, slow and sweet. "I like kissing you. And I have no problem admitting it," he said.

"Oh, goodness."

"You're so shy."

"I'm not shy."

"Then what are you?"

"I'm scared. I'm scared for you. Getting mixed up with me could get you hurt."

Dan shook his head. "You worry too much."

Finally the glue was dry. Letty slowly and methodically peeled away the layer of glue. Soon Dan had no spines at all in his skin.

"This should take care of all those spines. Just don't get tangled up with a cholla again. You should go wash your arm really well. As for me, I'm going now."

"Thank you, Letty, for our working date, and for treating me with desert rat medicine. I have to work today and tomorrow, too. I'll get off around seven in the evening tomorrow. Is it my turn now to ask you out? Or do you have another interesting idea for a date?"

"I'm sure we can come up with something. I had fun, too."

She leaned forward and kissed him briefly on his lips.

"Adios, mi novio."

She could hear Dan laughing as she walked to her pickup.

"Novio, novia, pinche, gordita," she heard him say. "I'm learning Spanish."

As she drove away, Letty had this oddly conflicted feeling. She was going to have to investigate a meth lab which wasn't going to be any fun. But what she really wanted to think about was Dan and his kisses. She felt happy thinking about him. It was a strange feeling. She couldn't remember being this happy for many years. And scared.

CHAPTER 19

The next morning, Letty took her usual run with Teddy. By the time she had arrived at her office, the late winter sky was an intense blue full of sunlight, not a cloud in sight. Frankie was already at his desk.

"Hey, Letty. I'm still working on finding who was in that platoon and if any of them resemble our studly groundskeeper."

"Studly? Is that a word?"

"Yes, that's definitely a word. Oh, I did find an interesting connection between Kellie Miller and Jen Kimball."

"What is that?"

"Those two went to the same high school in Scottsdale at the same time. They were both on the cheerleading squad together for two years."

"So they go way back."

Frankie nodded.

Letty sat down at her desk. Her phone rang.

"Señorita Valdez?"

"Yes. Señor Jimenez?"

"My English not so good. Por favor. We speak Spanish?"

"Yes, of course," Letty said. The conversation continued in Spanish.

"I found that man you are looking for. I have the license plate number for his pickup truck."

"Oh, that's really good news," Letty reached for paper and a pen. "Go ahead. I'm ready."

Jimenez gave her the license number. "Also, I followed him."

"Oh, no. Did he see you?"

"No. He looks at cars and girls, nothing else."

"What did you see?"

"This young man is renting a storage unit in Tucson. I was careful so he would not see me. But I can describe where the unit is located."

"Good. I'll write that down, too."

Jimenez proceeded to give her the name and street address of a storage facility in east Tucson on Tanque Verde Road. He described the specific row of units by number and an approximate location in the row.

Letty was considering what might be stored in these units. Packaged meth ready to sell? Or the chemicals needed to make the meth? Or both?

"Thank you, Señor Jimenez. This is very useful information. I'm so glad he didn't see you. We think he's dangerous."

"Yes, he looks like a cartel member."

"I don't know for certain about that, but I'm going to find out. By the way, did you get your family into Tucson safely?"

Jimenez's voice changed completely. He suddenly sounded light and happy. "We followed the road map given to us by your uncle Señior Antone. We arrived safely. We saw no Border Patrol."

"And how is little Juanito? My doctor friend thinks he needs a follow-up visit."

"He is doing very well. His leg is healing. I do not wish to disturb the doctor. My neighbor is what you call 'LPN'?"

"That's right. Licensed Practical Nurse."

"Yes, she is watching Juanito now. She says he is healing quickly. Please give my sincere thanks to the doctor. He was kind to us. You, also, Señorita. Thank you so much."

They said their good-byes.

"Frankie, I have a license plate number for you. I think I showed you how to look up the person who registered the license."

"Yes, you did. I'll get started." Frankie came into Letty's office, took her slip of paper, and went back to his computer.

Five minutes later, Letty's phone buzzed again.

"Miss Valdez, this is Jen Kimball."

Letty was surprised. "Hello, Mrs. Kimball. I'm sorry to hear about your loss. I saw the news reports Friday about your husband's death. I thought I'd wait a few days before I called you."

"Yes, well, uh....," Jen Kimball's voice was hesitant. Letty could tell she wanted to know something, but she didn't want to come right out and say what it was.

Finally she asked Letty, "Did you find anything? In your investigation, I mean."

Letty noted that Jen's question was open-ended. She did not ask if Letty found evidence of infidelity on the part of her husband. She wanted to know if Letty found 'anything.'" Letty knew that Jen and her pal Kellie had a lot to hide. They needed to know just how much Letty knew.

"My surveillance man watched your husband. There was no sign that he was meeting anyone secretly. As far as any other findings, I never received that financial information from you so I don't know what he might have been doing with your finances."

"Uh…well…yes…uh. I'm sorry. I just forgot."

Forgot? Letty thought to herself. Unlikely. The whole thing about finances, the bank deposit and withdrawal was most likely a big lie to throw Letty off.

"Are you interested in an investigation into your husband's murder? I'm available."

"No." Jen Kimball answered quickly. "The police are handling that."

"Okay. Is there anything I can do for you then?"

"No. I guess not. Send me a bill." She disconnected abruptly.

Well, okay, Letty thought to herself. Guess that's that. If she can't get any info out of me, then that will be the last I hear from her.

Letty called Alejandro Ramirez at his Tucson Police Department office.

"Hi, Letty, staying out of trouble?"

"So far, Alejandro. I told you I was hired to see if I can find anything about Edward Becker's death. Yesterday I went up into the foothills above Agua Caliente Park. I didn't find the sinkhole that Becker reported. But while I was there, the wind picked up. At one point there was a distinct odor of ammonia coming from downhill to the west. I also detected a couple of other smells. Acetone like in nail polish remover. Maybe a drain cleaner smell. Sulfuric acid maybe?"

"Ah. You know what this suggests, don't you?"

"Yeah, meth production."

"I'm going to need information about where exactly you detected those smells. We'll have to check it out."

"I think I know where the smells came from, but I can't be sure exactly. I'm going back out there and look for that sinkhole that I told you about. I hope to find some trash that will tell us what chemicals have been used. That will likely provide more evidence for meth production. Maybe forensics can find fingerprints. Also I have more to tell you about that Kimball case I was working on and the car bombing death of Scott Miller."

"You're finding connections?"

Letty filled Alejandro in on what Frankie found about SG Enterprises, the strong possibility of a relationship between the wives of the two murdered men, the house and RV on the east side of Tucson, and the Mexican-American groundskeeper who was also linked to Kellie and Jen.

"I think it's important for me to find the sinkhole that Edward Becker reported. I think there has to be connection to murders of Kimball and Miller."

"Okay. Then call me when you find something."

"Also I got a call this morning from a source."

"A source?"

"Yeah, an anonymous source. No tiene papeles."

"Hmm....undocumented. Right?"

"I don't really know for sure about him, but his wife and kids are undocumented. The cartels are after one of his kids, a thirteen-year-old girl. So let's keep him anonymous. I asked him to watch for the man in the dark blue pickup and try to get a car license plate number.

He did that, and he also followed the guy to a storage facility. You might want to check that out, too. If this man is producing meth, he may be storing the chemicals or finished packets of methamphetamines at this facility." Letty gave Alejandro the directions to the storage facility.

"I'll definitely look into that."

At that moment, Frankie appeared in the doorway to Letty's office.

"Hang on, Alejandro. I have something else."

Frankie showed her a photo. "I found him. His name is Augustín Padillo. He goes by Gus, or El Diablo. Here's his service record. Also I confirmed that he's the owner of that auto license plate."

Letty looked at the photo and read the information Frankie found. That strange almost-memory she'd had earlier came to her in a flash. She was almost certain that she'd seen Padillo at the bombing of Gordon Miller's car. He was some distance away, watching. He had a smile on his face. He never looked at Letty.

A minute later, she returned to her call with Alejandro.

"I told you about the Mexican-American groundskeeper who is having sex with both those women. Marv saw him both at Jen and Kellie's houses. His name is Augustín Padillo. He's known as Gus or El Diablo. He's a veteran of the Afghanistan War, U.S. Army, five tours in all."

"How is this connected?"

"Turns out Padillo is a trained Explosive Ordinance Disposal Specialist. The Army trained him to take apart those Improvised Explosive Devices known as IEDs."

"And what he takes apart, he can put back together. He knows how to start from scratch and build a bomb."

"Right. Not only that, on one tour in the Army he was trained and used as a long-distance sniper. He's quite a good shot with those specialized rifles that can take out insurgents from a distance."

"So he has the skills to have taken out both his lovers' husbands?"

"Yeah, but I'm not so sure you could call them 'lovers.' The way Marv described their encounters, it sounded more like sex for fun with no attachment or feeling. It is meaningful, though, that he knows how to shoot people from a distance and how to blow up cars and other things. I'm wondering now if he also knows how to cook meth."

"Do you think these women know what's going on?"

"Yes, I do. In fact, I bet it was all their idea. Padillo gets sex, maybe a big pay-off for the assassinations, and some or most of the profits from the meth production. The two wives get a hit man, and they don't have to get their hands dirty."

"The criminal creativity of some people never fails to amaze me."

"I'm thinking now that Becker may have stumbled onto the meth production, and Padillo took him out with a long-distance shot."

"Makes sense."

"The smell of chemicals on the wind isn't enough. That's why I'm going back out to see if I can find whatever Becker found. Some tangible evidence."

"Meanwhile, I'm going to get a search warrant for the storage facility and an arrest warrant or maybe three arrest warrants. I'll connect with the sheriff's department, too."

"Law enforcement has the bullet that killed Becker, right?"

"Yes, it's evidence from the autopsy."

"If we can find the rifle Padillo used, then we can match the bullets."

"Right. Ballistics. You're not going to get yourself shot, are you, Letty?"

"Not if I can help it. If Padillo shows up at the house, I'll disappear. Becker didn't know to watch out for him. I do."

"Got your gun on you?"

"Yes, I'll let you know what I find."

They disconnected. Letty reached into her desk and pulled out her holster and her Glock semi-automatic pistol. She stood up and attached the holster around her waist. She slipped the gun into the holster.

Letty walked into the front office. Frankie saw the gun right away.

"Oh, shit, Letty. This is the *not-fun* part, right?"

"I'm hoping I don't run into our bomber-sniper. So you hang in here and hold down the fort."

"I will."

"You've done a terrific job, Frankie. You're going to make a great detective."

Frankie's face turned a dark red.

"Thank you, Letty. Please be careful."

* * *

Letty drove east to Agua Caliente Park. As with her earlier trip with Dan, she drove past the turnoff to the big house owned by SG Enterprises. She continued to the next street which went into the residential area. She found a shady spot for her pickup under a big tree. She started her trek up the hill, staying behind a low ridge so she would not be visible from below. Within fifteen minutes, she was above the big house with the RV.

For more than an hour, Letty walked north, then south, then north again, systematically moving up the hill. She found nothing. No sinkhole. No sign of trash dumping associated with meth production.

She sat down and considered what to do next. She decided to move down closer to the house where the RV was parked. The dark-blue pickup was nowhere to be seen, and there was no sign of humans anywhere. She went closer, knowing that if anyone showed up, they would see her immediately.

Then she found it. The sinkhole. It was located to the southeast of the house and RV, not too far from where she had been searching. The sinkhole had been hidden from her view by some large rocks. She knew she was well within view of the house and RV. She approached and could see a patch of barren ground with no vegetation at all, not even the much maligned nonnative buffel grass that fed unwanted wildfires in the foothills.

She quickly found a crack visible in the earth between the rocks. It could easily be the entrance into the underground water, Letty thought. Pour chemicals into that crack, and they would disappear. Unfortunately the chemicals would likely reappear in groundwater farther downhill.

Letty looked around. If the groundskeeper Gus had been dumping chemicals, no doubt he'd left some trash nearby. Apparently, Edward Becker had not mentioned trash to anyone. Either he hadn't found any trash. Or he had not been familiar enough with meth to recognize that he was seeing the tell-all items signaling meth production. His focus would have been on the sinkhole and the potential threat to water.

She walked downhill from the sinkhole. Now she was just south of the house and RV and slightly below the patch with no vegetation where the sinkhole appeared to be. That also put her closer to the next house in the residential area farther to the south. And even farther southeast, she could see yet another residence. She was within sight of all three houses now. She couldn't help but feel vulnerable.

It didn't take her long to find the dump of meth trash. The dump was small in size, only about three feet across, but at least three feet deep, again located in a depression surrounded by rocks. Since each home in this residential area was located on a small acreage, it was possible to leave trash without it being seen unless a person was out walking and stumbled upon it.

She approached the dump, pulled a plastic bag out of her backpack, and she put on some latex gloves. It was all here: a medium-sized metal can marked "toluene," plastic bottles of household cleaner containing ammonia, plastic bottles of nail polish remover containing acetone, and empty blister packets that had contained cold and antihistamine pills. These contained the key meth-production ingredients of pseudoephedrine and ephedrine. She collected samples of each kind of trash and stuffed them in the plastic bag. The plastic bag went into her backpack. She hoped that police forensics would find finger prints and maybe DNA traces on the bottles and blister packs. She worked quickly.

Letty was acutely aware that she was within sight both of the house and RV and now within sight of the neighbors' houses to the south.

She had her gun holstered on her hip, but she knew it wouldn't help her at all when threatened by a sniper with a long-range rifle. She headed back to her pickup truck as quickly as possible.

* * *

Now back on the road toward Agua Caliente Park, she decided to stop off and call Agnes Olsen. She parked below Agnes's house behind the big boulder so her truck wouldn't be visible from the street. She phoned Agnes. They spoke briefly. Then she called Marv Iverson. He answered on the third ring.

"Hey, Marv. I'm coming over to your house. I'll be there in about an hour. I'm bringing someone to meet you. She's very attractive. I think you're going to like her. So get ready. One hour."

She could hear him start his bluster, but before he could say anything, Letty hung up. She was chuckling to herself when Agnes appeared behind the wheel of her Jeep.

"If you'll follow me to the park, I'll leave my truck there and ride with you."

Agnes picked Letty up after she'd parked her truck, and they headed to the veterinarian's office.

"Thanks, Agnes, for helping me out. I thought it might be hard for me to manage the dog and drive at the same time. I don't have a dog crate."

"I have a crate. It's in the back. I should thank you, Letty. I'm always glad to help out when it involves a dog. Also I don't know a lot of people here in Tucson, and I get lonely sometimes. So going along with you is an adventure and relieves the tedium."

"Actually I have an ulterior motive."

"What's that?" Agnes asked.

"I don't know if you knew this, but I served as an Army medic in Iraq. I was kind of a mess when I came home. I still have really bad nightmares."

Agnes nodded. "Yes, I understand a lot of vets were traumatized and still suffer the effects. In some ways, you're like us cops who see some bad things."

Letty nodded. "I stayed with my grandmother for a while. When I felt ready to work, I applied for a job as a private-investigator trainee with a guy named Marv Iverson. He's a gruff old curmudgeon who complains about everything and everybody. In reality, he's a teddy bear. Marv is the angel that gave me a chance at a new life. He trained me, and when he retired, he turned everything over to me. I worry about him because he's at home all the time watching sports on TV. I occasionally hire him to do surveillance for me. Other than that, he doesn't get out, doesn't get any exercise, and I think he needs a dog."

"He doesn't have a wife?"

"He told me once that he had a wife who was killed in a car wreck years ago. He made it clear he didn't want to talk about it."

"Wow. That's what happened to my husband, too. He was a cop like me. He was engaged in a high-speed chase when the perp turned around in the highway and smashed head-on into my husband's cop car. Suicide and murder at the same time."

"I'm sorry, Agnes."

"Yeah, it was nearly fifteen years ago. I still miss him. Sounds like your friend Marv is another lonely person."

"Right. A dog would help with both exercise and loneliness. I told him this but he said he didn't want a dog because they just die."

Agnes frowned. "Yes, they do. They die, and your heart gets broken."

Letty knew Agnes was thinking about her dog Moto who was killed in action.

"Marv had a dog, and it died when it was sixteen years old," Letty said.

"That's pretty old for a dog."

"He refuses to get another dog. I think Marv doesn't want to be hurt again."

Agnes glanced at Letty and nodded.

"You're right though. There's no friend like a dog even if they don't live as long as we do."

"I was out here hiking the other day with ...." Letty hesitated, "with my boyfriend. On our way home, we came upon this injured dog, a Golden Retriever named Maizie. She's at the vet's office now. We're going to pick up the dog and take her over to Marv's and leave her there. He's going to resist me so you have to help me convince him."

"We could tell him that it's temporary. He'll just be fostering her."

"Knowing all the while that he's going to fall in love with Miss Maizie? And he'll have a companion for life? Are you in?"

"You bet. I'm in."

They picked up the dog and headed to Marv's house. They placed Maizie in her crate behind them on the sidewalk, and they stood shoulder to shoulder at Marv's door. Letty knocked.

Marv opened the door. His eyes grew wide.

"Hi, Marv, this is my friend Agnes. She's a retired cop from Milwaukee who moved to Tucson recently. She was with the police canine unit there. She knows a lot about dogs."

Agnes stuck out her hand.

"Hi, Marv, I've heard all about you. Letty really admires you."

They shook hands. Marv turned pink and mumbled something about how Letty was a good detective.

"We need you to do a favor for us," Letty said. She and Agnes stepped aside, and Marv could see Maizie in her crate.

"No, Letty. I told you. I'm not getting a dog."

Agnes smiled and said in calm manner, "Marv, her name is Maizie. She has a dislocated hock joint in her back left leg. There's a cast on it now. She needs a foster parent to watch over her until she heals. That's all. Just a foster."

"She didn't have a microchip or tags. Only a collar with her name," Letty added.

"Once she's okay and can get around again," Agnes said, "you can take her to the animal shelter to be adopted. Or one of those adoption events."

Marv was frowning. Then he looked at Agnes and turned pink again.

"Well, I guess you better come in."

Letty bent down and opened the door to the crate.

"Come on, Maizie."

The dog lifted herself and gingerly limped out of the crate. She headed straight for Marv, wagging her tail.

Marv led them into his house. Maizie followed him and stood next to him. She began leaning against Marv's knees.

"Sit down," Marv gestured to the couch. Both women sat. Marv sat in his recliner chair.

"Oh, I forgot to tell you. Maizie is a Saints fan." Letty said.

That brought a slight smile to Marv's face. "Bullshit."

"Truth."

"I don't know about you, Letty Valdez. What am I going to feed this dog?"

"We brought some dog food and a bowl for water. You have an old dog bed, don't you?"

"Yeah, I still have that." His hand had drifted down to Maizie's head. He began to stroke her. She looked up at him with adoring eyes.

"I thought if it's okay with you, I might come back tomorrow and help you get her up and moving around. She'll heal faster." Agnes said.

"Okay," Marv said. "Tomorrow morning?"

"Fine." Agnes replied.

Letty stood. "Okay, time for us to go. Take her out every few hours to pee. Go slowly because she's limping. Make sure she gets enough water. I'll bring in the dog food now."

A few minutes later, Letty and Agnes were back on the road headed back to where Letty could pick up her truck.

"I think we just made a match," Agnes grinned.

"Yep, no way is Marv gonna let that dog go. He's such a softy."

"I like Marv," Agnes said.

Letty smiled. Hmmm...maybe they'd made two matches.

CHAPTER 20

Back at her office, Letty hid the bag of trash she'd found at the sink-hole in her tiny closet.

"Frankie, I found evidence to support the idea that meth is being produced in that house or the RV. I think that's what Edward Becker found, and that's what got him killed."

"What are you going to do now?"

"It's about time to turn this over to Tucson Police. I'm going to call Alejandro Ramirez right now."

Just as Letty finished her sentence, the front office door opened. In walked Gus Padillo, the Mexican-American former Army sniper and explosives expert that she and Frankie had been looking for since Marv photographed him at Jen Kimball's house. Letty stood up from her desk and walked to the door between her inner office and the front office where Frankie sat at his desk. She and Frankie both recognized Padillo instantly from his tattoos and the U.S. Army photo Frankie found earlier. Letty glanced over at Frankie. He looked terrified.

Padillo was a good-looking young man, medium height, and fit. He obviously worked out. He was clean-shaven, and his dark hair was long enough to be captured by a small band at the back of his neck. He stood at the door, weight on one hip, with an insolent look on his face. His arms were crossed in front of his chest. His eyes fell briefly on the gun in its holster around Letty's waist.

"Hello, I'm Letty Valdez. Can we help you?"

"Yeah, I know who you are." Padillo turned to Frankie. "Who are you?"

"Francisco," Frankie's voice was faint.

"And who are you?" Letty asked.

"El Diablo," Padillo turned to Letty. He glared at her, daring her to speak.

"So you're a couple of Mexicans pretending to be investigators, huh?" Padillo's attitude was confrontational.

"Yes, I'm an Arizona-licensed private investigator. He's my trainee." She nodded at Frankie.

"Well, I think you're sticking your nose into places it shouldn't go."

"What are you talking about?"

"I saw you with that boyfriend of yours up above my house. You two shouldn't be there. Stay away from my place."

"We were just out hiking, and we were well away from houses. We were so far up we may have been in the national forest."

"I don't give a damn. You stay away from my place. Or maybe you'd like to see your boyfriend end up with a bullet in his head?"

This last comment made Letty feel sick to her stomach and angry, too. Shit, shit, shit, she said to herself. She should never have taken Dan with her on that search for the sinkhole. What an idiot. She'd put him in danger. And all that kissing had just been a distraction. She hadn't been watching. She hadn't been doing her job. She let herself get caught up in the moment. She couldn't let that happen again. She couldn't let anything bad happen to Dan. She glared at Padillo.

"You're not the only one with a gun, Diablo." Letty could feel the weight of her Glock on its holster on her hip.

"Yeah, but that little handgun won't shoot very far, will it?"

His arrogance and insolence permeated the air. His eyes were half-closed, as if he were bored. He was dismissing Letty. Padillo reached casually to open the front door.

"How did you know that was me anyway?" Letty wanted to know as much as possible.

"A little birdie told me. I described you, and the little birdie told me your name."

Jen Kimball, Letty thought to herself. Or maybe Kellie Miller. They knew who she was and what she'd been working on. Gus described her, and one of them told him who she was.

"I'll be going now. Just remember. I'm watching you." He jutted his chin out with these words.

Letty had an instant flash of inspiration and insight. Maybe it was time to rev things up. Turn on the heat. Bring things to a boil. Give El Diablo something to think about other than shooting Dan in the head.

Letty crossed her arms in front of her chest and cocked her head. She looked at Padillo with the same level of insolence.

"You are so being played, Gus Padillo."

"What are you talking about?"

For the first time, Padillo looked unsure of himself.

Now she was going to up the ante.

"Those two women you've been banging. They are so playing you." She sneered back him.

There. She'd said it. Told him she knew his name. Told him she knew he was doing something illegal. Told him that she knew about Jen and Kellie. Told him that she knew about his relationship with those two women.

A mixture of emotions passed over his face. Surprise. Shock. Fear. Anger.

"What two women?"

"You know very well what two women. We've been watching you. You get regular pussy and money from selling the meth. You do the dirty work for them. You're their hired hit man. Meanwhile, those two women fix things so that there's no connection between you and them. You get left holding the bag. They become the grieving widows, two widows with fat bank accounts. You get a prison cell. If you're lucky that is. The state of Arizona still has the death penalty. That sounds about right for a paid assassin."

Padillo was scowling now. "You don't know shit, Valdez." He jerked the office door open, stomped out, and slammed it behind him.

Letty turned to Frankie.

"Call Alejandro Ramirez in the Homicide Unit at TPD, Frankie. Tell him that everything is going down now. He should send a squad car, or two or three, to the house I told him about east of Agua Caliente Park. And tell him to call the sheriff, too."

She ran out of her office and jumped into her pickup. She was certain that Padillo would go back out to the house and RV and frantically look for anything that might tie him to the crimes. Then he would get in his truck and drive away from Tucson as fast as he could. Maybe go across the border into Sonora, Mexico. Or north to Phoenix. Dump the truck and get a new vehicle. Head west to California or north or east. Anywhere but Arizona. Disappear. Escape. Write off the whole thing. Take his rifle and his money and escape.

Letty threaded her way as fast as possible through the early-afternoon traffic. It seemed that she was stopped by every red light between her office and the road out to Agua Caliente Park. Only once did she see Padillo's dark-blue pickup about ten cars ahead of her at the big intersection of Kolb Road and Tanque Verde Road. As soon as he made the turn onto Tanque Verde Road, he zipped away heading east. She could see him weaving from lane to lane around cars, going fast. Maybe a cop will stop him for speeding, she thought. She shook her head. Probably not. She couldn't get that lucky.

It took her only twelve minutes to go the length of Tanque Verde Road. She turned onto Soldier Trail, going so fast that her rear wheels spun out as she went from east to north. Far ahead of her, she could see Padillo turn east again on Roger Road which went past Agua Caliente Park. When she made the turn, she couldn't see him at all. He'd gone far enough, fast enough that he'd already turned into the residential area where the big house and RV were located.

Letty knew that for her to drive up to the big house was a bad idea. Gus would hear her coming almost immediately, and turn his rifle on her. She'd be a sitting duck. So she pulled off at Agnes Olsen's house. She drove her pickup truck a short distance into Agnes's driveway just far enough to pull behind the big boulder that sat at the end of the driveway. Above her, she could see upslope to Agnes's house with her Jeep parked in front. Agnes was nowhere in sight, probably inside her house.

Letty left her truck and began the trek on foot up the hill. She just hoped that Padillo would be so distracted that he wouldn't notice her. Soon she was high enough up the road so that she was now even with the driveway leading to the big two-story house and the RV parked behind it. There was a luxury Lexis SUV parked in the driveway that Letty had never seen there. No way did this vehicle belong to Gus Padillo.

She crept into the shadowed area under the second-floor over-hang. Around the corner, she could see Gus's old pickup parked next to the RV. Loud sounds were coming from inside the RV. She could hear banging and thudding, as if the interior of the RV was being torn apart. She could hear Padillo cursing inside.

Gus came out of the RV and around the other side to face the big house. Letty was hiding in the shadows, but he couldn't have seen her anyway because he wasn't looking her way. He was looking up at a deck on the second story.

"What did you bitches do with my rifle? And you owe me money. I did the two jobs for you. Took those two men out nice and clean. Where's my money? And my rifle?" He was yelling now.

Letty could hear giggles and whispering.

A voice that sounded very like Jen Kimball said, "Now, sweetie. Don't get upset."

"Don't tell me that. What did you do with my rifle? I want it *now!*"

Then there was another voice, a woman, someone Letty didn't know. A voice she had never heard.

"Gus, hold your voice down."

"Kellie, give me my fucking gun. And pay me. Then I'm leaving. I've had enough of your games."

"Okay, here's your gun."

There was a loud, low popping sound with a slight echo. A nine millimeter from the sound of it, Letty guessed.

The bullet went directly into Gus's chest. Gus fell backwards into the dirt and rocks. The bullet must have hit his heart because Letty could see regular bursts of blood emanating from his chest every second. The bursts were strong at first then they grew weaker and thinner. Finally the blood stopped.

"Well, that shut him up," Kellie said.

"Kellie, you shot him," Jen said. She sounded scared.

"Him or us, Jen."

Letty heard one of the women moving down some steps from the overhung above. It was Letty's first view of Kellie Miller. She looked rather like Jen Kimball, only slightly thinner and with bleached blonde hair cut a little shorter than Jen's. She was wearing plastic gloves. A nine millimeter gun was in her right hand. Letty recognized it as a Beretta.

Kellie leaned over Gus and put the gun in his hand.

"You were good, baby, but not that good," Letty heard her say.

She's trying to make this look like a suicide, Letty said to herself. That's not going to work. He was shot from too far away for the shot to be self-inflicted. Plus there won't be gun powder residue on his hand indicating that he'd shot himself. And most important, there were two witnesses to the murder. Jen Kimball and Letty Valdez.

Kellie turned back and looked up to the second floor.

"Time for us to get out of here." She started up the stairs again.

"I'll bring our purses," Jen said.

"I'll get the rifle."

Letty could hear them coming down again but this time on a different staircase at the downhill side of the house. The staircase led to the Lexus. She moved around the corner of the house, still in the shadows, so they wouldn't see her when they appeared on the lower level. Both Jen and Kellie climbed into the SUV. Just before Kellie got in, she tossed a big rifle with an elaborate scope into the back seat. This was Gus's sniper rifle.

Kellie started the engine, and the two women took off down the hill. They didn't drive fast. No need to hurry. They didn't want to attract any attention although that was unlikely. Hardly anyone would notice two well-dressed matrons driving away at a measured pace in an expensive SUV, Letty thought. Not many people were home in the neighborhood anyway at this time of day. Most people were still at work.

Letty ran to Gus. He was dead. No breath. No heartbeat. He was already starting to turn a pale whitish color. Sad, Letty thought. He lived a life that ended in this deadly path. At least you don't get to carry out your threat against Dan, she whispered to his body. She turned back to the house.

Letty waited until the two women and their SUV were out of sight, then she started her trek back down the hill. She ran as fast as she could without losing her balance and tumbling down the steep incline.

She arrived even with Agnes' driveway.

Suddenly Kellie stepped out from behind the big boulder at the end of Agnes's driveway. Kellie had parked the SUV out on the main road to Agua Caliente Park. The SUV was pulled off the road, hidden from Letty's view by mesquite trees and creosote bushes. Jen was waiting in the SUV for Kellie.

Kellie moved into position at the end of Agnes's driveway. She had Gus's rifle resting in one arm as she confronted Letty. She shifted it into her two hands so that the muzzle pointed directly at Letty.

"Miss Valdez, so finally we meet."

Letty stared at Kellie and said nothing. She had her gun still in her holster. She knew it wasn't much use now. The rifle was pointed at her chest. All Kellie had to do was pull the trigger.

"You know, you were just supposed to look into Jen's philandering husband. But you seemed to have gone much further."

"I found no sign that Scott Kimball was seeing anyone at all. I don't know about your husband, though. I never got a chance to see what he was up to."

"Oh, that son-of-a-bitch has a couple of girlfriends. Or he *had* a couple of girlfriends, I mean. During our entire marriage, he saw other women. I lost count a few years ago of just how many."

"Why send Jen to me?"

"We had this idea that hiring you would deflect attention away from us. And there was always the possibility that you'd actually find that Scott had some other woman on the side. That was back when we were just going to divorce these rats and take them for every penny we could. But we decided that Gus was a better option for us. He's very skilled, you know. We decided to use Gus to get rid of both of the husbands so we could inherit everything."

"Are you and Jen lovers?"

"No, not that it's any of your business. You might say we're partners in crime." Her laugh was humorless. "We just had no idea that you would investigate us, too."

"I often do a background check on my clients. It happens that clients lie a lot."

"You thought Jen was lying?"

"I couldn't tell. Let's just say I was being extra careful. I decided to look into her and her husband. That led me to SG Enterprises and to you and your husband."

"Big mistake on your part. You should have stuck to business. You were out of bounds to be investigating either Jen or me."

"What I don't know is which one of you killed Edward Becker?"

"Who the hell is Edward Becker?"

"He's this older man, an environmental activist and volunteer. He was checking mountain springs not too far from this place when he found signs of chemical dumping. Someone shot him long-distance with a rifle. I think it was Gus."

"Oh, that moron Gus. Yeah, he killed that guy not long after he arrived here." Kellie looked and sounded very annoyed.

"So he was making meth all this time?"

"It wasn't enough that Gus got all the sex he could handle with two women. He got greedy. Not long after he arrived here, he came upon this stash of pseudoephedrine that had been owned by a drug dealer who later died of an overdose. Gus just couldn't resist. He wanted to use up the stash making meth and sell it before he left Arizona. We went along with him and even volunteered to help him sell the stuff, especially after we found out about his special skills." Kellie snorted in disgust.

Letty knew 'special skills' meant his sniper and bomb-making abilities.

"We let him park that RV behind the house, too. That's where he produced the meth. Inside the RV. We promised to pay him the tidy sum of one hundred thousand dollars, too. All he had to do was take out Scott and Gordon and then leave town. But no. Now you're telling me that you found out about him killing that old guy. Gus was trying to protect his meth lab. I should have shut him down right away. What a dumb shit he was."

"Becker was trying to protect the water resources in Agua Caliente Park."

"So you were working on that, too? The murder of this old guy?"

"Yes."

Kellie exhaled, irritated.

"You're into our business way too far. That means you're in our way now. I think the best thing for Jen and me is to get rid of you now. It will look like Gus killed you. His fingerprints are all over this gun."

She lifted the rifle and pointed it at Letty.

Letty blinked and tried not to look at Agnes Olsen standing ten feet behind Kellie.

"Drop the gun!" Agnes Olsen yelled at Kellie. Agnes appeared silently from behind the big boulder at the foot of her driveway. Now she was in a classic cop stance, her feet apart, one slightly behind the other, arms outstretched with a semi-automatic Glock in her right hand, finger on the trigger, with her left hand steadying the right hand.

Kellie stepped back at the sound of Agnes's voice so she could see both Letty and Agnes. She gestured with the rifle for Letty to move closer to Agnes. Now she could shoot them both. There was no doubt. Kellie intended to shoot and kill Agnes first. Letty would be next. She wouldn't be able to get her gun out of her holster in time to stop Kellie.

Again Agnes yelled. "Drop the gun!"

Kellie lifted the rifle, now pointed at Agnes.

Before Kellie could shoot, Agnes pulled the trigger on her Glock. The bullet pierced Kellie's chest. She dropped the rifle and fell to the ground onto her back. Blood seeped out and stained her ivory-colored linen blouse.

Letty ran forward and pushed the rifle away with her foot. She bent down over Kellie.

Kellie's eyes were opened staring at the sky, but there was no sign of life.

At the sound of the shot, Jen Kimball jumped out of the SUV parked on the road below. She came running up the street toward Agnes's house. When she saw Kellie, she screamed.

Jen threw herself on the ground next to Kellie. She stayed on her knees sobbing and whimpering.

Letty could hear approaching police sirens.

"No. No. No. How could you? How could you? Oh, Kellie, what will I do without you?"

Jen looked at Letty, then at Agnes. She stood and began screaming again. She was hysterical.

Letty could hear the sirens coming closer toward them from the road. There were at least two sirens, maybe three. She figured the police units were about even with Agua Caliente Park now.

Ten seconds later, the first cop car pulled into the street where Agnes lived. It was a Pima County Sheriff's vehicle. By this time, Agnes had placed her gun on the ground and was standing with her hands in the air. Letty removed her gun from her holster and, like Agnes, placed it on the pavement. She raised her hands. A second Sheriff's Department vehicle pulled up, and then a Tucson Police car. Before the police got out of their patrol cars, Letty turned to Agnes and said, "Thank you, Agnes. You saved my life."

"Yeah. She was going to kill us both."

CHAPTER 21

Another police car pulled into Agnes's street and stopped across from her driveway. The sirens were off now, but the lights were still on. Two sheriff deputies exited the cop car and approached.

"What happened here?" His voice was rough and demanding.

"This woman," Agnes pointed to Kellie, "tried to kill both of us with her rifle. I shot her with my Glock."

Yet another police car pulled in line. This time Alejandro Ramirez got out and walked toward Letty. Then another police car appeared and pulled into line behind the other police and sheriff's vehicles.

"Letty," Alejandro nodded, but he was watching Agnes.

"Alejandro, this is Agnes Olsen. She's a retired police officer from Milwaukee. She recently moved to Tucson. She just saved my life." Letty turned to Agnes. "This is Alejandro Ramirez. He's chief of the Homicide Unit in the Tucson Police Department's Violent Crimes Section."

"Okay, ladies. Let's start from the beginning. You can tell me everything that happened."

Meanwhile, police were setting up a crime scene around Kellie Miller's body. Yellow ribbons stretched from one point to another. The forensics team had appeared, and team members were already examining Kellie Miller's body. Jen Kimball had been arrested, handcuffed, and placed in the back seat of one of the police cars. She hadn't stopped crying and moaning Kellie's name.

For the next couple of hours, Letty and Agnes gave statements to Alejandro and then stayed around to see if they could help out.

Letty took Alejandro up to the two-story house, and showed him the body of Gus Padillo, which led to another crime scene set up. She recounted everything she'd seen and done since she last talked to him on the phone earlier that afternoon.

"Did you see Kellie shoot this man?"

"No, but I know it was her because Jen called her name. I was down here under the overhang. Kellie and Jen were up on the balcony. Gus Padillo spent some time tearing apart the interior of the RV looking for his rifle. When he couldn't find it, he came out and started yelling at the two women. He demanded his rifle and also payment for killing the husbands, Gordon Miller and Scott Kimball. That's when Kellie shot him. I heard Jen say to Kellie those very words, 'Kellie, you shot him.' That's how I knew it was her for sure."

Alejandro nodded. "This cabrón got in way over his head with those two women, didn't he?"

"Yeah. He faced down insurgents in both Iraq and Afghanistan. But he couldn't manage these two. I think a big part of the problem was that he was having sex with them. A lot of men have this illusion that they are in control if they are having sex with a woman."

"Well, that's certainly not true. I discovered that when I was a teenager." He shook his head.

"No, Gus wasn't in control at all despite the sex. I think Kellie was the ring leader, and Jen was just following her direction. My intern Frankie found that they had known each other since high school in Scottsdale when they were both on the cheerleading squad. They used and manipulated Padillo from day one. My conclusion is that Kellie had a big plan. She was going to sell this house so they'd have some cash to live on until money came in from their dead husband's estates. I bet they wouldn't have stuck around here either. There are too many nice places to live if you have lots of money."

"Yeah, like an island in the Caribbean?"

"That would work for me. I bet Jen is going to tell you what they had in mind when you interrogate her. I think she'll be pretty easy to break. She'll tell you the whole story, especially when she finds out that she's facing a long jail sentence. All I can say is that I think Jen lied to me about everything when she came to my office. I think those two women were world-class liars and manipulated everyone in their path, especially Gus Padillo."

"Yeah. But it didn't end well for any of them."

"Nope. Not well at all."

* * *

Letty went back down the hill to Agnes's place. Agnes was hanging around watching the cops do their job. She had kind of a wistful look on her face, as if she missed doing the very thing they were doing now.

Letty came to stand next to Agnes.

"Miss being a cop?"

"Yes, I do miss it," Agnes paused. "I didn't realize how much until just now."

"I bet you were really a good one. I can't thank you enough for being here. You saved my ass."

Agnes nodded. "Mine, too. She was going to take us both out with that rifle."

"Are you doing okay? Shooting someone can be really hard on a person."

"Right. I'm sorry I had to kill her. But you saw how it was." Agnes sighed. "This isn't my first time. I had to kill once before and for the same reason, to save myself and another police officer."

They stood together in companionable silence for a few minutes.

Then Agnes spoke. "Letty, I've been thinking. I went over to Marv's to help him with his new dog."

Letty's mouth dropped open. "He agreed to adopt her?"

"Not yet, but he will. You're right about him. Marv's a real softy. A real sweetheart. I like him a lot. We have a lot in common. Not just detection and law enforcement. We're both big sports fans. I'm more selective than he is, though. He'll watch anything. My focus is on ice hockey and basketball. He seems pleased that I like sports. He even laughed when I told him no way was I going to watch cricket. I'm thinking about asking him out on a date. Maybe get tickets to a local sporting event. Do you think he'll agree to go out with me?"

"Goodness, he may fall over dead in shock to be asked on a date. I think after his wife died, he hasn't socialized much. But I think it's a great idea. I noticed every time he looked at you, he turned pink. He likes you. Your being a sports fan is a big plus. Just don't ever say anything negative about the Saints. Yes, I think he'll agree to spend time with you. Going to a game, any game, is the best kind of date for Marv."

Agnes nodded. "Also, what do you think about this? I mentioned this to you before. I'm seriously considering starting a training school for dogs. I know a lot about canine units. I could train dogs for law enforcement, and maybe even Border Patrol. From what I hear, most of the illegal drug shipments coming across the border are found by their narcotics detection dogs. What do you think?"

"It's a great idea, Agnes. Training dogs would be a great service."

"Thanks for your opinion. That's very reassuring. I think I'll ask Marv's opinion, too."

Letty's phone buzzed. It was Frankie. She caught him up with everything that had happened that afternoon.

"Letty, you're totally freaking me out. I don't want you to get shot."

"I wasn't shot. I'm just fine. It's all over now. Go home, Frankie. You did a great job today, and you deserve some free time. Take a couple of days off. Paid days off."

Letty made a quick call to Professor Anselm. She left a message. "Steve, I found Becker's killer. I'll call you, and we'll catch up next week." Letty said goodbye to everyone and headed for home.

* * *

Back home again, Letty came in to find her brother Will and Clarice loading the car with camping equipment.

"Hey, Letty," Will said, grinning at his big sister. "We have a couple of days off from school because of some holiday or conference or something."

"We decided to go up on Mount Lemmon and go camping," Clarice added.

"Sounds like a good idea," Letty answered.

"Is it okay with you if we take the dogs?"

"Sure. They'll love that. Just don't let them run around loose and attract the attention of a mountain lion or a park ranger."

Will nodded. "They'll be good. We'll keep them close."

"When are you coming home?"

"Not tomorrow but the day after that. We'll come home early because I have to work at the bike shop." Will gave Letty a hug. Then Clarice gave Letty a hug.

Letty waved as Will and Clarice drove away. Teddy and Millie sat in the back seat looking pleased with the world. She walked back into the house and found her cell phone.

Dan answered on the second ring, "Hola, Novia," he laughed.

"Oh, your Spanish is so good," Letty said. "'Hello, Girlfriend.' That's two words you know now."

"I know more than just two words. I'm getting really good at Spanish. Don't forget 'pendejo' and 'pinche.'"

"That's terrible. You are already cussing in Spanish, and you only know a few words." She chuckled. "I'll have to teach you how to speak properly. You need to learn proper manners."

She imagined Dan in the hospital, dressed in his scrubs with that white doctor's coat on top, a stethoscope around his neck, dark hair ruffled, those beautiful blue-green eyes shining, a grin on his face. He was so sexy. Oh god. So that's it. She didn't want to admit it, but she found him irresistibly attractive.

"Learn proper Spanish? Sounds like a good deal. How about this evening? Are you free? What have you been doing today anyway?"

Letty hesitated. She didn't really want to tell him about watching Gus Padillo being murdered, or how Kellie Miller ended up dead, too. Worst of all, she didn't want to talk about how Kellie had almost shot and killed Agnes Olsen and her, too, with Gus's rifle.

"Uh…well…uh…not much really," Letty finally managed to say. "My case has been turned over to the Tucson police. I don't have anything to do now."

"Oh, so you *are* free. That's great, Letty."

"Are you free, too?"

"You bet. Want to come by the emergency room around seven? That's when I get off work. Wait for me out in the front waiting room."

"Okay. I'll be there at seven to pick you up."

"How do you say 'give me a kiss?' in Spanish?"

"I'll show you later. Sometimes it's better to show and tell. Not just tell."

"I so agree. Show is better than tell. I can't wait to see you."

"I'll be there at seven." She disconnected her phone.

* * *

Letty showered, ate a sandwich, and then headed to the hospital. She had no idea what she and Dan would do this evening. They seemed headed toward a closer relationship, perhaps even an intimate one. This scared Letty. It had been a long, long time since she'd been intimate with a man. She didn't know how to act.

She parked her car in the parking lot. The evening sky was dusky now. She could see bands of light from the setting sun streaking across the Catalinas, turning the mountains into a copper color that transformed into a deep red color. So beautiful.

Letty walked into the waiting room and sat down at the end of a row of chairs against the far wall. She was close to the door where employees usually emerged when they headed home. That's where Dan would be coming from at seven when his shift as an emergency room doctor was over. Across the room to her right, she could see the reception desk and a wide door beyond that led to rooms where patients were examined. To her left across from the reception desk was the front glass-door entrance to the waiting room and, outside those doors, the parking lot where she'd left her pickup truck.

There were only a couple of people in the waiting room. One person was behind the reception desk working at a computer.

Letty looked down at her phone. There was a text from Clarice. She and Will had arrived at the campground and were setting up their camp. All was well.

She looked up.

Across the room just inside the glass entrance door, a man was standing there staring at her. Letty realized with a start that the man was Rigo, the homeless vet with whom she'd had a couple of very hostile interactions at the encampments. The last one was especially tense because Rigo was looking for the missing vet Kenny Wilson. He had repeatedly blamed Letty for Kenny's disappearance. No, Kenny was not just missing. Kenny was dead, a suicide by drowning in Agua Caliente Park's big pond. Letty suddenly felt very tense.

Rigo stood there with both hands in the pockets of his outer jacket. He was glaring at Letty.

"So here you are, Valdez. I finally found you."

Rigo pulled a handgun out of one pocket. He waved the gun at the receptionist and the two people sitting in the waiting room. "Get out!" he yelled.

The two people waiting quickly exited through the glass doors behind Rigo. The receptionist disappeared as well.

Letty stood up and faced Rigo. She moved slightly to her right so that her back was against the wall. She was acutely aware of the fact that she'd left her gun at home.

"What do you want, Rigo? You're scaring everyone."

"You're the one who should be scared, Valdez. Kenny is dead, and it's your fault."

"Rigo, Kenny killed himself. He left a suicide note. The cops told me that he apologized to his family and everyone."

"I served with Kenny in Afghanistan. He was my best bud. But I could see when he came home that he was in big trouble. Depressed all the time. He couldn't shake the war, all the violence, seeing guys get shot, seeing little kids blown up. His family was a problem for him. He felt guilty, and he couldn't face them. I didn't understand this. Why so much shame? Then I found out his dad had been some hotshot military officer who won a bunch of medals in Vietnam. Kenny felt like a failure. He couldn't live up to his dad's reputation. He couldn't face his family. He felt like a loser."

"Rigo, a lot of us came home from those wars with problems. That includes you and me both. I don't know why you blame me for Kenny's problems."

"You stupid bitch. You're the one who caused all this. You came to him with a demand that he contact his family. He had to face the fact that they weren't going to leave him alone. He couldn't go home and be around them. He was at a dead end. That's why he killed himself. Because of you. You started this."

"I didn't demand anything. I just told him that they were worried about him and wanted to know he was okay. I told him that I wouldn't tell them where he was. It was up to him to decide if he wanted to contact them or not."

Was it her imagination or did she see a police car pull up to the curb in front of the main entrance to the emergency room? Sirens and lights were off. Rigo didn't notice the cop car. She focused on what he was saying.

"Yeah, but if it weren't for you," he said, "Kenny wouldn't have been forced to face his family. He couldn't bear the shame."

"Kenny needed help. You do, too, Rigo. You can't just go around trying to beat up people or waving a gun around to solve a problem."

Just as Letty completed her words, the doors to her right swung open, and Dan stepped into the waiting room. He was looking at Letty with all his attention. He was smiling.

"Hi, Letty," he said. But he quickly saw that her focus was on something across the room. Dan turned and saw Rigo standing there.

Rigo lifted his gun and pointed it at Letty.

"No!" Dan yelled. He threw himself in front of Letty, arms outstretched, just as Rigo pulled the trigger. "No!"

The bullet slammed into Dan's left side just below his rib cage. He fell back against Letty, and they slid down to the floor together. Her arms were around him as he slumped back against her. He turned his head up and back toward her. He looked at her and whispered, "Letty…" Then his eyes rolled back in his head, and he collapsed.

CHAPTER 22

Everything erupted in chaos.

Rigo dropped the gun to his side just as two police officers entered the front door of the emergency waiting room, their guns already drawn.

Someone called the cops, Letty thought vaguely. She was intensely aware of Dan's warm body against hers.

A security guard came through the door next to the reception desk, his gun in hand, too.

"Drop the gun!" yelled one of the cops.

Rigo grinned at Letty. "So now you know what it's like to lose someone you love."

He lifted the gun and pointed it at the cops. Both cops fired. Rigo's body convulsed violently as several bullets slammed into him. He was dead before he hit the floor.

Suicide by cop, Letty thought to herself.

Letty looked down and saw a red bloom of blood seeping out of Dan's side, staining his white coat and dripping onto her pants and shirt. She pulled off her outer shirt, pressed it hard against the wound, and she cried out, "Medic! Medic! I need help."

At that exact moment, several of the emergency room staff pushed through the doors closest to the reception desk. She could see a doctor, a couple of nurses and two attendants pushing a gurney and running toward Letty and Dan. Within seconds, they pulled Dan up and onto the gurney. The last thing Letty saw was one of the nurses jumping onto the gurney and straddling Dan. The nurse started chest compressions.

Letty gasped and tried to not sob. Chest compressions meant his heart wasn't beating. The nurse was trying to bring Dan back to life.

She sat back against the wall. A hospital attendant came over and asked if she'd been wounded.

"No," she said weakly. Then she stood and made her way across the waiting room and out the front door. The cops were so focused on Rigo that they failed to notice her.

This great cloud of white light began to descend over Letty. She stumbled out of the emergency room and to her pickup truck in the parking lot. She fought back the glaring white light enough to drive herself home. She was more than numb. She couldn't feel anything at all. She couldn't hear anything. She couldn't speak. She was enveloped by the cloud of white light. She could barely breathe. She could barely see.

She had only one thought in her mind. The thing Letty feared most about Dan was that loving him meant that he would be killed. It was like that with Chava. She loved Chava, and he died. And now Dan was gone. Her fault. She was toxic, and she knew it. She should have stayed away from Dan.

Letty went home. She found a blanket and went out onto her back porch. She wrapped the blanket around her, sat down, and the white cloud enveloped her.

* * *

Evening turned into night, night passed, then a day, then another night, then morning came. Will and Clarice came home early.

Will called out, "Hey Letty. We're home. We're late. I have to hurry to get to work. We had a great time."

Clarice opened the back door to let the dogs out. That's when she saw Letty.

Will and Clarice gathered around her. Letty looked at them when they spoke to her, but then she turned away. She did not respond. The white cloud was too much to overcome.

Will and Clarice went back into the house.

"Something is really wrong," Will said. "She's not responding to us at all."

"I bet something bad happened. Let's call Seri. Maybe she can help."

Time passed. Letty didn't know how much time.

She looked up, and there were her friends Seri and Zhou sitting in chairs across from her.

"Letty, talk to me," Seri said in a demanding voice.

Letty looked at Seri. She turned away.

Seri reached out and took Letty's hand. "I'm not going away, girl-friend. You better talk to me or there will be hell to pay. You know I can be a pain in the ass so talk to me."

Letty looked at her.

"It's my fault, Seri. Dan is dead, and it's my fault."

"Oh my god. Is that what you think? Dan is *not* dead. They operated on him, took out the bullet, and put him in a hospital bed to recuperate. He's asking for you."

"He's not dead?" Letty's voice wavered.

Zhou spoke. "Letty, Dan is not dead. He is a hero. Yes, I would say he is a hero. He prevented you from being shot and killed."

"That's right," Seri added, "Dan took a bullet for you. He's definitely a hero in my books."

The white cloud began to lift, and the morning light appeared. The light seemed strange and unfamiliar. Letty shook her head.

"He's not dead?"

"No. He's alive. Here's what you're going to do, Letty Valdez." Seri was Letty's best friend. Letty had saved Seri's life when she'd been kidnapped by a criminal and thrown down into a hole to die. But Seri was in the habit of giving orders, and she figured now was the time to give Letty an order.

"You're going to get up, take off those bloody clothes, take a shower, get dressed, and eat something. Then I'm taking you to the hospital to see Dan."

"I can't do that. He'll just die if I see him again."

Zhou spoke now. "Letty, you show signs of your PTSD from the wartime. This idea that you are a danger to Dan is not accurate. I have seen cases like this myself in law enforcement. You must focus on the present, and give up your incorrect thinking. You will not cause Dan's death."

"Yes," Seri added. "This notion that loving Dan will kill him is your PTSD talking. It's like a venomous snake. It bit you with a bad idea."

"He's not dead?"

Zhou said firmly. "I spoke to Dan on the phone. He is not dead. He is alive. He wants to see you."

"He's asking for me?" Her voice was weak.

"Yes, and you don't want to disappoint him, do you?" Seri asked.

"No. I don't want to disappoint him."

"Okay, so get up and I'll help you get ready to go to the hospital."

"Clarice and Will are making a sandwich for you," Zhou added.

Seri and Zhou led Letty back into the house. As Seri and Zhou passed, Will and Clarice both whispered, "Thank you, thank you, thank you."

* * *

Letty knocked lightly on the hospital door. There was no answer so she slipped quietly into Dan's hospital room. There were two beds in the room. The first was empty. Dan was lying propped up in the bed closest to the window. He opened his eyes and looked at her when Letty sat down on his bed next to him.

"How are you?"

Dan was pale and subdued.

"I'm okay." He looked despondent, a sadness that Letty had never before seen in him.

"I have to apologize to you for taking so much time coming to visit you. I thought you were dead."

"I'm not dead. You thought I was dead?"

"Yes. I'm so relieved. I really and truly thought you were dead. When I found out you were alive, I felt really scared. I'm still scared."

"Scared of what? Of me?"

Letty took a deep breath.

"I have something serious to tell you, Dan. I don't want to be your girlfriend. I want...."

Dan sighed, dejected. "I guess I'm not really surprised. When you didn't show up, I figured you were calling it quits." He frowned and looked out the window. He looked so sad.

"No," Letty struggled not to let tears take over. Her voice was barely above a whisper. "You're misunderstanding me. I have a different idea of how things should go. I want to be your lover, not your girlfriend."

Dan's eyebrows went up. His head jerked toward her.

"Lover? Really?"

"I'm bat-shit crazy about you, Dan Ennis. I have thoughts about you the way a man thinks about a woman. I mean the way a woman thinks a man. Oh, you know what I mean." She struggled to contain her tears. "Dan, I want to come in for a nuzzle."

"Oh, Letty, sweetheart." His voice was gentle. "Don't cry. You know you're my little filly." He reached out for her.

"I need to tell you this to help you decide if you want to be my lover or not."

She sat up straight and took another deep breath.

"My friends Seri and Zhou helped me to realize that I've had this irrational idea for a long time. I thought that if I cared for a man, he would end up dead. I've thought of myself as toxic. Then you were shot and that just confirmed my worst fears. All this time I've been afraid for you and for your survival so I thought I should stay away from you for your own sake. Seri told me that was the PTSD talking. She said that I needed to deal with my fear and not be such a coward. On the way to the hospital, Seri reminded me of this old Spanish proverb. 'Vivir con miedo es como vivir a medias.'"

"What does that mean?"

"To live in fear is to live half a life."

Dan nodded. "My teacher in the monastery would agree with this proverb."

"I have to admit to myself now that I have PTSD, that I have nightmares about the war, that I have irrational fears and anxiety about living every day. It's made me work all the time so I won't have to feel the fear. I won't allow myself any pleasure because it makes me scared. I'm good at martial arts and at being an investigator, but otherwise, I'm a total mess."

Dan looked at her tenderly and held her hand.

"I want you to know what happened." She took a deep breath. "I had a boyfriend, a lover, named Chava. He was a Chicano dude mixed up with a gang in East LA. He got caught doing something criminal when he was seventeen years old. The judge gave him a choice – either the Army or jail. He chose the Army. He was on his third deployment when I met him. He liked the Army, and he was thinking of making a career of it. On the day this happened, his time was up in Iraq, and he was on his way to the airport to fly out and go on leave back home. I was due to go home myself in ten days. We were going to meet once we were both back in the States. On this day, we were in a convoy on the way to the base airport. I was in a vehicle four trucks behind his. His truck hit an IED, and the explosion blew the truck apart. Chava was one of three guys in the truck. The convoy stopped. I got out of my truck and ran forward. I was screaming, 'Chava, Chava.' That was when I got hit by that bullet, when the insurgent shot me, but I continued running forward."

Letty took a deep breath.

"His truck was a mangled mess. The driver had been blown out of the truck. I saw the driver sitting on the ground with his back against a wall. His head was gone. The guy who had been in the back seat was missing. They found his body later about a half a block away. I ran forward looking for Chava. Then I saw his boot. I picked it up. His foot and half of his lower leg were still in the boot. That was all I could find. The sand around me everywhere was red with blood. The guys in my unit came and pulled me away. I was bleeding so they took me in to get care for my bullet wound. They told me later that the IED explosion pretty much tore apart Chava's body. They found Chava's head and part of his upper torso and not much more."

Dan shook his head. "Oh, man. That's bad. I'm so sorry, Letty."

"What you need to know is that I fell apart. I became…well, it was like I was in this white cloud. I couldn't hear or see anything. I stopped talking. I couldn't remember anything."

"Perfectly understandable. This would be a traumatic event for anyone. I think they call what you experienced a 'dissociative fugue.'"

"Yeah, I guess so. They sent me home. I was in the VA hospital for while then I went out and stayed with my grandmother on the reservation. After a while with my grandmother, the cloud started to lift."

"And that was, what? seven or eight years ago."

"Yes. But I want you to know that the cloud came back when I thought you were dead."

Dan frowned. "I'm so very sorry. Seeing me get shot was traumatic for you, especially if you thought I died."

"Yes. I'm still terrified really. I'm scared something will happen to you. But you're too good to pass up. I don't want to live in fear anymore. I don't want to live half a life. It's time for me to let go of Chava. It's time for you now. What do you think? Would you like to be my lover? It means we would have an intimate relationship. I want to go out with you and have fun with you. I want to laugh with you. I want to stay home with you and share secrets and cuddle with you. I want to make love with you. I mean sex. You know what I mean? Want to have sex and make love with me?" Letty found a tissue and wiped her eyes and nose.

Dan's face was relaxed now, and he was smiling. "Are you sure?"

She took his hand and kissed his palm. "Yes, I'm sure."

At that moment, a doctor came into the room. Letty stood and retreated to stand in the corner.

"How are you doing, Ennis?" the man said, looking at papers on a clipboard. He looked down at Dan, then at Letty, then back at Dan. He smiled.

Letty noticed his nametag. Dr. Joaquín Salazar.

"Looks like you are doing well. Your color is better."

Dan nodded in agreement. He was smiling, and he was no longer so pale. Talking to Letty made a big difference.

"Let's take a look." Dr. Salazar, a middle-aged man with graying hair, pulled back the sheet and opened Dan's cotton hospital top to look at the bandaged wound. He pulled the gauze and tape away on both the front and back of Dan's body, just enough to inspect the wound.

"Hmmm….healing nicely. I think you can go home soon. Maybe in three days."

"No. I don't like being a patient. I want to go home now."

"Most doctors don't like being in the hospital. But today is too soon. By the way, Ennis, all the nurses are talking about your tattoo. What's the deal with the tattoo?"

Letty strained to see Dan's chest, but the doctor was in the way.

"This is so embarrassing," Dan's face had turned a ruddy red color. "When I was in Kabul, this big bomb went off in the market. The explosion killed a bunch of civilians and injured even more. We did our best to help them. We worked on them for a long stretch, maybe sixteen hours or so. When everyone had been taken care of, I met up with my Aussie mates. We went out for a drink together. We all got shitfaced. It's the most drunk I've ever been in my life. I'm lucky I didn't poison myself. I totally passed out and stayed passed out. My mates thought it would be hilarious to get me tattooed when I was out of it. I woke up the next day with the worst hangover of my life, and with this tattoo on my chest."

"The nurses are saying it's very sexy."

"Sexy? But it's a Hello Kitty tattoo meant for Japanese school girls." The doctor shrugged.

"I don't understand women," Dan said.

"Welcome to the club," said the older doctor. He turned to Letty. "You're that private investigator Letty Valdez, right? You're probably observant and a good judge of people. What do you think of his tattoo?"

Letty came closer and took a good look. Sure enough, a Japanese cartoon Hello Kitty with a bow stuck on the side of its head was inked onto Dan's chest.

Letty crossed her arms in front of her, trying to suppress a grin. She said in a serious tone of voice, "I agree with the nurses. I would say that a man who has this tattoo is self-confident and usually gets what he wants. A less macho guy couldn't pull off a tattoo like this, but Dr. Ennis can." She turned to Doctor Salazar and smiled. "The nurses are right. That tattoo is smokin' hot, and so is Dan Ennis."

The doctor laughed.

By this time, Dan was grinning. "I don't understand women, but I like them."

Dr. Salazar shook his head in agreement. "Yeah, we can't live with 'em and can't live without 'em."

"Please discharge me today. Letty can take care of me."

"Let's make a deal. I'll order your discharge for tomorrow, but not today or, as I prefer, two or three days from now. Tomorrow check-out time is two p.m. Go home. Rest. Watch for infection. Then come back to work. We need you in the ER."

The doctor started to leave then turned to Letty, "You'll take care of him?"

"Yes, sir. I was a U.S. Army medic. I know the basics."

"Good. Just don't wear him out." The doctor laughed again as he walked out.

Letty came to sit next to Dan again. She took his hand in hers.

"Letty, I have something to tell you now. It's kind of crazy. But I want you to know everything."

"Okay. Can't be any crazier than what I just told you."

He shrugged. "We'll see. Here it is. I first encountered you eight years ago at Al Asad Airbase in Anbar Province."

"*What?*" Letty was shocked. "I don't remember you."

"You never met me. I think you never even saw me. I had been working for a couple of hours on the wounded after a surprise attack and an explosion. I needed a rest so I went over and collapsed in a folding tent chair near the back wall of the tent. The medics brought in a couple of injured soldiers. One of them was severely wounded. The other docs worked on him and did what they could, but it was clear he was unlikely to live more than an hour or two. So they put him on a gurney and pushed him over to the back where I was resting. In cases like this, we do our best, but we figure a person is either going to make it or not make it. Our medicine isn't the deciding factor. I'm not sure what is. I don't know why some survive and others don't."

Letty nodded.

"I heard one of the guys call out, saying that the wounded man was a Native American and they should go find that Native medic. About five minutes later, you came in. They led you back to the wounded soldier. You never looked at me. Your focus was on the soldier."

"I remember. He was Diné. A Navajo."

"I watched you help him die. You spoke poetic words to him that were so reassuring. He was smiling at the end. You were saying something like, "in beauty we walk.""

"It's actually a prayer, part of the Navajo's Blessing Way."

"I listened and watched as you held his hand. You said this long prayer with him about walking in beauty and beauty all around. He died smiling. But you didn't let go of his hand. After a while, one of the soldiers came to get his body. You said he wasn't gone yet, and we should wait."

"His spirit was still there."

"I waved them away. Finally you let go of his hand. I was so impressed by your serenity. When I thought of you, and I thought of you many times in the intervening years, I decided the best word to describe you was 'soulful.' A soulful woman."

Letty shrugged. "I don't know."

"Not long after, they called me to work on a guy with a seriously-injured leg. When I was done, I looked for you. I didn't know your name. When I asked, no one knew who you were. For the remainder of my two tours, I asked about you everywhere I went. Finally in Afghanistan, this grunt told me that he knew who you were, but he didn't know your name. He just knew you were a Native American from Arizona."

"You looked for me?"

"Yes, I looked for you everywhere. Later when I was in the monastery, I thought a lot about you. I came to realize that I had been looking for someone to save me. I thought I needed a soulful woman to save me. I already told you about losing my friend Preed and about my drinking and all that."

Letty nodded again.

"I finally realized in the monastery that no one could save me. I had to save myself. I told myself that I would probably never see you again, but I promised myself that if I did, I would try to be a good person for you. I wouldn't expect you to save me. But I hoped you would want to know me better."

Letty smiled. "I do want to know you better. What you said makes sense. You can't save me either. I have to deal with this white cloud myself. I have to confront my fear, or else I'll be living half a life."

He nodded. "When my teacher released me, I started looking for a job. Nadia told me about the opening in Tucson. I applied, and I got the job. I remembered that soulful Native woman from Arizona, but I figured it was unlikely that I would ever find you."

Dan shook his head. "Then there you were on the river trail. When I found you there after you'd been attacked, it felt like this incredible miracle. I told myself I was going to be my best person from that moment on and hope that you would want me in your life."

"That's why I'm here."

"You know what I sang all the way home that day?"

"No. What did you sing?" she asked.

"The Beatles song 'Got to Get You Into My Life!'"

Letty squeezed his hand.

"Then when I returned to Tucson from Puerto Rico, I was trying to figure out how to get on your radar again. That's when Teddy found me up in the tree."

"Teddy is a good dog." Letty said.

"You turned out to be much better than I ever dreamed."

"I think that about you, too."

"So hearing all this, you don't think I'm weird?"

"You already know that I think you're weird."

"Weird charming?"

"Nah. More like weird lovable." She was smiling at him now.

"Really? Weird lovable? Wow! That's even better."

"So what do you think? Do you agree to be my lover?"

"Absolutely yes for sure without a doubt. Yes. One hundred percent. For sure. Definitely. Count me in. I'm up for it." He began to laugh. "Ouch." He grimaced. "Don't make me laugh. I just want you to know that I do definitely agree to be your lover."

"Even though you had to get in bed with me out on the reservation and hold me when I was having one of my Iraq nightmares?"

"You were awake?"

"Yes."

"Why didn't you say anything?"

Letty fell silent. Finally she said, "I was afraid you would leave."

"I won't leave you, Letty. I won't ever leave you."

"Okay. Then we agree. We're going to be lovers starting tomorrow. Of course, you are hurt now so we'll have to go slow. You need time to heal."

"Sure, but I'm stronger than you think. Want to start today? We could be lovers right now."

"Here in the hospital? I don't think so. You told me you are a patient man. So be patient and wait for one more day. Also I have something else to tell you. I went to see that doctor you recommended."

"Nadia Ochoa?"

"She did just as you predicted. I was examined, poked and prodded and scanned. She gave me vaccine injections. She reprimanded me just like you did for not taking better care of myself. Also she tested me for sexually-transmitted diseases, and the results were negative."

"Me, too," Dan said. "I was tested before my last volunteer gig. I'm negative, too."

"Also we …uh…well, let's just say that I have birth control now, too."

"Really? You asked for that? You were anticipating?"

"No. I was too scared to even think about that. When I told Dr. Ochoa that you were calling me your novia, she laughed and said it was just a matter of time that you and I would become lovers. She said I was going to need some birth control unless I wanted to get pregnant. She asked me to trust her. So I did. I have birth control now."

"Ah, so you know what that means, don't you?"

"What?"

"No need for condoms. We can have naked sex."

Letty felt herself blushing. She covered her cheeks with her open palms.

"I'm embarrassing you again?"

Letty nodded.

"Okay. I'll shut up now." With two fingers, he made the motion across his lips of a zipper closing. He winked at her.

Letty said, "I'll be back tomorrow, and I'll help you check out. Then we'll go to your place away from Will and Clarice and the dogs. We'll have some privacy. I'll stay with you and take care of you until you are a lot better. So if you'll give me your keys, I'll buy some groceries and get everything ready for us."

He pointed to a bedside stand, and she retrieved his keys.

"Come here, sweetheart. Give me a kiss before you go," Dan said. He pulled her to him for a lingering kiss.

Letty stood and headed for the hospital room door. She turned back.

"One more thing. I think I love you, Dan Ennis."

Dan grinned. "I *know* I love you, Letty Valdez."

When she was gone, Dan whispered to himself. "Thank you, Letty, my soulful woman."

* * *

Letty went home. She first called Seri and Zhou and thanked them for coming to talk with her and for helping her so much. True friends. She called Frankie and told him that she was taking a few days off. Call if there's an emergency, she said. She let Frankie know that she trusted him to take care of everything.

Next she got some much needed rest. She slept ten hours. The following morning, she told Will and Clarice that she would be taking care of Dan for a while. She gave them both a hug. Then she went to the grocery store and selected food items that she thought Dan would like and that he could manage to eat. She went to Dan's house to stock the kitchen and tidy his house. There wasn't much to do. His house was amazingly neat. She didn't know if that's because he was a neat person naturally, or if he just wasn't home enough to get things messy. I guess I'll find out, Letty said to herself.

Letty returned to the hospital in the early afternoon.

"I'm here to help Dr. Dan Ennis check out."

There were two nurses behind the desk. Almost immediately, they were joined by several other members of the staff. There were a couple of doctors, attendants, and more nurses. One of the doctors was Joaquín Salazar. They all smiled at her.

"We don't know what you did to him, but Doc Ennis has been singing since you left yesterday," one of the nurses said. "He's sung all the Stevie Wonder songs, and one tune in particular. You know that one about how lovely and wonderful and precious she is? We figured he was singing about you. We're getting a little tired of hearing the same song." The nurses laughed.

Letty felt herself growing warm. She looked behind her. Dan was in a wheel chair at his room door waiting. He was smiling at her.

She went to him, stood in front of him, and bent down so that her face was near his.

"Haven't changed your mind, have you?" she whispered. "Still want to be my lover?"

Dan grinned. "I want you, Letty Valdez!" He grabbed her shoulders and pulled her to him. He gave her an ardent kiss.

All the staff members behind the desk laughed, cheered, and clapped their hands.

"Come on, Dan," Letty Valdez took control of the wheel chair and steered him toward the hospital exit.

Dr. Salazar shook his finger at Letty and mouthed, "Don't wear him out." Then he laughed, too.

Everyone called out, "Bye, Doc Ennis. Get well soon!"

Dan looked up at her, a happy smile on his face.

"Let's go home, Letty," he said.

"Yes, Dan. Let's go home," Letty answered.

Thank you from the Author:

Hello Reader! Thank you for reading *Daemon Waters*. I hope you enjoyed accompanying Letty Valdez and her friends and family on all their adventures. Please leave a review of this book on your favorite book vendor website. By leaving a review for others to read, you can make it much easier for mystery readers everywhere to find Letty. A new Letty Valdez Mystery is being written now. To learn more, go to www.cjshane.com, sign up for my monthly newsletter, and feel free to email me with comments or questions.

About the Author:

C.J. Shane is a writer and visual artist based in Tucson, Arizona, U.S.A. She has traveled widely and lived and worked in Mexico, the People's Republic of China, and in the U.S. She has worked as a newspaper reporter, freelance writer, academic reference librarian, and ESL teacher. She is the author of eight nonfiction books. Her first work of fiction, *Desert Jade: A Letty Valdez Mystery* (2017), was followed by *Dragon's Revenge: A Letty Valdez Mystery* (2018). See more at www.cjshane.com or www.RopesEndPublishing.com

Made in the USA
Las Vegas, NV
17 December 2020